THE CHRISTMAS TRESPASSERS

WITHDRAWN

Titles by ANDREW J. FENADY

The Christmas Trespassers

Black Noon

Range Wolf

Destiny Made Them Brothers

THE **CHRISTMAS TRESPASSERS**

and 3 Bonus Stories *told by*
THE WISE OLD MAN OF THE WEST:

The Stranger Who Limped

Blazing Guns of the Bible

The Bravest Soldier

ANDREW J.
FENADY

PINNACLE BOOKS

K

www.kensingtonbooks.com

PINNACLE BOOKS are published by

Kensington Publishing Corp.
119 West 40th Street
New York, NY 10018

Copyright © 1999, 2018 Andrew J. Fenady

The Christmas Trespassers was originally published as *The Runaways* by Berkley Books in 1999.

All Kensington titles, imprints, and distributed lines are available at special quantity discounts for bulk purchases for sales promotions, premiums, fund-raising, educational, or institutional use. Special book excerpts or customized printings can also be created to fit specific needs. For details, write or phone the office of the Kensington sales manager: Kensington Publishing Corp., 119 West 40th Street, New York, NY 10018, attn: Sales Department; phone 1-800-221-2647.

PINNACLE BOOKS and the Pinnacle logo are Reg. U.S. Pat. & TM Off.

ISBN-13: 978-0-7860-4291-3
ISBN-10: 0-7860-4291-5

First printing: October 2018

10 9 8 7 6 5 4 3 2 1

Printed in the United States of America

First electronic edition: October 2018

ISBN-13: 978-0-7860-4292-0
ISBN-10: 0-7860-4292-3

For

The Two CLINTS—
WALKER *and*
EASTWOOD

The Two DUKES—
WAYNE *and*
FENADY

The Two DANS—
BLOCKER *and*
"DANDY" DON MEREDITH

and, of course,

The One and Lovely
MARY FRANCES

Contents

THE CHRISTMAS
TRESPASSERS

Prelude

December. Month of the longest nights. But since he'd returned to the Shenandoah Valley and then left the valley and the graves behind, all the nights had been long and bleak and infinitely lonely.

Inside the cabin, the log in the fireplace had long since turned to ash. Once again Shad Parker had gone up against the bottle and once again the whiskey had failed to erase the memories or ease the pain.

He had memorized the letter—all of her letters—but somehow felt nearer to her when he held it in his hand. The last letter she ever wrote.

My dearest darling:
   I pray this letter finds you safe. The children and I are well and think of you every moment.
   It is still impossible for me to understand and countenance the madness that has torn you—and the other men of our valley—away from us.
   You who never raised a hand in anger—so gentle and compassionate—whose heart and mind recoiled

at the very thought of slavery—turned into a machine of war.

And why? Because we are Virginians. Because other men—farmers like yourself who love the soil of their Ohio or Massachusetts—would devastate our valley.

If only our Blue Mountains were walls to shut them out and let us live in peace.

But the war draws closer to us. You can sense it in the air. Even the doves have left the valley.

And now, as the time we celebrate our Savior's birth is near, I feel another life stirring within me, too. I know you want a daughter—and may it be God's will to grant her to us.

I pray that next Christmas we will be at peace, together, our family . . .

But long before the next Christmas, General Philip Sheridan's army had put the Shenandoah to the torch.

Shad Parker's sons—Sean, age six, Shannon, age four, his wife, Molly, and their unborn son or daughter were all dead. His farm and everything he ever loved destroyed.

He vowed that he would never again be touched by another living thing. Never again would he lose anything he loved, because he would never allow himself to love anything or anybody.

Shad Parker moved west. The cabin on the hardscrabble little farm near the outskirts of Gilead, Texas, was in grim contrast to the gracious structure in the lush, green valley in Virginia, but it suited Shad Parker—what remained of him.

He gently placed the letter in the tin box with Molly's other letters, took up and drained the tumbler of whiskey, then set it on the table next to the gun. For a long time he stared at the Colt, and then as he had countless times before, he took it in his palm, with a hand that knew well the shape and feel of a gun, a hard hand with deep creases and strength from working the soil, but a hand that once held his wife close and gently. Once again his thumb tripped back the hammer, once again the gun moved closer to his face. Once again he thought about the one certain way to erase the memories, not just to ease the pain, but end it.

This time he meant to do it. But he had meant to do it many times before.

From outside once again came the clarion call of the rooster telling the world it was time to start another day. Shad Parker eased the hammer into place and put the Colt back on the table.

Shad Parker had lived through another night without sleep—and now faced another day without purpose.

Chapter 1

It was a no-good time to be in Texas.

Just over six years ago, on February 1, 1861, Texas had seceded from the Union—the former Union—and joined the glorious Confederacy. But the machinery of war grinds exceedingly ingloriously and is lubricated by blood and money.

The War for the Confederacy drained Texas of both. By April 9, 1865, when General Robert E. Lee surrendered the Army of Northern Virginia to General Ulysses Simpson Grant at Appomattox, Texas was bankrupt, and in the two years that followed things had gone from bankrupt to worse.

Cattle by the thousand swarmed all over the plains, valleys, and slopes of Texas. But there wasn't any market for beef because there was a lack of money in Texas . . . and everywhere else in the South.

But Deek Keeshaw knew of one place in Texas that had money. A bank in Gilead, whose owner, Amos Bush, had been conservative in his financial dealings as well as his patriotism.

While the other banks in Texas had backed the

Confederacy with every resource at their command, Amos Bush had played the game close to his ample vest.

Deek Keeshaw, who had never made a deposit in Amos Bush's bank, or any other bank, had planned to make a withdrawal, a substantial withdrawal, with dynamite. But at the moment, Deek Keeshaw was inside a formidably enclosed wagon on his way to the Oklahoma Territorial Prison.

Deek's two younger brothers, Tom and Bart, were strategically poised, waiting to unburden the formidably enclosed wagon of part of its living cargo, the part called Keeshaw. The deed would take some doing and some dying, but not on the part of the Keeshaws.

They were good at making sure that it was the other people who died. The best way to make sure was to back-shoot, or ambush.

The Keeshaws learned that lesson from Quantrill in Kansas when they rode alongside Frank and Dingus, the Daltons, and all the other young rebels who never charged a fortified position in military formation or maneuvered in open combat. They struck mostly in the dark and at the defenseless. What was left of Lawrence when they rode out testified to the merciless efficiency of William Clarke Quantrill's tactics and gave new emphasis to the epithet "guerrillas."

But for this ambush Tom and Bart needed daylight. They had to make sure of their targets. And they made sure of every other advantage. Concealment. Elevation. Surprise. Those advantages added up to death. For other people. Not the Keeshaws. And Tom would also get a chance to use just a little of the new dynamite they had lately acquired. Tom had been taught by Deek that it was dynamite, and not faith, that moved mountains—and banks.

Tom believed everything that Deek said. So did Bart. And Deek had said that their fortune was not west, but south. Mexico. All they needed was a stake. That stake was in the safe of the Bank of Gilead. Dynamite would also move that safe. But first they needed Deek to show them the way.

Tom studied the narrow road that snaked through the rocky terrain below. The December day was clear and windless. He aimed the rifle barrel down a long road toward an imaginary moving target. He squeezed the trigger but not hard enough to fire the rifle.

"Bam!" he whispered.

Tom Keeshaw smiled and looked north toward another vantage point across the leaden landscape.

Bart Keeshaw, skulking behind a boulder, held a rifle that would deliver the deadly crossfire when the moving target would no longer be imaginary. The wagon with the driver and guard would be advancing directly into the sun, another calculated advantage set forth by William Clarke Quantrill.

Of the brothers Keeshaw, Bart was the youngest, thinnest, tallest, and the best-looking, except for the vacancy no longer occupied by two front teeth. All three Keeshaws were porcine in appearance, but Bart's boniness and height made him look the least piggish.

Bart smiled back at his brother, letting a current of cold December air seep through the gap in his mouth. He took a cheap watch out of his frayed vest pocket and looked at the timepiece. He held it up to his ear. Silence. A look of disgust passed across his face. He tapped the edge of the watch against a rock a couple of times and listened again. Silence. He banged the watch a couple more times and listened once again. Still tickless. But Bart heard another sound, from a distance.

He buried the watch back into his pocket and made ready with his rifle, at the same time nodding toward Tom, who was already aiming his long gun.

A two-up wagon appeared from around the shoulder of rock on the hard, narrow road that lay below, between the two brothers. Hoofbeats and rattling traces echoed and bounced across the basin and the sound of squeaky music cut through the rhythm of the rolling wheels.

The driver held the reins in both hands, but the shotgun guard wasn't holding a shotgun. The 10-gauge was straddled between his legs while he did his best to make music with the mouth organ without damaging his teeth. The potholed roadway didn't help.

The wagon was completely enclosed except for a small opening striped with iron bars on the locked door in the rear of the seal-tight carriage. Lettering along both sides of the wagon spelled out:

OKLAHOMA TERRITORIAL PRISON

There were Christmas wreaths nailed across both signs.

The tune the shotgun guard was playing bore

some resemblance to "God Rest Ye Merry, Gentlemen," but not much.

"Jake," the driver said, "for Chrissake will you give it a rest?! You been playing that damn tune for twenty miles."

"You want me to play somethin' else?"

"I want you to keep your mouth shut and your eyes open. You make me nervous."

"Curley, you got no Christmas spirit."

"It ain't Christmas yet. Just save it till we deliver them two." Curley nodded back toward the wagon. "Then I'll drink my Christmas spirit. You hear me?"

"I hear you. Godalmighty, you'd think we was still in the army, the way you . . ."

"Jake, just shut up!"

"Okay," Jake started to pocket his harmonica, "but I just remembered somethin'."

"What?"

A barrage of shots rang out from two directions, ripping into both men. The driver fell dead between the team of horses. The harmonica dropped from the guard and he slumped lifeless in his seat. The smell of blood and death was already in the horses' nostrils as they stopped in their tracks.

Then one of the horses whinnied at the sound of hoofbeats.

"What the hell's goin' on?!" came a voice from inside the wagon.

Tom and Bart rode in from either side. Tom was leading an extra horse, saddled. A buckskin. The brothers reined up close to the wagon.

"Deek?!" Tom called. "You in there?"

"Where the hell you think I'd be?" came a second voice from the wagon. "Get 'em both?"

"Yeahbo." Bart grinned.

"Guard's got the keys." Deek's face came up against the iron bars.

Bart, still grinning, rode forward, pulled up the slumped and bloody guard, and lifted out a ring of half a dozen keys. As he did, Bart noticed a heavy gold chain across the dead man's vest. He reached over and tugged at the cold, gleaming chain. Attached to the end of it was a gold watch. Bart ripped the watch and chain from the vest. He pressed the stem and the lid flipped open.

"Hurry it up!" Deek commanded.

Bart tossed the ring of keys to Tom, who was off his animal. Tom caught the keys and hurried toward the locked door. Bart held the gold watch to his ear and listened to the staccato ticking of the timepiece.

"Ain't that purty," he muttered, snapped the lid shut, and attached the chain to his own vest while he threw away his played-out turnip.

Tom unlocked the door and two men handcuffed to each other jumped out. It was easy to tell which one was a Keeshaw.

Deek held up one of his cuffed hands, which forced the other man to do the same.

"Get 'em off."

"You bet, brother," Tom said as he tried to insert the right key into the eyelet of the handcuffs. The second try turned the trick.

"Johnny," Deek said to the other prisoner, a sunny-faced youth two months shy of twenty, "meet my brothers, Tom and Bart."

"Hallelujah!" Johnny exclaimed. "Pleased to meet you fellas. Special under these circumstances. I thought we was goin' to spend Christmas in jail."

Deek and Johnny were both free of the shackles. Tom tossed the cuffs onto the ground.

"Nope," said Deek. "Gonna spend it in Texas." He swiftly took a gun from Tom and slammed the barrel across Johnny's forehead. As Johnny dropped, his head hit the iron rim of the wagon wheel. But he didn't feel it. He was already unconscious.

"Bring my pipe and tobacco?" Deek inquired.

Tom pulled a pipe and pouch from his coat pocket and handed them across to Deek.

"Matches?" Deek asked. "Guard wouldn't let us smoke. Afraid we might try to burn down the wagon."

"That'ud be a shame." Tom smiled as he pulled a handful of matches from another pocket and dropped them in Deek's palm.

"Unhitch the animals." Deek nodded toward the wagon team. As he started stuffing the discolored pipe with the dry hard flakes of tobacco, Tom and Bart proceeded to execute Deek's orders, as they always did.

Deek walked casually to Tom's sorrel, paused long enough to fire up his pipe to his satisfaction. It took three matches to satisfy him. He opened a saddlebag and looked inside at the collection of dynamite sticks. He took one of the sticks with him and walked back toward the buckskin. Deek and Tom mounted. Bart rode up alongside, slipped his freshly acquired watch out of his pocket, and proudly displayed his new possession to his kin.

"Ain't it purty?" He pressed the stem and the lid flipped open. "Real gold. Nothin' purtier than a gold watch."

"I can think of somethin'." Tom grinned. His two front teeth looked like they should be on a rabbit.

Deek took the pipe from his mouth and lit the wick of the dynamite from the bowl. He stuck the stem back through his thin lips into his mouth, then tossed the lit stick through the open rear door into the wagon.

Bart snapped the lid of his gold watch shut and the Keeshaw brothers went to their spurs.

Six seconds later the blast, even at the distance they had covered, sent splintered debris spraying down on the happy little band of riders.

William Clarke Quantrill would have approved of the operation—and its execution.

Chapter 2

The next three days were short on daylight, but the Keeshaws rode from first light past sunset, stopping only for a cold noon meal of jerky and hardtack and when the animals puffed and slavered and shuddered beneath the riders. Straight south through East Texas, no-place country, raw with red flanked hills, unblessed, infertile land, grassless, ungreen, and winter grim. South toward a speck called, God only remembered why, Gilead.

During the days they rode mostly silent, but at night, by the flickering light and inadequate warmth of a mesquite campfire, while Bart admired his newly acquired timepiece, Tom urged Deek to tell them more about what lay ahead for them in Mexico. Deek spoke about women, wealth, and tequila just as if he had been there. Tom closed his eyes and listened, just as both younger brothers had listened to Deek since their daddy died drunk, stomped to death in a barn by a bay. They buried their daddy next to their long-dead mother, who had expired giving birth to Bart.

They shot the bay, stopped by to say "so long" to

Frank and Dingus, who had a nearby farm in Clay County, Missouri, and rode off to join up with Quantrill, flower of Southern knighthood.

A few months later Frank and Jesse also joined up. The war was the worst thing that ever happened to bleeding Kansas, but the best thing that ever happened to the Keeshaws. But all good things must come to an end. For Quantrill it ended with a mortal wound near Taylorsville, Kentucky, in May of 1865.

Frank and Jesse went into the railroad and banking business, investing with lead and dynamite. For a time the Keeshaws rode along, but splintered off when Jesse started taking too many chances and giving orders for his band to take even more chances.

The Keeshaws decided to go into business for themselves. They hadn't exactly prospered. But things would be different in Mexico after they stopped off in Gilead. Deek told them so.

And the brothers believed everything Deek said.

Midmorning of the fourth day the three riders topped out on the crest of a hill curved along a moody sackcloth sky.

They paused at the rim and drank from a canteen in the order of their birth.

"Wish it was tequila," Bart said as he passed the canteen back to Deek.

"Soon will be," Deek said, and took another pull. Then he saw something on the road down below and pointed.

In the distance, a two-up wagon, a buckboard. One of the rear wheels had fallen off. The buckboard was empty except for the driver, who was just climbing down. He walked toward the fallen wheel, which had rolled a few feet away.

"Looks like that man's had some bad luck," said Deek.

"Better him than us," said Bart, checking his time-piece again.

"Let's go down."

"What for?" Tom asked.

"Why, it's our chance to play the 'Good Samaritans.'"

Deek rode off toward the wagon.

"What's that mean? Sam-mar-samarisons?" Bart asked.

"Don't know."

"Well," Bart grinned through his absent teeth, "I guess we'll soon find out."

Tom rode after Deek. As always, Bart followed.

Shad Parker rolled the wayward wheel close to the wagon.

And as the three riders, first Deek, then Tom and Bart, came closer, they sized up the man they approached. It wasn't hard to see that he was a powerful man, with buffalo shoulders and thickset arms under the gray jacket he wore, now faded to a washed-out bone gray. His face a sullen, dangerous mold. His eyes bleak, weary, bitter. From under the black, sweat-scalloped, flat-crowned hat, jutted twists of coarse dark hair grained with irregular ridges of gray. His cheekbones were high and hard. In spite of his powerful structure, he moved with a pantherine grace and ease. The barrel of a Walker Colt inched out of its holster from beneath the edge of his jacket against his dark serge pants. Without moving his head, Shad

Parker's eyes appraised the approaching riders, but he went on with his task.

The Keeshaws were now in an almost straight line just a few feet from the wagon.

"Howdy," Deek greeted as pleasantly as he knew how.

There was no response from the man, who went on working.

"Deek Keeshaw," Deek said after a silence. "My brothers. Tom and Bart."

Shad paid no attention. He dropped the wheel near the rear axle, then proceeded to remove a pickax from the bed of the wagon. He placed the pickax on its head so the handle stood straight up near the rear of the tilted wagon.

"Looks like you need a hand," Deek tried again. "We'd be happy to help you, mister."

Shad ignored the offer. The three men let the silence settle in, then looked at one another.

Shad Parker squatted so the bed of the heavy wagon rested on his shoulder.

"Maybe he's deaf and dumb," Bart whispered to Deek.

Deek didn't reply. His eyes fastened on to the man and what was happening.

Shad Parker strained for just a moment, then the tilted side of the wagon started to rise, slowly, steadily. It almost appeared that the man could have flipped the wagon over if he wanted to, but he didn't. Shad walked the wagon back, one, two, three steps until the rear end was directly over the ax handle.

The Keeshaws were justifiably astonished. Bart pushed the brim of his dirty hat back over his hairline and swallowed some cold air.

While Shad started to lower the wagon, one of the two horses hitched to the wagon nickered.

"Easy, Nell."

"*Whatever* he is," Tom said, "he ain't deaf and dumb."

Shad gently lowered the bed of the wagon so it rested on the pickax handle that now acted as a jack. He lifted the wheel without much strain and slipped it onto the axle. He still hadn't even glanced at the three horsemen.

"Looks like you *don't* need a hand." Deek smiled. "If you're heading for Gilead, we'd be happy to buy you a holiday drink."

By now the Keeshaws didn't really expect an answer. They didn't get one.

"Come on, boys," Deek said to his brothers, "I calculate that Gilead is just beyond that next turn." The Keeshaws rode off toward the turn about a quarter of a mile south.

A few vagrant flakes of soft snow drifted uncertainly out of the amber sky but melted instantly on whatever they touched.

It wasn't until the Keeshaws were halfway to the turn that Shad Parker looked in their direction.

Chapter 3

The croaking Conestoga with weathered buffalo hides stretching over the iron ribs groaned to a stop along the road within sight of Shad Parker's spread.

A man who called himself "Buffler Jones" held the reins of the four-up. Whoever designed his face had never heard of handsome, and growing older while letting a crop of spiky hair cover most of what went under his hat hadn't helped much.

Next to Buffler sat an Indian, older and homelier, but hairless, at least the hide on his face was hairless.

"All right, young 'uns," Buffler looked back inside the wagon, "I said I'd take you far as the first farmhouse we come to. Ain't hardly much, but this appears to be it."

After waking up the youngest, the three of them crawled over the seat and jumped down on the ground.

First the oldest, a boy, Austin Coats, age eleven, but older inside than out, gaunt, with defiant pinwheel eyes, a knife blade mouth, long rankled yellow hair, half-sad, half-insolent but comely. Clothes torn and dirty.

Next a girl, Peg, a year and a month younger than her brother, in the same slattern condition, but with wider, more tragic eyes.

And finally, a six-year-old boy, Davy, rope thin, in about the same condition as his brother and sister, except still sleepy.

"Thanks, Mr. Jones," the little girl said. "Me and Austin and Davy appreciate your help."

"I'd admire to do more." Buffler rubbed his spiky beard. "Grub, or some money, but ol' Moondog and me is busted flat. Gonna have to kill what we eat till we hook up with the railroad. Well, so long, young 'uns, and good luck."

The wagon pulled away and left them standing there.

They had met the old man and the Indian the night before when the three of them had walked toward the campfire and found themselves looking into the barrel of a Sharps buffalo rifle, held by the old man with a carved piece of wood for a left leg and an Indian standing beside him.

"Just the three of you young 'uns?" the old man asked.

All three nodded.

"Hungry?"

"All three nodded again.

"Eat." The old man pointed toward what was left of a rabbit they had cooked for supper.

The three of them went to work on it until there was nothing left of the animal but a few bones, and they sucked them clean.

While they ate and long after, the old man talked. Austin, Peg, and Davy never heard anybody talk so much in all their lives. He didn't ask many questions, and they were glad of that.

"Family? Ma and Pa?"

"Dead," said Austin.

"Orphans, huh?"

Peg nodded.

"They have places for orphans."

"Not for us," said Austin.

"Why not?"

"They kept trying to split us up," Peg said.

"So you run away?" That was just about the end of the questions, but not the conversation. It wasn't exactly a conversation, more like an oration.

Buffler Jones appeared eager to spill out his story while Moondog sat, seemingly asleep with his eyes open, and never spoke a word.

"Moondog ain't long on talkin'," Buffler observed. "Some days he don't even grunt." But the old man made up for his friend's silence.

The children listened, partly because they were fascinated by the story and partly because they hoped the old man might take them along to wherever he was going, he and Moondog, north to the plains to hunt buffalo for the railroad.

Buffler told them how he began to hunt the beasts when he was a boy little more than Austin's age. It was no great task to kill buffalo with a rifle. For years the Indians had done it the hard way on foot and horseback, with bows and iron-tipped arrows. The beasts had bad eyesight and were short on brains, but they were big and strong and brought down many ponies and braves with hoof and horn.

But they were no match for rifles. Buffler said that he and the other white hunters who smelled of death and old guts all the time would come upon a countless herd two to four hundred yards away and pick off 150 buffalo a day apiece. Their skinners stripped the animals, whose tongues were smoked and sent back East as a culinary delicacy, while the hides were sold as lap robes.

The heaps of meat lay rotting. There weren't enough buzzards in the world to consume what was left behind.

And, said Buffler, there was a time when he thought there weren't enough rifles and cartridges in the world to decimate the herds. But now he wasn't so sure. But they'd last his lifetime and that's all that mattered to him because there was no other way he knew how to make a living.

"I tried after I lost my leg last year. Ol' Moondog and me, we went to farmin'. But we weren't cut out to be no farmers. Went flat bust, so it's back to the buffalo. You know, boy," he said to Austin, "I could take you along, you're old enough to go to skinnin', I'd teach you how, but there wouldn't be any place for the younger 'uns."

"Thanks anyway," said Austin. "We'll stick together."

"Suit yourself. Well, time to turn in. We'll take you far as the first farmhouse tomorrow then me and ol' Moondog'll turn north. At least the railroad eats the meat. Still, if there's another world after this 'un, and if there's ghosts of buffaloes up there, I got a heap of explainin' to do."

Austin, Peg, and Davy watched the wagon move away then turned toward the farmstead. The structures consisted of a squat main cabin, a barn, a smokehouse, a chicken coop, and a hog pen. There was a well between the cabin and the barn.

Part of the spread had been fenced, plowed, and planted. Part of it was still studded with rocks, especially along the bottom of a soaring hillside.

In front of Austin, Peg, and Davy there was a sign nailed to a post.

NO TRESPASSING

"What's that sign say?" Davy asked.

"It says 'No Trespassing,'" Peg answered.

"What's that mean?"

"It means what it says," came a voice from behind them.

All three turned and saw a man aboard a mule. He was tall and lean, with a long face and musing eyes.

"We don't mean no harm, mister," said Austin. "Is this your property?"

"No, it's not. Haven't got any property, not anymore. But I stopped by once to water my mule. Least, that's what I intended to do. Man who owns this property had other intentions. Didn't include being hospitable, or even civil. Probably poke a hole in a blind man's cup."

"Doesn't appear to be anybody home," said Austin.

"Then, that's the time to leave, before he gets back."

"We don't mean no harm," Austin repeated.

"You already said that, and I said you better get to gettin' before he gets back. And that's all I'm saying."

And that *was* all he said. Then he and the mule left.

"I still don't know what that word means." Davy pointed to the sign.

"It means," Austin said, "'keep off.' 'Get away.'"

"And that's just what we're going to do," Peg remarked. "Isn't it, Austin?"

"I'm getting hungry," Davy said. "Listen to all them chickens. Where there's chickens, there's eggs."

"They don't belong to us, Davy," Peg said. "I think we better do like the man said and get away from here."

"We will," Austin replied. "But let's take a look up that hill first."

"What for?" Peg asked.

"Well, for one, we ain't got nothing else to do. For another, I think I see somethin'."

"What?"

"Yeah, what do you see?" Davy said. "Somethin' to eat?"

"Just follow me and you'll find out."

Chapter 4

South of the Red River that separated the Oklahoma Territory from Texas, west of the Sabine that divided Louisiana and Texas, and east of the Brazos that threaded down toward Galveston and the Gulf of Mexico, somewhere where the devil stomped the dust off his boots, there was a place where even wolves didn't have much of a chance.

Somebody chanced to call it Gilead. Not all that far from where some other Bible thumper thought it appropriate to christen some other boghole Palestine.

Not even "New" Gilead or "New" Palestine. Whoever named these places apparently was trying to pass them off as the genuine article. And apparently some citizens didn't know the difference—or care.

In the depressed post–Civil War Texas, bled of men and money, all anybody cared about was surviving.

There were traces of snow scattered along the streets, signs, and rooftops. But the day was crisp and clear in Gilead.

Despite the economic depression, the townsfolk of

Gilead had not forgotten that it was the Christmas season. They reminded one another and whoever might pass through by nailing up Christmas banners, wreaths, and assorted decorations.

Let nothing you dismay, these Texans seemed to be saying. *We'll survive. We'll prevail. We're tough. We're Texans. No matter where we came from, Tennessee, Ohio, Arkansas, Missouri, or Kansas—we're Texans here and now—and here and now we'll stay until things get better.* And some added, *They can't get any worse.*

Shad Parker's wagon rolled through the main street of Gilead and stopped in front of Inghram's General Store on the corner. This was the center of town. On the other three corners were a bank, a saloon, and a hotel.

Just south of the main street there was a church, Methodist. Actually it was little more than the size of an ordinary house with a small steeple stuck on top of it. But the little steeple did have a bell.

There were a few more citizens than usual, doing what passed for Christmas shopping, with whatever passed for money; coins, currency, barter, but more often credit. The youngsters were on Christmas vacation from school and that added some to the people on the street and to the noise.

Only one man paid much attention to Shad Parker as his wagon rolled by and pulled to a stop.

Sheriff Elwood Hinge, whose office was next door to the bank, leaned back on a Douglas chair, carving a small Christmas tree out of a chunk of wood. Lying across the sheriff's lap was a shotgun.

Elwood Hinge knew how to use it. Just as important,

he knew *when* to use it. Not too soon—and not too late—at least not too late for himself.

He didn't move fast. He didn't move slow. But he moved when he had to. Even without the shotgun or the badge he was the sort of man who commanded attention. With the shotgun and the badge he commanded respect.

He wore a trail hat, a mackinaw, a flannel shirt, and wool vest with canvas pants, and Justin boots with three-inch heels. He also wore a .44.

Elwood Hinge had a frontier face with shoulders to match. His eyes were the color of a December morn and just as cold. He was born on the eleventh day, of the eleventh month, of the eleventh year of the nineteenth century.

Shad Parker wrapped the reins around the brake handle and alighted from the wagon. He walked around the team and headed for the entrance to Inghram's General Store. He paid no attention to anything or anybody on the street.

A boy of ten or twelve stood near the doorway to the store. Two men were working in front of the livery stable next door to Inghram's.

"Merry Christmas, mister," the boy greeted Shad. "Can I water your animals?"

The two men in front of the livery looked up from their work.

Shad looked at the boy for only a moment.

"No." Then he walked on, opened the door, and went into the store.

The two workmen at the livery went back to their

work. The boy sat on the stoop in front of the store and turned up the thin, threadbare collar of his coat.

Pete Inghram and his wife, Martha, were listening to Mrs. Hinshaw, a woman of bulk who was trying to decide between three bolts of material, one of which would become curtains for her parlor. Evidently she had been busy at deciding for quite some time while the Inghrams stood by feigning interest in the matter.

". . . Mr. Inghram," Mrs. Hinshaw went on, "if I do decide on the green, will you promise that you won't sell anybody else the green for their curtains? Will you?"

"Well, Mrs. Hinshaw, I don't know if I . . ."

"I don't want everybody in Gilead, specially Margie Lou Reynolds, coming in here buying the same curtains for their parlor just because . . ."

"Excuse me, Mrs. Hinshaw. Martha, you finish up with Mrs. Hinshaw while I take care of Mr. Parker."

Shad had entered the store and walked up to the counter past a decorated Christmas tree that stood in the center of the floor.

"Well, it's good to see you again, Mr. Parker. What can I do you for this Christmas season?"

For answer, Shad pulled out a piece of paper from his shirt pocket and put it on the counter.

Inghram was in his late forties, pale and somewhat stooped. He and his wife looked more like brother and sister, rather than husband and wife. Same color hair, brown. Same color eyes, brown. Same lips, thin. Same nose, parrot. Same complexion, pallid.

Pete Inghram picked up the paper, studied the list for a moment, then winked at Shad.

"Uh-huh. Not too many of us around these parts can read nor write." Inghram nodded in the direction of Mrs. Hinshaw toward the rear of the store and waited for a reaction from Shad. There was none.

Inghram pushed a box of cigars toward his customer and opened the lid.

"Care for a fine ceegar while you wait, Mr. Parker?"

"I'll be back." Shad turned away from the counter.

"Have it all loaded on your wagon in just a few minutes. Yes, sir."

Shad was halfway to the door.

"Say, I was wondering, Mr. Parker."

Shad stopped. The boy outside had left the stoop and was peering through the window. Shad looked at him for a second then turned back toward Inghram.

"Since you're settled here now, would you like me to start carrying you on my books? Carrying most everybody else around Gilead."

"I'll pay cash." Shad turned again and walked out of Inghram's General Store.

"Mister . . ." said the boy as Shad walked past, but Shad Parker kept on walking toward the saloon on the corner across the street.

The two men at the stable took note, but kept on working.

On the other side of the street Sheriff Elwood Hinge kept on carving.

"Mr. Parker. Oh, Mr. Parker!" The man's voice came from behind Shad, who stopped and glanced back.

A tall, thin, elderly man who somewhat resembled Abraham Lincoln and dressed somewhat like him in a black frock coat, but with a flat-crowned hat instead of a stovepipe, and without Abe's beard, approached. Close behind him, a brittle woman about the same age.

"Mr. Parker, I thought that was you," the man said in a voice that seemed too deep for his lung capacity. "I'm Reverend Groves. This is Mrs. Groves. Merry Christmas."

Shad said nothing.

"We've been meaning to come out and see you."

"'Bout what?"

"Oh." Reverend Groves looked at Mrs. Groves. "Just to welcome you. See if there's anything we can do."

"There isn't."

"We understand that you're going to be a part of our little community. I, uh, don't know your religious persuasion—we're mostly Methodists here—have a nice little church—fine organist, that's Mrs. Groves. And we'll have a mighty fine Christmas service—if you care to join us."

"I don't."

Shad walked toward the saloon. When Shad was out of earshot, Reverend Groves addressed Mrs. Groves.

"Doesn't appear to be a Methodist."

"Or even a Christian," said Mrs. Groves.

Just before he entered the Appaloosa Saloon, Shad noticed three familiar mounts tied to the hitching post. The three horses had been ridden by the men who had offered to help him with the fallen wagon wheel.

Shad went inside.

A curling haze of smoke from cigarettes, pipes,

cigars, and the potbellied stove sought to escape from the room, but there being no exit except for the brief times the door opened and closed, the smoke curled and settled against anything it could find, the bar, the tables, the posts and beams that held the room together, and the people, all men, who stood at the counter and sat at the tables playing cards.

The floor had not been swept from the night before nor the week before. However, the proprietor or someone else had chalked a MERRY CHRISTMAS on the mirror behind the bar. There was a crude painting of what passed for an Appaloosa horse on one of the dirty walls.

Some of the players looked from their cards as Shad entered, but most of them studied their hands and smoked.

Among the patrons who glanced up, noticing Shad Parker as he entered, were the Keeshaw brothers. Directly upon arriving in Gilead, Deek, Tom, and Bart had made for the town's only saloon. They did their best to avoid appearing to be too interested in the bank across the street, but took note of the man with the shotgun in front of the sheriff's office who sat in a chair with a catbird look in his eyes. They had seen that look before, usually on a lawman or a killer. Sometimes both.

They would address the lawman and the bank in due course, but first they had to reconnoiter adroitly and then plan their strategy.

The two places to find out anything in any town were the bar and the barbershop. The Keeshaws preferred the bar. Bedsides, Deek hadn't had a drink

since his incarceration. There was something else he
had done without and he didn't waste much time
before inquiring of the bartender, a man who went by
the name of "Hooter," where the saloon women were.
Hooter said there were only three in town and they
mostly worked at night, and this being December and
the Christmas season, they'd been putting in some
long hours.

Deek then proceeded to buy Hooter a drink and
make friendly. That's when Shad Parker walked in.

"Why, there he be!" Deek smiled at Hooter and
waved his pipe toward Shad. "The fella I was telling
you about! Lifted that wagon like it was a crate of
mushrooms. Never saw anything like it in Louisiana."
He nodded toward Shad. "Howdy, friend."

"Whiskey," Shad said to the bartender.

"That's on me," Deek instructed the man behind
the counter.

"No," said Shad.

"Well, I'd admire to buy you a drink."

"Why?"

Hooter put a bottle and a glass on the bar. Shad
poured and drank before Deek came up with an
answer.

"Just to be friendly."

"Be friendly with somebody else." Shad poured
again. He drank again.

There was a heavy moment. All the card players
and other customers had heard. Deek looked at
Tom and Bart, then smiled, shrugged, and puffed on
his pipe. It was over. The players went back to their

cards, the other customers to their drinks. And most all of them went back to smoking.

"Say, Hooter," Deek called out. "Come on down here a minute, will you?"

Hooter moved a couple of steps closer to the Keeshaws. Deek pointed toward the window and across the street.

"That the best hotel in town?"

"That's the only hotel in town."

"Then that's our home away from home till we find what we come looking for."

"What's that?" Hooter asked, not really caring much.

"My brothers and me are looking for a spread to buy."

"That so?"

"You bet. Know of anybody wanting to sell?"

"Was I you, I'd talk to Amos Bush."

"Who's Amos Bush?"

"Banker. Amos'ud know of anybody looking to sell."

"That sounds like a good notion. Thanks, friend."

Shad Parker had helped himself to a couple more shots. He wiped his mouth and motioned to the bartender. Hooter made the trip back.

"Yes, sir," he said.

"I'll want to take along some whiskey."

"Bottle?"

"Case."

"A case?"

"Yeah. Can't you sell whiskey by the case?"

"Why, sure I can."

"Then bring up a case."

"That'ud be thirty dollars."

Shad reached into his pocket and pulled out a roll of bills. Just about everybody in the Appaloosa, including the Keeshaw brothers, reacted. Many of the patrons hadn't seen that much money since the War for the Confederacy. Some since before, or ever.

"Bring it up."

Shad laid three bills on the bar then pointed to the bottle he'd drunk from.

"How much for this?"

"Oh, that's on the h . . ." The bartender started to say "on the house," but looked at Shad and changed his mind. "Six bits."

Shad Parker reached into another pocket and brought out a handful of coins.

Bart Keeshaw took the gold watch out of his vest pocket and sprang the lid open to see what time it was.

Sheriff Elwood Hinge glanced up as Shad came out of the Appaloosa carrying a case of whiskey under one arm with about as much effort as if it were a loaf of bread.

Since Shad bought his spread he had made more than a half-dozen trips to Gilead, but never a word had passed between him and the lawman. Neither went out of his way to avoid the other, but neither went out of his way to make the other's acquaintance. Sooner or later they'd meet up and as long as Shad Parker didn't violate any law, Elwood Hinge was in no hurry. If either man would give it much thought, he'd conclude that they had many of the same characteristics, but neither man gave it any thought.

Shad proceeded across the street toward his wagon

in front of the store, where Pete Inghram was just finishing the loading. The ten- or twelve-year-old boy was helping. The boy spotted Shad, jumped down from the wagon, and ran over to him.

"Can I hep ya with that, mister?"

Shad ignored the boy and proceeded to the wagon. He placed the case of whiskey in the bed with the other provisions that already had been loaded. Pete Inghram handed the piece of paper to Shad.

"Here's your list back, Mr. Parker. You'll see everything's checked off. Oh, I was all out of dry peas—gave you lentils instead. Hope that's all right."

"Yeah. How much?"

"It's right there on the paper. Totals to thirteen dollars and forty cent."

Shad reached into his pocket, took out the roll of bills, and handed a couple to the storekeeper.

"I'll get your change and be right out, Mr. Parker. Won't take but a minute."

Inghram went into the store. Shad walked to the wagon, reached in, drew out a whiskey bottle. He uncorked the bottle and took a long pull. The boy stood by, watching.

As Shad swallowed a second mouthful of whiskey Pete Inghram came out of the door with some money in hand and a grin pasted across his pallid face.

"Here you go, Mr. Parker, and if I don't see you before Christmas . . . Merry Christmas."

Shad took the money with one hand and stuffed it into his pocket. The boy's eyes were still fixed on Shad.

"What you looking at?"

"Oh. Some of the customers," Inghram said through the pasted smile, "give the boy a penny or two . . . sometimes."

"Not this time." Then Shad snapped at the boy. "Get away from me."

"Just a minute!" came a hard voice from the direction of the livery. The two workmen, Dutch and Bub, were looking toward Shad. Dutch had called out. First he, then Bub, moved toward Shad.

"No cause to talk to the young 'un that way," Dutch said as he came closer. He was bigger and heavier than Shad. So was Bub.

"Boys," Inghram interceded, "Mr. Parker didn't mean no harm."

"What did *Mister* Parker mean?" Dutch growled.

"Now, fellas," Inghram continued to play the part of peacemaker, "there's no need to take offense."

"There's no need for the likes of him to be talking that way to my boy."

"Yeah," Bub added. "That's right."

Shad took another drink then addressed Bub.

"He your boy, too?"

"Nephew," said Bub.

Shad Parker turned toward the wagon, but Dutch grabbed Shad's shoulder, or tried to.

"Don't you turn away . . ." Dutch never finished.

Shad crashed the whiskey bottle across Dutch's head. Blood, broken glass, and whiskey dripped from Dutch's face as he fell against the wagon. Bub rushed at Shad, swinging. Shad backhanded him with a brick fist, then picked Bub up and threw him through Pete Inghram's Christmas-decorated store window.

From inside Mrs. Inghram screamed.

Dutch had regained his equilibrium, most of it. He wiped the blood and broken glass and whiskey, most of it, from his face and lunged at Shad. But Shad gripped him by the shoulders and smashed him against the wall—once—twice—three times. It seemed that every bone in Dutch was, or would be, broken. By then the boy was pounding at Shad and screaming.

"You're killin' him! You're killin' my daddy! Let him go! Let go'a my daddy!!"

But again and again Shad smashed Dutch against the wall—until the stock of a shotgun slammed across Shad's skull, stunning him.

As Shad spun around, Dutch dropped to the ground. Shad was dazed but ready to fight. But he was looking directly into the barrel of a shotgun in the experienced hand of a man with a sheriff's badge. And beside the sheriff stood a deputy—young, tall, also leveling a shotgun, this one also double-barreled, but sawed-off.

And by now there were dozens of spectators gaping at the proceedings, but at a far enough distance until the show was played out.

"That's all, fella," the sheriff said.

Shad Parker wiped at the blood leaking from behind his ear. For an instant, it looked as if he might spring at the sheriff.

"Don't give it any more thought, brother," said Hinge.

The curious citizens clustered closer to get a better look, now that it appeared the danger had passed.

Among the interested were the Keeshaw brothers and most everyone else from the Appaloosa, including Hooter. They whispered in puddles and appraised the damage, human and property.

Shad walked toward his wagon and the onlookers allowed him a wide swath.

On the porch Mrs. Inghram pulled the crying boy away from his unconscious father and put her arms around him.

"For heaven's sake," she pleaded. "Someone get the doctor."

By then Shad had climbed onto the wagon. Pete Inghram came closer to him.

"Mr. Parker, I'm sorry this happened. But the boy didn't mean to bother you."

Shad reached into his pocket, brought out some money, crumpled it into a wad, and threw it on the ground near the storekeeper.

"Get your window fixed." He whacked the reins and the wagon horses moved out.

Inghram picked up the money and walked over near the sheriff and his deputy, who were watching Shad's wagon roll down the street.

"Elwood," the deputy asked, "shouldn't we have arrested him?"

"Didn't like the odds, from what I saw," the sheriff said, then looked at the men from the saloon. "Go about your drinking, boys. That's all there is."

Deek Keeshaw had made his way next to Inghram.

"That man's stronger'n Samson." Deek said.

"And meaner'n a gut-shot grizzly," Pete Inghram replied.

* * *

Not much later, inside the Appaloosa, Deek Keeshaw bought Hooter a couple more drinks and plied him for information that could be vital in their strategy, while Tom and Bart listened.

"That there sheriff, what's his name?"

"Name's Hinge. Elwood Hinge."

"Well, from what I've seen so far, I'd say that Sheriff Hinge has the situation pretty much in control in the town of Gilead."

"He's the boss around here and if you don't believe it, you can ask them two he clapped in his jail just a short time ago. They're waiting to be escorted outta here by a federal marshal, and Hinge'll get the reward. Rumor is, he's gonna give part of it to Yellow Rose."

"Who's Yellow Rose."

"One of the women here—at night. Octoroon, from New Orleans way. But they're the lucky ones."

"Who?"

"The two in jail. The other two who rode in with 'em weren't so lucky."

"Why?"

"They're dead."

"What happened?"

Hooter looked at the empty glass in front of him.

"Have another drink," Deek said.

"Don't mind." Hooter poured.

"What happened?" Deek repeated.

Hooter proceeded to relate the recent adventure. It turned out to be a four-drink story.

Less than two weeks ago four men rode into Gilead just before sundown. They drifted into the Appaloosa, ordered a bottle, sat at a table, and asked Hooter about women, while making it known that they had plenty of money to spend. Sheriff Hinge's deputy, Homer Keeler, chanced to be there at the time. Deputy Keeler studied the strangers without making it obvious, then went across the street to Sheriff Hinge's office.

Yellow Rose, who would be a good-looking woman anywhere, and no doubt the best-looking woman in Gilead, was just walking out of Elwood's door. Homer had never seen her in the office before but returned her greeting without thinking much about it. He had other business on his mind.

"Elwood," Homer said with fervor, "you know who I think rode into town? Sitting in the Appaloosa right now?"

Sheriff Hinge said nothing.

"Elwood, you hear what I said? I said, do you know who's sitting in the Appaloosa right now?"

Sheriff Hinge pointed to four dodgers spread on the desk in front of him. The four wanted posters included names, drawings, and descriptions of four men wanted dead or alive for murder and bank robbery. Five hundred dollars each man. The leader was Frank Chase. The others were Red Borden and the two Reno Brothers, Johnsy and Charlie.

"How'd you know?" Homer was a little disappointed that he hadn't been the one to bring the news, but he was still excited. "Yellow Rose tell you?"

"Nope. Spotted 'em when they rode in."

"You spotted 'em from clear over here in the near-dark?"

"Homer, that's my job. I see the faces on every dodger we got in my dreams."

"Well, what are we gonna do?"

"We're gonna do our job. Bring 'em to their milk—and collect the reward. Dead or alive."

"You and me?"

"That's right, Homer. You and me. With a little help from a friend. Now, sit down, check your weapons, and listen . . ."

Homer Keeler sat down, checked his weapons, and listened.

Half an hour later all the lamps were turned off in the sheriff's office. Hinge and Keeler stood in the darkness and looked out across the street as Stella Bright, the homeliest of the three saloon women, walked unsteadily out of the Appaloosa's door with Charlie Reno's arm around her shoulder. Though Elwood and Homer couldn't hear her, she told Charlie she needed some fresh air before they went upstairs, then proceeded to vomit all over his boots. She excused herself, saying she had to go see the doc, and walked away. Stella Bright could make herself vomit anytime she wanted to.

Charlie Reno stomped his boots a few times and went back into the saloon. At the same time a buxom silhouette in the upstairs window of the Appaloosa moved a lamp away from the window and farther into the room. The silhouette belonged to Yellow Rose.

That was the signal.

With their badges out of sight beneath their coats,

Sheriff Elwood Hinge and Deputy Homer Keeler walked toward the Appaloosa, armed.

They entered from the kitchen and nodded at Hooter. Hooter took a fresh bottle of whiskey over to Borden and Charlie Reno, who sat at a table by themselves. Frank Chase was the leader and Johnsy Reno came second in the pecking order, so Frank had first call on Yellow Rose and Johnsy got Francine Needle, who was an obvious choice over Stella Bright.

Since Stella had bowed out, Charlie, who was third in the pecking order, had to sit down with Borden and wait his turn.

"This bottle's on the house," Hooter said to Charlie Reno and Red Borden, as he set it on the table in front of them. "Help yourselves till your friends are finished upstairs."

As Charlie and Red turned their attention to the fresh bottle, each of them was slammed across the back of the head by the butts of separate shotguns. Each was cuffed with their hands behind their backs, gagged, even though both were out cold, and relieved of their sidearms, which were given to Hooter, who in turn handed Elwood and Homer a key apiece.

Nobody in the place said a word as Elwood and Homer walked up the stairs.

Two keys turned in two locks. Two doors opened. Two naked men sprang for their holsters as two naked women rolled out of bed away from the open doors. There were blasts from two shotguns. Two men, Frank Chase and Johnsy Reno, died.

The other two, Red Borden and Charlie Reno,

were still in jail behind Sheriff Elwood Hinge's office waiting for a federal marshal.

That was the end of Hooter's four-drink story.

Deek, Tom, and Bart Keeshaw drank up their drinks and thought things over.

Chapter 5

It was almost dark as Shad Parker drove his wagon within sight of the NO TRESPASSING sign on the post in front of his property.

For an instant he had thought of lunging at the sheriff, who would have had no choice but to squeeze the trigger on the shotgun and blow the life out of his attacker.

That would have broken it to a finish. It would have been over, ended. The strife, the memories, the pain.

But he hadn't lunged. Something held him back. What?

Was he somehow punishing himself? Or was it because no matter how cruel the strife, how bad the memories, how deep the pain, the truth is that every living, breathing thing wants to go on living and breathing?

If he couldn't bring himself to end his life, why hadn't he let the sheriff do it for him?

The blood had now matted into his hair and dried along his neck. The blow from the sheriff's shotgun probably would leave a scar. One more visible scar to go with all the others his body had suffered, and with the scars that were not visible.

Alone again, Shad began to unload the provisions from the wagon. But he was not exactly alone. As the sun dropped beneath the rim of the hill, three young faces peered through the gathering darkness from the opening of a cave that nature long ago had carved high near the crest.

Austin, Peg, and Davy watched until it was too dark to make out the figure of a man they had never met.

Not yet.

Chapter 6

Shad Parker sat like a colossal stone statue in the big chair facing the fireplace. In his grasp, a whiskey bottle half-empty. He stared at the crackling blue and yellow flames, as he had done so many nights before, until the fire burned itself out and the memories burned deeper.

Some nights the visions of Molly and the children prevailed. Those were the worst times, and other nights, nights such as this, the battlefield of his mind recalled the bloody battlefields that claimed the men of blue and gray and smeared and seared them both with red.

Geography and fate destined the Shenandoah Valley to be among the bloodiest of battlefields. The valley, more than 150 miles long and 10 to 20 miles wide, was nourished by the Shenandoah River, winding 170 miles, rising in two main forks, flowing northeastward, uniting near Front Royal and then onward to the Potomac at Harper's Ferry. The Virginia valley, rich in farmlands, orchards, and pastures, between the Blue Ridge on the east and the Alleghenies on the west, was a region of varied scenery and natural wonders.

Unfortunately, it was also the ideal avenue of approach between the forces of the North and South. The Shenandoah Valley was the passport to victory or defeat for both sides.

Ironically, many of the generals from both sides were Virginians; most prominent of those who chose to fight for the Confederacy were Robert E. Lee, Joseph E. Johnston, and Thomas "Stonewall" Jackson. But not a few Virginians remained loyal to the Union, including Winfield Scott, George H. Thomas, and David G. Farragut.

Thomas Jonathan Jackson had served with distinction under Winfield Scott in the Mexican War, then from 1851 to 1861 taught at the Virginia Military Institute. In May of 1861 he was given a brigade in Johnston's army and made a Confederate brigadier general. Shad Parker was part of that brigade.

At the First Battle of Bull Run, Jackson's stand earned him the sobriquet "Stonewall" and a promotion to major general. Lieutenant Shad Parker was with him and earned a promotion to captain. Captain Parker was also with Stonewall Jackson when they routed Banks at Front Royal and Winchester, driving him across the Potomac.

And Parker was with Jackson and the famous "Foot Cavalry" against Pope late in August 1862, which set the stage for the crushing victory at the Second Battle of Bull Run, and in the Antietam campaign, and helped seal Lee's victory at Harper's Ferry.

But Shad Parker was also with Stonewall Jackson at Chancellorsville, where Jackson, in the coarse darkness, was mortally wounded by the fire of his own men. Major Parker helped to bury his fallen commander, then joined General Jubal A. Early at Cold Harbor.

Jubal Anderson Early, another Virginian, graduate of West Point, Indian fighter against the Seminoles in Florida, and veteran of the Mexican campaign, studied law and practiced at Rocky Mount, Virginia. Early had voted against secession at the Virginia Convention in April 1861, but when war broke out he accepted a commission as colonel in the Virginia troops. He won victories and promotions at Salem Church, in the Wilderness Campaign, and defeated Lew Wallace in the Battle of Monocacy.

Parker was with him when Early burned Chambersburg after the Pennsylvania town refused to pay a ransom.

In September of 1864 General Philip H. Sheridan moved against Early at Winchester and Fisher's Hill, driving Early, with Parker, deep into the valley, and at Cedar Creek what was left of their small force was overwhelmed and broken by General George Custer of Sheridan's army.

That opened the way for Sheridan's holocaust. Philip H. Sheridan was a small man, with the largest part of his head forward of his ears. He was restless, combative, and not politic in language. He had the reputation of being sharp and peppery, a self-reliant man of courage and decision. He had decided that in order to end the war the Shenandoah Valley had to be destroyed. He made rubble of the principal towns, Winchester, Front Royal, Luray, Staunton,

Waynesboro, and Lexington and laid waste the fertile countryside.

In his report Sheridan stated "even a crow flying over the Shenandoah would have to bring his rations with him."

General Philip Henry Sheridan was not prone to exaggeration.

The flame in the fireplace had burned out. The empty bottle had fallen from Shad Parker's hand.

This night he had fallen asleep.

Chapter 7

It was still dark when Shad awoke. Predawn, December-morning dark. Reb, the rooster, had not yet cackled reveille. The cabin squatted peaceful and silent, soaking up the night juices.

The time of the night creatures—the owl, the bat, the possum, and the raccoon—more mysterious and arcane than the daylight denizens—was nearly done. They had crept and crawled, flown and hunted—and were hunted. The survivors had filled their stomachs and were returning to their daylight sleeping places, to rest the day and return to the business of survival another night.

Soon the day creatures would stir, cat and bird, bird and insect, snake and rodent, fish and worm, and every hunter with tooth and claw would begin the daily adventure of eating and avoiding being eaten.

To these hunters every day was the same, a dangerous game of life or death. But the nights were longer and colder in autumn and winter.

Shad knew it was close to Christmas. He didn't know exactly how close, nor did he want to know.

Holidays and other special days—anniversaries, birthdays, and the like—only boiled up the memories and heated up the hurt. He seldom if ever looked at a calendar. He didn't keep one in the house. He didn't want to be reminded of the dates that he and Molly and later, the boys, celebrated together. His and her birthdays, Christmas, Easter, Thanksgiving, the Fourth of July, the day they were married—the thirtieth of June—the days that the two boys, Sean and Shannon, were born—the twenty-first of March and the first of October—two and three years later.

He wanted all the days remaining in his lifetime to be the same, just the same as are the grains of sand in an hourglass—and just as indistinguishable. He wished his life were an hourglass, that he could turn it over just once and watch the grains drop into the bulge below—and know how much time he had left, instead of waiting and wondering how many times the hand of fate would turn over the hourglass of his life while he endured, until that inevitable, merciful hour.

For the first time in three days Shad Parker washed and shaved. As Reb roused the feathered inhabitants of his domain, Shad walked shirtless across the chill, first light of the farm to the well with soap, razor, and towel in hand and used them in that order after he brought up a bucket of stone-cold water from twenty feet below.

He washed his face and hair, getting rid of the dried blood on both. Then shaved without benefit of mirror, with the long-since unsharpened razor causing more blood to appear on his cheek and throat. He soaked the soap and water and blood from his face with the towel, then hung it out to dry in the clear, cold light of dawn.

After collecting the daily quota of eggs, Shad scrambled up four of them and fried six fat strips of bacon that he had sliced. The coffee was black and strong, the last two cups laced with a couple dollops of whiskey. Then Shad began the day's work.

Austin had heard Reb's wake-up call. He rubbed the sleep from his eyes and took a second or two to recollect just where it was that they had slept. In fact, Peg and Davy were still sleeping, huddled close together facing the jagged wall of the sheltering cave.

In the days and weeks since they had run away from the Faith, Hope, and Charity Orphanage under the command of old Miss Stritch, Peg, Davy, and Austin had slept most of the nights without roof, except for a couple of barns and twice under wagons. The thought of old Miss Stritch sent a chill through Austin's already chilled bones.

"Old Miss Stench" is what the kids called her— but not when she was within earshot—or "smellshot" as they sometimes said, also out of earshot. She was a string-thin old woman who appeared brittle, but was stone hard and with a voice like scratching chalk. She was seldom seen without a yardstick that she seldom used to measure anything except the number

of whacks some wayward child could endure before
tears would appear.

Old Miss Stritch had aversions to children and
bathing, so naturally she was put in charge of the orphanage by her brother Silas, the mayor of Palestine.
Old Miss Stritch was not yet forty, but to the children
of the orphanage, most of whom were not yet ten, she
was an old woman—a smelly, mean, old woman. Her
hairline was well above the upper curve of her forehead and the bone of her skull shone through the
frizzled palomino-colored fuzz that poked out of her
head.

Old Miss Stritch, being a "miss," of course never
had any children of her own. That being the case, it
was a puzzlement to all the children at the orphanage
how she came to dislike other people's children so
much. She seemed to go out of her way to find fault
with the "inmates," as she called them, and to make
corrections with the ever-present yardstick. She had a
knack for finding bare skin with that yardstick even
in the wintertime when the inmates wore heavier
clothes. She managed to whack uncovered arms,
necks, and the sides of little skulls, sometimes apply-
ing punishment to two inmates simultaneously.

Even though it was obvious that she felt no affection for her little charges, she seemed to resist letting
them go. Several times she had talked potential adop-
tive parents out of going through with the adoptions.
Once Austin was sure that a nice-looking couple,
Mr. and Mrs. Ketchum, had made up their minds to
take him and Peg and Davy home with them, until
old Miss Stritch had a long talk in private with the

Ketchums, then they left the orphanage without even saying good-bye.

Another time a couple seemed willing to adopt all three and after conversing with old Miss Stritch they decided they wanted only Austin—until he made such a commotion, even acting crazy, talking gibberish, and pulling out his hair, so they changed their mind about him, too.

Finally the children figured out that old Miss Stritch was protecting her job. If there were no orphans, there would be no orphanage, and if there were no orphanage, there would be no place for old Miss Stritch to work, so she had to keep enough inmates at Faith, Hope, and Charity to keep the orphanage operating.

Faith, Hope, and Charity wasn't all bad. There was food enough, such as it was, and in the winter there were blankets, worn as they were, and also there was Mrs. Grady, a widow who volunteered to teach the children to read and write and do their sums. And best of all to tell stories about knights and dragons and the magic kingdom, where, at the end of each story things would always come right and everybody lived happy ever after.

But there wasn't much happy ever after with old Miss Stench around, and after she whacked Davy again with the yardstick, this time busting his lip because he was slumping in his seat, Austin decided that they had had enough and the three of them took off in the middle of a moonless winter night.

Somewhere there must be a better place for the three of them. Davy kept asking if they were going to find the magic kingdom. Both Peg and Austin avoided a direct answer. And now it was nearly Christmas and the three of them had spent the night in a cave without food or blankets.

Davy woke up cold and crying.

Peg's arm was around him, her other hand wiping the tears from his cheeks.

"It's all right, Davy, don't cry. We're all here together and everything's all right. Did you have a bad dream?"

Davy nodded.

"Well, it was just a dream. Nothing bad's going to happen. See, Austin's right over there and we're way far away from old Miss Stench and pretty soon we're going to find a place to stay and stay together. Isn't that so, Austin?"

Austin nodded, but not very emphatically.

"I'm hungry." Davy ran the back of his hand across his eyes. "We didn't have no supper."

"Didn't have *any* supper."

"That's what I said."

"Look what I got." Austin pulled an object out of one of his pockets.

"What?" Davy asked.

"What's it look like?" Austin held the object closer to Davy.

"Looks like a potato."

"Yep, that's what it is, all right. It's also breakfast."

"A potato for breakfast?" Davy questioned.

"Sure. People eat potatoes for breakfast all the time."

"How you going to cook it?" Davy inquired. "We don't have no fire."

"Not going to cook it." Austin then pulled a pocket-knife from another pocket. Knives weren't allowed at the orphanage, but Austin had managed to hide it from old Miss Stench. "Going to peel it and eat it raw. Tastes good."

"It does?" Davy wondered.

"Sure it does. Pa used to eat raw potatoes all the time . . . before you were born . . . Didn't he, Peg?"

Peg hesitated.

"Didn't he, Peg? Before Davy was born, didn't Pa used to eat raw potatoes? You remember." Austin nodded toward Davy.

"I guess." Peg nodded, also not too emphatically.

"Sure he did." Austin started to peel.

"Austin?" Peg looked at the potato.

"What?"

"Where'd you get it?"

"Get what?"

"The potato."

"Oh, that. Well, Mr. Jones give it to me . . . for us . . . just before he left . . ."

"Austin . . ."

"Well, actually it was that night, after you and Davy went to sleep. He said him and the Indian had rifles and cartridges to hunt food with and since we didn't . . . have any rifles and cartridges, that is . . . he give me the potato and . . ."

"Austin . . ."

"Well, he would've . . . if he'd thought about it. Here. Eat." Austin had finished peeling and had cut the potato into three slices. He gave a slice each to

Peg and Davy and took a bite out of the third slice. "It's good. Eat."

Peg and Davy took tentative bites from their share of the potato. The potato was cold and crisp and didn't taste bad at all.

"You know," Austin added as he chewed, "when it comes right down to it you can eat the peels, too . . . sometimes Pa used to do that . . . eat the peels and all. You bet."

Peg took another bite from her slice of the potato and said nothing further on the subject.

Shad Parker's rifle leaned against a rock. Shad swung the pickax sure and deep into the hard brown earth near a large, sharp-cornered stone. He pulled the blade loose from the clinging ground, raised up the pickax in a smooth, powerful motion over the arches of his shoulders, and sliced down again near the half-buried rock.

From the field he intended to cultivate, he had, for days and weeks, and for almost two hours this day, unearthed a great many rocks, varying in size from cantaloupes to boulders. He swung the pickax again and again. Then took up the shovel stuck in the ground nearby and dug around the rock.

Shad stooped, reached out his oversize hands, grasped at the stone, his fingers clinging like claws, pulling at it with brute strength, until the rock was torn loose from the earth, and rolled it over, exposing in the gaping ground a community of hundreds of worms, crawling crazily all over one another, seeking shelter from the menace of the naked light.

Shad Parker picked up the shovel and the pickax and moved on to the next half-buried rock. He stabbed the shovel into the ground and started swinging the pickax near the base of the rock. Then abruptly he stopped his work and listened. The sound came from a nearby tree. The plaintive song of a male and female dove.

Shad stood motionless for just a moment. He reached down, picked up a stone, and hurled it at the tree in a single, continuous motion. The stone whistled through the branches, terrifying the doves and sending them flying into the somber sky.

Shad Parker went back to his task.

Concealed from Shad's view, just inside the cave, Austin watched as the man worked below. Austin had been watching for the better part of an hour, trying to make up his mind what to do. A couple of times he had made up his mind to approach the stranger, but there was something about the way that the man wielded the pickax, even the shovel, that scared Austin.

"Austin."

He turned toward Peg's voice. She and Davy stood just behind him.

"Austin, are we going to stay up here all day?"

"No, we're not. But you two are."

"What do you mean?"

"I mean, you two stay up here till I get back."

"Where you going?"

"I'm going out to see what I can find."

"Find something to eat," said Davy. "'Cause I'm not going to eat them peels."

"You won't have to. And I'll get us some matches so we can build a fire."

"You going to talk to the man who owns the farm?" Peg asked.

"Nope. Goin' in a different direction. Keep outta his sight. When he goes inside, gather up some branches, anything that'll burn. I'll be back soon as I can."

Chapter 8

At midmorning Tom and Bart were on the porch of the Eden Hotel, Tom sitting on the rail and Bart leaning against a post, as Deek, stuffing tobacco from a pouch into his pipe, walked out through the lobby door.

"Morning, boys," Deek greeted his brothers, struck a match against a post, and lit up.

The "boys" just continued to look across the street. They were looking at Sheriff Elwood Hinge, who sat on a Douglas chair, carving the small Christmas tree out of a chunk of wood, with the shotgun lying across his lap.

Somehow all three Keeshaws had the feeling that even though the sheriff wasn't looking in their direction, he was aware of their presence. It appeared that Sheriff Elwood Hinge was aware of just about everything and everybody that fell under his jurisdiction. That had become even more apparent after last night.

When Hooter had finished his four-drink story

about Sheriff Hinge, Yellow Rose and the four strangers—two living and two deceased—the Kee-shaws checked into the Eden Hotel. As Deek was signing the registry on behalf of his brothers and himself, a woman walked across the lobby and up the stairs. All three Keeshaws stared at the woman from the time she entered the door until she was out of sight at the top of the stairway.

"Is that who I think it is?" Deek Keeshaw inquired of the man behind the counter.

"Depends, Mr. . . ." The man looked at the names on the registry. ". . . Keeshaw."

"Depends on what?" Deek smiled.

"Depends on just *who* you think it is. By the way, my name's Mr. Peevy. I'm the owner of Eden." From a distance Mr. Peevy had the appearance of a well-dressed scarecrow. From closer up his appearance didn't change much.

"Glad to know you, Mr. Peevy—nice place you've got here. I thought from Hooter's description, that might be Yellow Rose."

"Might be."

"She's a mighty fine-lookin' . . . woman."

"Not much doubt about that."

"Works over at the Appaloosa, ol' Hooter said."

"That's right, too."

"I was just wonderin' . . ."

"What?" Mr. Peevy arched a pencil-thin eyebrow.

"Well, if you could arrange . . . you know . . . for me to go up and . . ."

"And what?"

"And pay her a visit up to her room."

"In the first place I ain't in that business. In the

second place *Miss Rosalind DuPree lives* here, *Yellow Rose works* at the Appaloosa. You'll have to make your arrangements over there. *When* she's receiving. But Miss DuPree don't receive no visitors at Eden."

"I didn't know the rules, Mr. Peevy."

"You do now, Mr. Keeshaw." Mr. Peevy shoved a set of keys at Deek. "Room 216. I hope the three of you'll be comfortable."

Deek Keeshaw smiled again and took the keys, started to walk away, but turned back.

"Mr. Peevy. They say that for every rule there's an exception."

"Who's 'they'?"

Deek Keeshaw shrugged and walked toward the stairs. Tom and Bart followed.

After dark the Keeshaws had gone back to the Appaloosa. It was Deek's intention to visit Yellow Rose during working hours. He stopped by the barbershop, had a haircut and shave, and told Tony the barber to pour on the toilet water. Tony did. Then Deek walked over to the Appaloosa and joined his brothers, who were at a table, sharing a bottle of rye.

It was still relatively early. Francine Needle and Stella Bright stood at separate tables doing the best they could to display their visible means of support, while watching separate poker games. As Deek swallowed his second shot of rye, Yellow Rose walked down the stairs.

She had done the same, for many, many nights at just about the same time, and the reaction all those nights, and tonight, was the same. Everyone in the

Appaloosa turned away from his drink or his cards or his conversation and watched as Yellow Rose walked.

Yellow Rose didn't exactly walk. It was almost a sort of flotation. She seemed to glide, from her narrow waist downward to the swelling of her hips and upward to the canopies of her breasts and the broad, clean curves of her naked shoulders. She had deep, dark dovelike eyes, scarlet-ribboned lips, though not much makeup, a straight, classic nose, and an expressionless face that defied anyone to guess what she was really thinking. Her skin was a warm, cream color and her soft hair dark as a raven's wing.

Her eyes swept the silent room. Defiance. Disdain. Then the slight trace of a smile, the sort of smile a royal feels obliged to bestow. A nod acknowledging their adulation, but telling them it was time to go back to their common business.

They did. Drinks, cards, and conversation.

All except Deek Keeshaw. He had never seen a woman as compelling as this. He was about to rise when two gunshots rang out just in front of the Appaloosa and glass shattered.

Now all eyes including Deek's were fixed on the batwings. Two men slammed through. The first was big, bearded, and dirty. The second was almost as big, beardless, and almost as dirty. Both were just about as drunk.

The first man, Pete Tillashut, held a gun in his hand. The second man, Willard Krantz, held an almost-empty whiskey bottle.

"Evenin', folks," Tillashut boomed, waving the .44. "Name's Tillashut, Pete Tillashut. This here's ol'

Willard Krantz. Me and ol' Will just spent three months up on a line shack for the Bar 9. Ain't seen nothin' human in more'n ninety days and nights. Got three months' pay and a powerful cravin' for whiskey, and . . . well, well, well . . ."

Tillashut was looking at Yellow Rose. Up and down.

"You want to stay in here," Hooter barked from behind the bar, "put that gun away, Tillashut."

"Sure, sure, sure," Tillashut grinned, "just havin' a little fun." But the gun stayed in his hand. "Speakin' of fun," he walked closer to Yellow Rose, "you got to be Yellow Rose. Some of the boys at the Bar 9 was singin' your praises."

Yellow Rose looked at the dirty man and said nothing.

"I'll say this," Tillashut pointed at her with his left hand, "they didn't exaggerate none. You're prime cut if I ever seen it."

"Tillashut!" Hooter called from the bar.

"Bring out a bottle there, bartender," Tillashut kept looking at Yellow Rose, "me and ol' Yellow Rose is goin' to have a drink . . . for openers."

"No, we're not." She spoke softly, but everyone heard. There was a moment of silence. Then Tillashut laughed.

"Sure, we are, honey. You know how much money I got in my pocket?"

"Not enough," said Yellow Rose.

No one had seen him come in, but Elwood Hinge stood inside the batwings.

"You," said Hinge. "Loudmouth."

Both Tillashut and Krantz turned toward the voice at the entrance.

"Leather that gun. For openers."

"Who're you?" Tillashut grimaced.

"Name's Hinge. Elwood Hinge."

"That don't mean nothin'." Tillashut looked at his companion. "Does it, Krantz?"

Krantz emptied the whiskey bottle and set it on a table.

"It will," said Hinge.

Silence.

"Now, first off, you're going to holster that hogleg. Then you're going to pay for the damage outside. Then you and that donkey next to you are going to mount up and ride in any direction you choose. But ride out, you will."

"Maybe I got a different mind."

"Change it." Hinge walked, not fast, not slow, closer to Tillashut.

Almost imperceptibly, Tillashut's gun hand began to rise.

"Lift that hand another inch and I'll kill you."

"With what?" Tillashut grinned.

The sheriff's gun was still in its holster as Tillashut's right hand started to rise. It never got above his belt.

Hinge had drawn and he slammed the barrel in one sure stroke across Tillashut's forehead, then the gun was pointing at Krantz before Tillashut hit the floor.

"All right, donkey. Left hand. Lift it out and put it on that table."

Krantz followed instructions.

Hinge stooped, rolled Tillashut on his back, took

a wad of money out of his pocket, selected a couple of bills, and handed the rest to Krantz.

"Now, drag him out, mount him on his animal, and ride in any direction you choose. You hear?"

"Ye-yess," Krantz stammered. "Yes, sir."

Again, Krantz followed instructions, much to the amusement of the saloon spectators. Then they went back to their drinks and cards and conversation.

Hinge walked close to Yellow Rose.

"Evening, Rose."

Rose nodded and smiled. Her right hand held a pearl-handled derringer.

"Care for a drink?" Hinge inquired.

"No, thanks," she said. "But you can walk me home. Think I'll call it a night."

"Yes, ma'am."

After Hinge and Yellow Rose left the Appaloosa, Deek Keeshaw had to be content with the companionship of Francine Needle, but as he looked across the street this midmorning, he couldn't help wondering about Yellow Rose and Hinge and the old saying about "an exception to every rule." Deek's thought was interrupted by the sound of Tom's voice.

"I don't like it."

"You don't like what, Tom?"

"The setup."

"You like money, don't you?"

"Sure, but . . ."

"But what? You didn't think they were just going to hand it to us like a Christmas present, did you?"

"No, but . . ."

"You're full up with 'buts' this morning. We'll get what we come for."

"Sure, but . . . I mean . . . all day long either him or his deputy sitting there cradling a scattergun. And you seen how he can handle himself."

"I seen."

"Deek," Bart spoke for the first time.

"What? You got some 'buts,' too?"

"Hell no. You're the boss."

"That's reassuring."

"I was just wondering," Bart said, "what do you think we ought to do? Can't just stand around all day long. People, specially that there sheriff, will go to wondering what we're here for."

"You're right, Bart. We're going to take care of that right now."

"How?" Bart asked.

"We're going to walk over and talk to Amos Bush." Deek strolled off the porch of the Eden Hotel. Tom and Bart followed.

The foot and horse traffic in Gilead was about the same as it had been yesterday and so was the weather. The same chill and the same remnants of snow scattered along the streets, signs, and rooftops. As nearly as the Keeshaws could tell, the same people as the day before, no strangers. Not since the two last night.

Deek nodded and smiled at several of the townspeople as they passed, even greeted some with a "merry Christmas" and they greeted him back. Tom and Bart also nodded and smiled but let Deek do all the verbal greeting.

These were the good citizens who had put their

trust and money in Amos Bush's bank. If the Keeshaws had their way it wouldn't be a very happy New Year for Bush or his depositors after the three brothers left town.

Deek had heard about Amos Bush's bank from a former resident of Gilead whom he had met in prison. The former resident, Gotch Hill, had planned to return to Gilead, either when he had served his sentence or managed to escape, and relieve the bank of all its liquid assets. Gotch had sought to enlist Deek in the scheme, because of Deek's self-proclaimed ability with dynamite. Deek had listened and agreed to participate. But Gotch Hill neither served his sentence nor did he escape. He died from a knife wound in his liver. His murder was never solved and not much mourned.

When Deek rejoined his brothers he decided to dedicate the campaign to the memory of Gotch Hill as they drank a toast to the enterprise.

And now here they stood, directly in front of the bank, whose door was adorned with a Christmas wreath.

Just when it seemed Deek was about to reach for the knob, he paused, glanced toward Elwood Hinge as if he had noticed him for the first time that day, and beamed a broad, friendly smile and walked toward the lawman. Tom and Bart followed.

"Howdy, Sheriff."

"Howdy." Hinge looked up from his carving as if he had noticed the Keeshaw brothers for the first time that day.

"Chill in the air," said Deek.

"Not unusual this time of year."

"Uh-huh," Deek responded, then glanced toward Inghram's General Store, where two workmen were replacing the window. "Had a little excitement around here yesterday."

"A little."

"I see they're patching up the place."

"Yep."

"How're them two fellas," Deek pointed toward the livery stable, which was closed, "feeling?"

"Poorly."

"Yeah, I expect they are."

Silence.

"Had some excitement last night, too," said Deek.

"Some."

"You surely laid one on that Tillashut."

"Just as hard as I could."

"Could've been worse, I guess. You could've shot him."

"No need to."

It was evident that the sheriff didn't have anything else to say. He went back to his carving.

Deek looked at his brothers a moment, then back to Elwood Hinge.

"We need to talk to Amos Bush." Deek pointed toward the entrance to the bank. "Know if he's in?"

"He's in."

"Much obliged." Deek started a step back but paused. "Deek Keeshaw. My brothers, Tom and Bart."

"Yep."

"And you're Mr. Hinge. Elwood Hinge."

The sheriff nodded.

"Been sheriff here long?"

"Not too long."

"We're thinkin' on settling here, me and my brothers."

Deputy Homer Keeler, carrying his sawed-off scattergun, came out of the office door.

"There's worse places," Hinge replied to Deek.

Deek Keeshaw smiled and walked toward the bank. Tom and Bart followed.

Elwood Hinge rose and brushed the shavings from his pants. Deputy Keeler assumed possession of the chair.

"Worse places than where?" Keeler asked.

"Gilead," Hinge replied.

Deputy Keeler seemed like he was thinking that over.

"Prisoners et?"

"They et."

The sheriff removed a kerchief from his rear pocket and blew his nose.

"Where?" Keeler asked.

"Where what?"

"Where's a worse place?"

"Ever been to O'Donnel?"

"Been there and back."

Sheriff Hinge nodded with satisfaction and walked into his office. As he proceeded toward the chair behind his rolltop desk, a voice called out from one of the cells in the back.

"Sheriff, is that you?" The voice belonged to Charlie Reno.

"It's me."

"Come on back here."

"What for?"

"Let me out."

"When the federal marshal gets here, you'll get out."

"I mean, I need to go to the outhouse."

"Use the chamber pot."

"It's near full. I got to go out and take a dump."

"You eat too much."

"I mean it, Sheriff. I got to go."

"You'll go later."

"How much later?"

"When the deputy comes in."

"When'll that be?"

"Before supper."

Sheriff Elwood Hinge took the four dodgers stacked on his desk and pinned them back onto the bulletin board. Frank Chase, Red Borden, and the Reno brothers, Johnsy and Charlie. Two men living and two deceased. But dead or alive worth a total of two thousand dollars on the hoof.

Hinge had been a lawman for a long time and had collected other rewards. But this would be the biggest payday of his life. Enough to do just about anything he wanted.

Trouble was, he wasn't sure just what he wanted.

The orange December sun was nearly noon high in its winter arc above Shad Parker's farm.

Without stopping even for drink of water or thought of time, he had labored with pickax and shovel and with the grip of his powerful hands to wrest from the stubborn earth the stones that had in scores and scores of years become a part of it, the barren, brown, unforgiving Texas earth, bleached by a white-hot sun in summer, numbed by the cold bleak nights of winter.

How unlike the rich, dark, fertile soil of Virginia Shad Parker and his family before him had worked with care and pride for more than a century.

The Parkers of Virginia.

There were Parkers there ever since there was a Virginia. And there was a Virginia before there was a United States. Virginia played a large part in the creation of the United States. Washington, Jefferson, Madison, Henry, Monroe. Would there have been a Declaration of Independence, a Constitution, a United States without them?

Since the birth of Virginia and the United States the Parkers had been there. Farmers and fighters. Soldiers of the soil. Parkers had fought and bled and died in the French and Indian War, the Revolution, the War of 1812, the Mexican campaign, and in the carnage of the War for the Confederacy. With Wolfe, Washington, Jackson, Scott, and finally Lee, always in the ranks there had been one or more Parkers bearing arms, sometimes far away, but returning always, those who survived, to their Shenandoah Valley in Virginia.

But as he toiled this day near noon Shad Parker knew that he would never go back. Someday the scabs would fall and the scars would fade. Someday the valley would bloom and bear fruit and flower and leaf. Someday the farmers of the Shenandoah again would work the land with care and pride. For some, that work already had begun. But not for Shad Parker.

Shad Parker would dig into the hardscrabble earth of Texas and curse the fate and cause that killed his wife and children and spared him. But now he had stopped the digging and thought again—he knew not for how long—of three graves far away—until he felt a presence.

Shad looked up and saw the tall, lean man with musing eyes, sitting on a mule.

"You all right, mister?" the man inquired.

Shad looked at the man on the mule but didn't answer.

"You looked, well, I don't know," the man said. "You looked like you was about to faint . . . or somethin'. You all right?" the man repeated.

Shad nodded.

"Well, that bein' the case . . ." the man on the mule pointed toward the NO TRESPASSING sign ". . . I'll move on." The man's heels lightly nudged the ribs of the mule.

"Just a minute."

The man held back the mule and turned his face toward Shad.

"You . . . you need to water your mule?"

The man's expression changed into a near-smile.

"No, thanks. Just stopped by the creek a ways back. But thanks anyway, and . . . merry Christmas."

Shad Parker did not answer.

The man on the mule moved east toward Gilead.

Shad watched for a moment, wiped the cold sweat from his face, stuck the pickax and the shovel into the ground, picked up his rifle from a nearby rock, then walked toward the cabin and his noon meal.

From the hillside above, but hidden near the face of the cave, Peg and Davy watched as the man went inside the cabin and closed the door.

They had been watching, on and off, ever since Austin left that morning. Davy dozed in the cave part of the time but now he was becoming restless.

"When's Austin coming back?" he asked.

"I don't know, Davy, but now's the time we're going out and do what Austin said."

"What was that?"

"Don't you remember? He said to gather some firewood when the man down there went inside. So, come on. While he's eating let's get to the other side of the hill and see what we can find that'll burn." Peg took hold of Davy's hand and led him away.

"Probably went in to eat," said Davy as they walked.

"Probably. I never saw a man work so hard for so long without stopping, or even slowing down. He just kept digging, and shoveling and wrestling with those rocks. I used to think that Pa worked hard, but I never saw anybody work like that man down there."

"Yeah, but at least he's eating now and I'm hungry."

"I know, Davy."

"Why can't we go down there and ask him for somethin'? You saw all them provisions he brought in last night."

"Sure, and you heard what the man on the mule said yesterday about him, about how mean he was and how he didn't cotton to strangers."

"Yeah, but today the man on the mule stopped and talked to him, didn't he? You saw him."

"I did. But I didn't see him get invited in to eat. Did you? So, for all we know he's lucky he didn't get chopped in pieces with that pickax and buried under some rock with that shovel."

"Cut it out, Peg. You're just tryin' to scare me."

"No, I'm just trying to teach you to do what you're told for your own good . . . until you're a little older, Davy."

"I know. Look!"

"What?"

"Over there!" Davy pointed. "A dead ol' tree. All fell apart. We don't have to look no further."

"Any further."

"Right. Hope ol' Austin brings back somethin' to cook."

So far ol' Austin's expedition had been pretty much in vain. Except for the matches.

He had met a peddler named Herman who had unhitched his team of horses and was letting them rest for a time, after which he intended to hitch them to the heavy wagon again and proceed on his journey to Prescott. Mr. Herman intended to start up a general store in Prescott and then send for his wife and four children. After Austin volunteered and undertook to help Mr. Herman with the hitching, Mr. Herman offered Austin a couple strips of dried beef jerky.

"If it's all the same to you, Mr. Herman, could I just take one strip of jerky . . . and a few matches?"

Mr. Herman looked at the boy and smiled.

"Or, I'll just take the matches, please," Austin added.

"You want to start a fire, my boy?"

"Yes, sir."

"Why?"

"To keep warm tonight. We . . . I mean, I've got a cave and it's cold at night?"

"You live in a cave?"

"For now."

"Alone?"

"I got a brother and a sister."

"Older? Younger?"

"Younger."

"Both of them?"

"Yes, sir."

"Well, I couldn't take you all to Prescott."

"I know."

"Too bad. You're a good worker. I could tell by the way you hitched those horses. All right, my boy, here's a strip of jerky. Eat it now. And here's three more strips for you and your brother and sister later. And here's matches so you'll be warm in that cave."

"Thank you, sir."

"Do you have a destination?"

"What's that?"

"A place to go. Relatives, maybe?"

"Oh, yes, sir," Austin lied, since he saw no point in telling the truth and dragging things out. "We'll be fine soon as we get there. So you see I couldn't go to Prescott anyhow."

"Yes, I see. Well, *auf Wiedersehen*, my boy."

* * *

From the moment the Keeshaws had entered the bank there was no doubt about which one of the people inside was Amos Bush.

He sat in a big leather chair behind a big oak desk with a triangular wood-and-brass nameplate.

AMOS BUSH
President

The desk was located in the left forefront of the bank near a windowed corner, an area separated by a three-foot-high wooden rail with a set of hinged gates.

President Bush's staff consisted of a teller and a clerk behind a cage that bisected the room. The most prominent object in the room was the bank's safe. It looked like a small fortress. Formidable. Impenetrable. Except to him who possessed a privileged sequence of numbers. Or dynamite.

Bush was busy with a man who sat on the edge of a chair near the big oak desk and appeared frightened. It did not seem that Amos Bush was doing anything to allay the man's fears. The man was a farmer, wearing his Sunday suit and workaday fingernails.

In any sort of physical contest the man could have crushed Bush to a pulp. But this contest was not physical. It was financial. And the man seemed to wither while awaiting Amos Bush's decision.

Amos Bush seemed in no hurry to render his verdict concerning the farmer's future. He had interrupted his cigar smoking and the stroking of his jowls when the Keeshaws walked in and stood by.

"Good day, gentlemen," Bush had proclaimed. "If you're waiting to see me, it'll be just a few minutes."

"Thank you, Mr. Bush," Deek had replied, and went about the business of relighting his pipe.

More than just a few minutes had since gone by. Deek had twice more relit his pipe and listened to parcels of the conversation. It wasn't exactly a conversation, because the only one doing any talking was the banker. The farmer was just nodding and moving closer to the edge of his chair.

Bush was a man in his fifties, gray-haired, pale, and gone to flab. His features, still handsome, but soft, with small eyes the color of currency, his voice smooth and confident, he droned on between puffs and swills of cigar smoke.

But Deek and Tom and Bart weren't interested in the monologue; their interest was elsewhere. Without being overly obvious they were sizing up the layout of the bank, and most particularly the dimensions and impregnability of the safe.

Just above the safe a banner hung from the ceiling.

START YOUR CHRISTMAS SAVINGS ACCOUNT
FOR NEXT YEAR . . . NOW

That's just what the Keeshaws intended to do. Bart pulled out his watch, checked the time, and gave the stem a couple of winds.

The man sprang out of his chair and reached for Bush's hand.

"Thank you! Thank you, Mr. Bush! I sure do appreciate it! So does Emmy Lou and the kids, we won't forget. No, sir. Where do you want me to make my mark?"

It almost seemed as if the man was about to kiss Amos Bush's hand.

"That's all right, Seth," Bush said grandly. "Glad to help. You just come in tomorrow and we'll have the papers ready for you to make your mark."

"Thank you, sir." Seth shook Bush's hand even more vigorously. "And merry Christmas, sir. You sure have made it a merry Christmas for the whole lot of us."

"Yes. Merry Christmas, Seth."

Seth rushed through the hinged gates and past the Keeshaws with a "beg pardon."

"Well, gentlemen," Amos Bush addressed the Keeshaws, "sorry to keep you waiting. Come in. Sit down. What can I do for you?"

Hands were shook while Deek did the introducing, then proceeded with his ploy.

"We're looking to settle hereabouts. Want to buy us a spread, with hard cash. Been told you're the man to see."

"Well, I guess that's true." Bush smiled. "What made you decide to come to Gilead?"

Tom and Bart tried not to look at the safe.

"Friend of ours . . . in the army . . . Confederate, of course, said this place had . . . a future."

"That so. Where's your friend now?"

"Dead, unfortunately. He died bravely on the field of battle. Told us just before he died."

"Yes, well, Mr. Keeshaw, I s'pose I can give you the names of three or four people might be interested in selling."

Bush placed the still-smoking butt of his cigar in an ashtray, reached across, and took up a piece of paper and pencil.

"Sounds like a proper start." Deek grinned and nodded toward his brothers, who nodded back.

"These are hard times and if you've got hard dollars . . . well . . ."

"We've got that, all right. Pa died a short while back . . . rest his soul . . . and left us fixed better'n most."

"I'll draw you a map so's you can find your way to these spreads . . . They're all close by." Bush went about his mapmaking.

"You're being very cooperative, Mr. Bush," said Deek. "We won't forget, will we, boys?"

The boys' attention snapped back from the safe and they nodded again.

"In the meantime," Bush looked up a moment from his map, "I expect you'll be wanting to make a deposit."

That was something the Keeshaws hadn't counted on.

"How's that?" Deek cleared his throat.

"Well, that 'hard money' we been talking about. Not safe to carry it around, specially in these hard times. So, like I said, I expect you'll be wanting to make a deposit."

Tom and Bart were helpless, but Deek showed the stuff that made him leader of the brotherhood.

"Yeah, well, you see, Mr. Bush, we got another brother . . . Maynard . . . he's still back in Louisiana.

He'll come with the money, all of it, soon's we find the right place."

"Yeah . . . Maynard," Bart interjected. "He's got the money."

"I hope it's in a bank."

"Oh, sure," Tom said. "Big bank . . . strong . . . just like this one."

"Good." Bush went back to his map.

"That's a handsome safe you got there, Mr. Bush," Bart added.

"Made in Chicago, Illinois. Now, let's see. Here's the road leading outta town to the west . . ."

"We'll get a fresh start tomorrow." Deek rose, struck another match, and glanced back at the safe as Amos Bush went on with his directions.

". . . follow your noses till you get to Dirty Creek . . . that's about a mile and a half. On the other side, the road divides. Bear to the left and . . ."

Chapter 9

What was left of the orange hump of the sun threw long, gloomy shadows across Shad Parker's property.

It was too dark to work, almost too dark to read the NO TRESPASSING sign. But Shad Parker had done more than an honest day's work. From sunup to sundown he had labored to smooth out this tiny patch of the planet, and there was a discernible difference in the area he had covered. Dozens and dozens of rocks and stones, part-stained from the soil where they had been buried, lay in no particular pattern waiting to be made into a wall.

Shad Parker's purpose was twofold: To clear the land so it could be cultivated. To build a wall as further evidence of his desire for self-seclusion. Actually there was a third purpose, to busy his body and brain and try to keep from remembering, at least during the days.

It was easier to accomplish the third purpose during the days, but there was no way to busy himself at night. The only balm, and it seldom worked completely, was to dull the brain with whiskey.

Shad Parker moved amid the field of overturned rocks, stones, and boulders, hoisting the shovel and pickax over his shoulder. He walked to where his rifle leaned against a rock, picked up the rifle, and started toward the cabin, past the chicken coop, where a covey of chickens clucked, scratched, and scampered. He made his way past the hog pen and barn, then stopped at the well.

Shad set down the tools and rifle and started to lift out a bucket of water.

From a slanting distance of just over a hundred yards, a pair of hands pushed back part of a bush and a pair of eyes peered toward the man at the well.

Shad Parker walked, carrying the bucket of water, the rifle, and the tools, toward the cabin. He left the tools on the porch, but took the water and the rifle inside.

Austin allowed the shrubbery to spring back into place. Since leaving Mr. Herman and taking along the jerky and the matches, he had had no luck in scavengering anything to bring back for Peg and Davy except for a few roots and berries. But Austin had plans. It was still too early to implement them, but he'd be back later.

He started up the shadowed hill toward the cave and Peg and Davy who were waiting for something to eat.

The Keeshaw brothers were dining on thick, well-done steaks at the New Heidelberg Restaurant adjacent to the Eden Hotel. It was the only restaurant in Gilead. The restaurant was run by the Sweissgood family—Curt, Erika, and their well-bred, well-fed twin daughters, Heidi and Hanna, and son Ralph.

Deek Keeshaw's mind was not on his meal. At a distant corner table Yellow Rose sat alone, not eating very much of the chicken dinner the Sweissgoods had prepared and served.

"If you're not gonna finish up that meat," Bart said through his missing teeth, "I'll do it for you . . . else I'm gonna order me another steak."

Deek shoved his plate toward Bart and proceeded to light up his pipe, looking through the smoke rings toward the distant corner table.

"What you got in mind for tonight?" Tom asked, looking from Yellow Rose back to Deek.

"Thought we might head over to the Appaloosa, show these locals how to play a little poker."

"That all?" Tom grinned.

"Maybe not."

"I thought so."

"Now, listen," Deek instructed. "Don't pull anything fancy. Just play straight, honest poker, win or lose. We're here for higher stakes than some dumb poker game, you hear?"

"Sure, Deek," Tom said. "But how much longer we gonna wait?"

"Till I say."

Yellow Rose got up from her unfinished chicken dinner and walked toward the door.

Deek watched, fascinated.

But he didn't know that Yellow Rose wasn't going to the Appaloosa. She was going back up to her room.

Yellow Rose was thinking about packing up and leaving Gilead, sometime after Christmas.

As she walked out of the door, young Ralph Sweissgood entered, carrying a tray of empty dishes. He had returned from taking supper over to the sheriff's office and jail.

"Sheriff," Charlie Reno spoke from his cell to Elwood Hinge, "anybody ever break out of your jail?"

"That's an idea worth ignoring," the sheriff replied.

"That's not an answer." Charlie grinned and looked toward Red Borden in the next cell.

"The answer is . . . nobody has, and nobody will."

"Oh, I don't know about that, do you, Red?"

"We busted outta Fort Smith," Red said. "That's a lot more prison than this."

"Yeah, you're plenty bad boys. Real killers. But from what I heard, Frank Chase was the brains of the outfit . . . and he's currently a corpse."

"Maybe you heard wrong, huh, Red?"

Hinge started to walk away from the cells.

"Say, Sheriff," Charlie called out. "That was a damn fine meal. How about if we smoked some?"

"Sure. If you got something to smoke."

"You know we don't."

"Then you won't."

"Sheriff."

"What?"

"You know we got nothin' to lose . . ."

"By trying to bust out, you mean?"

"That's what I mean. They're gonna hang us anyway."

"That they are."

"You already got a thousand comin' for Frank and Johnsy. That's a lot of money. There's a couple of dead men back in Arkansas. They tried to stop us, they thought they was brave. You think you're brave, Sheriff?"

"There's no brave men." The sheriff shrugged. "There's just men who're forced to do brave things, sometimes."

"Like I said, Sheriff," Charlie smiled, "we got nothing to lose."

"Look at it this way, boys. It's a long way back to Fort Smith. You can take your chances with a federal marshal out in the open, or you can take your chances with me. You're worth five hundred a piece to me. Dead or alive. And to me, either way . . . it makes no never mind. Good night, boys."

At the Appaloosa the Keeshaws had been in a poker game for more than two hours. Deek usually won. Usually when he played poker his mind was on the game. Tonight he wasn't winning. His losses didn't amount to more than a few dollars, but both his brothers, who weren't as good at poker, or anything else that Deek was, observed him making a couple of purely dumb plays. He had just made another one. A fellow named Chris was raking in the pot.

"Deal me out a couple of hands, gentlemen," Deek said as he rose. "Going to give my hip a rest and change my luck."

"Draw. Jacks or better." It was Tom's turn to deal.

Deek proceeded to the far end of the bar and

nodded at Hooter, who grabbed a bottle and followed behind the counter.

"Have one yourself." Deek smiled.

"Don't mind." Hooter poured rye into two glasses.

"A woman should be held by the waist, a bottle by the neck, or—?" Deek asked, "is it the other way around?"

"Depends on the woman, I reckon."

"You married, Hooter?"

"Nope. The way I see it, marriage is all right for women and that's that."

"Speaking of women," Deek got around to the core of the conversation, "I don't see Yellow Rose here tonight."

"No, you don't."

"How come?"

"I expect she don't feel like comin' in."

"Have another drink."

"Don't mind."

"Mind if I ask you something?"

"Ask."

"Who owns this place?"

"I do. Partly."

"Well, it seems you take an awful lot of stick from her."

"How so?"

"It just seems she pretty much comes and goes as she pleases."

"She does."

"The other girls don't."

"Nope."

Francine and Stella were upstairs.

"Is that because Yellow Rose is so much better-lookin'?"

"That's some of it."

"What's the rest?"

"I said I was the owner, partly. Yellow Rose owns the other part."

"I see."

Hooter poured Deek another shot of rye.

"Have one on me . . . and Yellow Rose."

Rosalind DuPree lay naked atop her oversize, canopied bed. She had, with Mr. Peevy's permission, and at her own expense, converted two of the rooms into a parlor-bedroom suite at the Eden Hotel. She had at her own further expense installed antique furniture unlike any other in Gilead, or Palestine, or anyplace in Texas.

One of the bedroom walls had been turned into library shelves, well stacked with well-read volumes. Philosophy, history, fiction—chiefly romantic, and much of it Dumas and Dickens, the complete works of Shakespeare. But the majority of Rosalind DuPree's bedroom library consisted of poetry. Chaucer, Drayton, Donne, Herrick, Milton, Shakespeare, Lovelace, Pope, Byron, Shelley, Keats, Browning, Blake, Hood, dozens of others.

Not a day or night went by that she didn't take one or two of the books down from a shelf and reread a passage, a page, or a hundred pages before and after her stint at the Appaloosa Saloon.

She alternated from one escape to another. From

the past to the present. She was running away from both but going nowhere.

But more and more she had abstained from the Appaloosa. It was just a matter of time before she would leave the Appaloosa and Gilead and probably Texas behind as she had, at other times, left other places, and most often, other people; different but the same. Ordinary people, predictable in everything they said and did . . . and wanted. Predictable as her life had been since St. Louis.

Soon, she would move to another place, probably San Francisco, take along her books and furniture and leave the ordinary, predictable people of Gilead behind.

But there was one man in Gilead who was neither ordinary, nor predictable.

Her head lay on one of two large goose-feathered pillows and she could see the curves and planes of her bare, seductive body stretching forward almost to the foot of the bed. Her face, framed with long, softly coiling locks, was as beautiful as it had been when she left New Orleans more than a decade ago, before the War for the Confederacy, the beloved Confederacy, but not her beloved Confederacy. Her body, too, was still as firm, yet pliant and desirable as it was that day in Paris when she looked into the dressing mirror and realized that at the age of sixteen she had become a woman.

She was in Paris to become a lady.

Rosalind had been sent there by her mother, Marie, who remained in New Orleans, having moved there from Charleston when Rosalind was an infant. Marie DuPree never spoke of her dead husband, who had left them enough money to provide for all the necessities and most of the luxuries that the two of them would ever need and desire.

Then the letter came.

From Marie DuPree on her deathbed to her daughter in Paris. The letter that revealed the dark legacy bequeathed from Marie to Rosalind.

For hours, then days, Rosalind never stopped crying. Again and again she looked into the mirror for any physical trace of her bloodline, on her face or body. The eyes, nose, hair, her lips, the nails on her fingers. There was nothing to expose the secret. She was the same Rosalind DuPree that she had been before the letter came.

She decided the secret would remain a secret. She returned to the antebellum South, visited her mother's gravesite, then listened as the lawyer read her mother's will. There wasn't as much as Rosalind had been led to believe, but there was the house, the furnishings, and more than enough to keep the three servants until Rosalind married one of the several beaux who had pursued her even before she went to Paris.

But for Rosalind DuPree there was only one beau. She knew that she would marry Wade Hammond from the first moment she saw him when she was thirteen and Wade was almost sixteen. Carriage rides, cotillions, moonlight walks along the river, and the promises both of them made to each other the night before she left for Paris.

The Hammonds of Louisiana had the largest, finest plantation for over a hundred miles in any direction, and the most slaves. The Hammonds had helped to settle and develop the state of Louisiana since Thomas Jefferson negotiated the purchase of the territory from France.

Wade Hammond made it official. Six months after Rosalind returned from Paris, after what was considered a suitable period of mourning, he asked Rosalind to marry him. Her reply was prompt and eager and positive. They broke the news to Wade's mother and father.

Mrs. Hammond smiled a curious smile and said nothing. But she did something. She hired a law firm in Charleston. The assignment, to find out everything possible about the family DuPree.

The law firm of Rutledge, Smathers and Smathers earned its fee and a bonus.

The engagement was broken off, and somehow, it wasn't all that difficult to figure out how, the revelation of Rosalind DuPree's background became common knowledge throughout New Orleans society.

Rosalind and Wade met only one time after that, accidentally. He stuttered and stammered and never once looked into her eyes.

She left him and New Orleans and went to St. Louis. She swore she would never fall in love with another man. She also swore that she would make no secret of her grandmother's African heritage.

Four years later she read in a St. Louis paper that Wade Hammond had died valiantly for the Confederate cause . . . of typhoid fever.

How many times had she been asked by how many men . . . "How did a girl like you . . . ?"

Her answer was never the same. And never the truth. Except once.

Elwood Hinge had not asked.

But for some reason, one night she told him everything. He never said a word. He held her close to him and kissed her gently and never said a word.

She looked at the canopied cover of her bed and thought again of the verse that she first read shortly after she had gone to St. Louis, and thought of so often since.

I traveld thro' a Land of Men
A Land of Men & Women too
And heard & saw such dreadful things
As cold Earth wanderers never knew

Chapter 10

The cabin was illuminated only by the kerosene lamp on the table. Also at the table, a plate of food half-eaten and a bottle of whiskey more than half-empty, and Shad Parker, who had fallen asleep with his head resting on his loglike forearms.

The day's work and the whiskey had brought temporary surcease. If he were lucky he would be unconscious for another hour, maybe two, and then as he had done so many nights before, he would slowly awaken, desperately conscious and infinitely alone.

But not this night.

Suddenly his head bolted up. Eyes alert. His body turned toward the cabin door and the sound, the sounds outside. Faint, but there.

He rose swiftly and silently from the chair and moved in the direction of the door. He took up the rifle leaning near the entrance, turned the knob, and opened the door a crack.

He looked through the darkness toward the sounds and caught sight of a fleeting silhouette that leaped over the fence of the chicken coop and blended into the chocolate night.

Shad waited just a beat, then opened the door wider, walked out, and closed it noiselessly behind him. He walked across to the chicken coop, looked toward the point where the silhouette had fled, then followed.

His mind was clear, his reflexes and rifle ready, as on the battlefield. He stalked through the brush toward the high curved horizon of the hillside. Step by silent step, until the hunter's instinct commanded him to stop.

He whirled and automatically aimed his rifle. Then lowered it.

For just a moment he looked at the owl less than fifteen feet away. And the owl looked back at him, with one eye closed, the other insouciantly glinting in the cold faint moonlight.

He turned and walked again and saw it near the top of the rise. A flickering glow. He moved ahead, this time with a fixed destination.

He made his way to the entrance of the cave, a small irregular hachure that fronted a natural hollowed-out portion of the hill. Shad flattened out near the entrance and listened.

Silence.

He moved his head to get a look inside. There was a feeble fire, barely burning but throwing off an erratic glow against the uneven walls of the miniature cavern.

Still no sound, except for the occasional crack of dead wood blistering in the tiny fire.

Whoever was there had to be crouched in the

darkness. He might have caught sight of the hunter with the rifle in pursuit. From what Shad had seen of the figure running away, he didn't appear to be armed. At least not with a long gun. But whoever it was, armed or not, he must by now have known that he was cornered. Shad Parker didn't hesitate any longer.

"Don't budge," he said as he stepped inside, rifle at the ready. "All right now. Whoever you are, you know what I came for. Don't do anything sudden. Slow and easy. Now, one foot at a time, step out into the light and keep your hands low."

Shad, rifle pointed, watched as the small figure emerged from a black corner.

"Slow and easy," he repeated.

Through the shadowy firelight Shad saw a gaunt, dirt-smudged face with defiant pinwheel eyes, hatchet blade mouth, long rankled hair, and an insolent expression.

Along a torn trouser, a dirty, sinewy hand clenched a fat dead chicken. Austin Coats said nothing.

Shad Parker didn't know what he had expected to find, but it wasn't what stood before him.

Austin had seen the man who owned the property only from a distance. Standing there in the cave just a few feet away the man looked taller and more terrible. He looked like he had risen from hell with his hair on fire. He leaned with his shoulders forward as if he was going to leap. There were deep creases on either side of his narrow mouth, and his eyes flashed danger.

"What you doing up here?" Shad asked.

"You don't own this cave." Austin was surprised at his own defiance, or maybe it was stupidity.

"I own that hen, thief. Drop it."

Austin dropped the lifeless hen.

Shad Parker looked at the dead fowl whose neck had been wrung.

"I ought to twist your neck." Shad said it as if he just might.

"We're hungry," Austin blurted.

Shad raised the rifle again. His eyes darted into the dark recesses of the cave.

"Who's 'we'?"

Silence.

"Your pa send you down to steal my chickens?"

Austin made no answer. Shad moved the barrel of the rifle across the cave.

"Step out, mister, before I let some lead fly around here."

Shad watched as another figure stood out from the shadows. She appeared to be a year or so younger than the boy.

"Brother and sister," said Shad, "by the looks of you." He started to lower the rifle, but stopped as he heard another footstep.

The third one was smaller yet. A boy about six, ropelike arms and legs, with an unmistakable resemblance to his brother and sister.

Shad ran the fingers of his left hand through his thick, whorled hair. The small boy stopped at the side of his sister. She took hold of the boy's hand and looked straight at the man across the cave.

"That all of you?" Shad asked.

"That's all of us," Austin replied.

They did not cower, the three of them facing the tall and terrible man. They were afraid, especially the younger two, but all three of them, dirty, ragged, and hungry, faced the stranger in the eye. They didn't plead or cry. They were ready to take their punishment.

Shad observed and approved of that, at least. They had the look about them of having been punished before. Of having learned that pleading and crying didn't make matters better, and sometimes worse. Shad looked at them a moment in an effort to determine if he had ever seen them before.

"You kids from around here?"

Austin shook his head slightly.

"Runaways, huh?"

This time there was no answer, nor any sign from any of them.

"How long you been up here in this cave?"

Peg and Davy were waiting for Austin to answer, but as yet Austin hadn't decided to say anything further.

"Your folks'll be looking for you. Why'd you run away? You do something wrong?"

Silence.

"You'll go back home when you get hungry enough."

"Nobody's looking for us. We haven't got any folks."

"Orphans, huh?"

"That's right . . . and we ain't leavin'."

"We'll see."

A cruel, vagrant wind swept into the cave. The meek fire gasped and tried to stay alive, but died. The night and the cave turned even colder. Shad took a couple of steps closer to the dead fire and picked up the hen, then turned and started toward the opening.

"Mister."

Shad stopped. Austin's voice was flat, almost matter-of-fact.

"We been living on roots and berries."

"So?"

"That hen ain't gonna lay no more eggs."

Shad looked at the hen, then back to the boy.

"No, she ain't. Thanks to you."

"Someone," Austin said, "might just as well eat her."

"Yeah. Me."

"What about us?" Austin looked at his brother and sister, then back at the man.

"Roots and berries."

Shad Parker stepped out of the cold, dark cave into the cold, dark night. He heard the girl's voice from behind him.

"Good night, mister."

Chapter 11

Back in his cabin, and now in his bed, Shad Parker did his best not to think about the three children in the cold, dark cave. They were not his concern, primarily because he would not allow them to be his concern, and besides they were in no mortal danger. Even though they were cold and hungry they would survive the night and in the light of day they would find someplace, someone who would provide food and shelter.

He wanted to discourage them and everyone else from intruding on his life—what was left of it. And without Molly and his own children, as far as he was concerned, there was nothing left—nothing worthwhile.

Molly.

To him she was always Molly O.

Ever since that Fourth of July picnic at Fair Oaks Hollow between Cross Keys and Port Republic, where annually several hundred friends and neighbors, all Virginians, all Americans, gathered to eat, drink, play, and celebrate the birth of the United States of America.

Part of the "play" included a wrestling contest. That year Shad Parker had been persuaded by his many friends, and particularly his best friend, Ben Warren, to challenge Tub MacGrudder, who had won the contest six years ago and had since beaten every challenger easily in two out of three falls. In fact, for the last six years there never had been a necessity for the third fall. Tub always had defeated the succession of contenders in the first two falls.

Wrestling, a sporting contest between two unarmed men, involved grappling and gaining body grips in order to secure a fall, which meant pinning the opponent's shoulders to the floor—or ground. The sport probably went as far back as prehistoric man and was a popular and honored event among several ancient peoples, especially among the Greeks. The pancratium, involving wrestling and boxing, became part of the Olympic Games in 648 B.C.

Later, the Romans changed in some ways the rough-and-tumble Greek style, thus originating the Greco-Roman wrestling. The tournaments were frequently conducted through medieval Europe, gained headway in England, and were then introduced early in the United States. By the mid-nineteenth century a form of wrestling, Americanized into "rassling," which combined upright *and* ground action, took root in the American frontier, including the Shenandoah Valley.

Tackling, tripping, slugging, leg holds, and assorted rough features—the rougher, the better—were allowed and encouraged, and this form came to be called "catch-as-catch-can rassling" in the United States, including the Shenandoah Valley.

Everyone at the Fourth of July picnic, men, women, and children, watched as Shad Parker, stripped to the waist, waited and looked across at the taller, heavier, homely Tub MacGrudder, who was also naked to the hips, but coated with what appeared to be some kind of grease. Tub MacGrudder scowled from the other side of the makeshift ring as the referee Goose Dunker, who looked like his name and was rumored but never proved to be a relative of MacGrudder's, made the announcement.

"Ladies and gents, boys and girls, once again, the annual Fourth of July catch-as-catch-can rasslin' contest for permanent possession of ten dollars in cash and temporary possession of the champeenship trophy, the Little Green Jug filled with the finest sour mash whiskey in the state of Virginia. The champeen also gets to drink the whiskey and keep the Little Green Jug until next year when the jug goes up for grabs again.

"Over there the challenger this year, who at the present time is upright and conscious, though some say is a damn fool and not in complete possession of his faculties for entering this bout, the young, popular, and foolhardy Shad Parker."

More than half, closer to two thirds of those present, clapped and cheered their approval and encouragement.

"Over on the other side stands the six-time winner, never defeated, never felled champeen rassler of these parts, that mountain of a man, part-grizzly, part-human, all-powerful Tub MacGrudder."

Perceptibly fewer cheers and hand claps.

"Just a minute," Ben Warren hollered out. "I want to talk to you, Goose."

Goose Dunker strolled toward Ben and Shad.

"I'm lodging a formal protest . . ."

"What about? Your man hasn't lost . . . yet." Goose almost doubled over at his own wit.

"That big son of a bitch . . ." Ben pointed toward Tub.

"I heard that!" Tub roared from across the ring.

"I said it so's you'd hear, you son of . . ."

"Watch your language, there's women and young-sters in earshot." Goose pointed a crooked finger at Ben.

"I'll get you later, you squirt!" Tub hollered, and smacked a huge fist into his palm. "I'll break both your legs."

Tub MacGrudder was notorious in the leg-and-arm-breaking business both in rassling contests and in barroom fights, which he initiated with frequency. A mean, angry man, sober or drunk, his anger was tempered by the sound and feel of somebody else's bone snapping. Two years ago he had broken a man's back. Jim Riggins hadn't walked since. Rig-gins's wife, Loretta, took a shot at MacGrudder a year ago. Loretta was a good shot with a rifle, but it was getting dark and she missed. Most people thought, and hoped, she'd try again in broad daylight.

"Never mind, Tub, I'll handle this. Speak your piece," Goose said to Ben.

"That big son of a bitch is coated with bear grease, makin' him slippery. Not fair! I protest!"

"Protest denied!" Goose exclaimed.

"Like hell, I . . ."

"Forget it, Ben," Shad said. "It's all right."

"Like hell . . ."

"One more word and you're banned from these proceedings. Two out of three falls! This here contest is gonna get started when I count to three! One! Two!"

Unfortunately, that was when Shad Parker first caught sight of her. She stood next to another young girl across the ring.

The other girl was comely.

She was beautiful.

Tall, perfectly proportioned. Nineteen or twenty. Even from this distance her green eyes sparkled, her flowing red hair blazed in the sunlight, her full crimson lips turned downward with a touch of terror at what was about to take place. In that moment Shad Parker was stunned by the sight of what he instantly perceived to be the most beautiful creature he had ever seen on the face of God's earth.

"Three!" Goose Dunker hollered.

Shad stood paralyzed as Tub MacGrudder sprang, shrinking the distance between them.

Ben Warren, with all his strength, pushed Shad forward, nearly knocking him down, but instead, directly into the big, bonding arms of Tub MacGrudder. Tub grunted, grasped Shad, lifted him off the ground by the throat and belt, then above his head, whirled three times, and slammed Shad onto the ground. The ground seemed to shudder. There was no question that Shad did. His back and head hit the hard surface with a sickening impact.

If Shad was not unconscious, he was skin close to it. Without hesitation, or mercy, Tub leaped on the smaller man, swung an elbow into Shad's face, and pinned both Shad's shoulders flat against the ground.

Not ten seconds had elapsed.

"One, two, three!" Goose counted, slapping the palm of his hand against the earth. "Fall! First fall!" he proclaimed.

Some cheers, but mostly gasps, misgivings, and dread from the spectators.

Ben rushed out and dragged Shad toward the sideline. Most people doubted that Shad could recover, at least until sundown.

"One minute between falls!" Goose announced. "If your man can continue. Or do you care to concede the contest?" he addressed both Ben and the barely conscious challenger.

"Shad?!" Ben slapped at Shad's bruised face. "Can you go on? Or do we give up?!"

"N . . . no," Shad stammered.

"No?! What does 'no' mean? Fight? Or give up?"

"F . . . fight!"

"We fight!" Ben yelled at Goose.

The crowd roared.

Tub grinned.

"You got thirty seconds till we start the second fall." Goose also grinned.

"Who . . . who is she?" Shad muttered.

"Who's *who*?!" Ben growled.

Shad managed to point across toward the beautiful, green-eyed, red-haired girl who had most of her face hidden in revulsion with the palm of her hand.

"You know her, Ben?"

"I sure do."

"Start at the count of three!" Goose yelled.

"Who . . . who is she?"

"One! Two . . ." Goose was counting again.

"If you don't beat that son of a bitch," Ben said, "you'll never find out!"

"Three!"

Ben pushed Shad into the ring again.

Shad wanted to find out. He never wanted anything more in his life. And this time he was ready. But Tub MacGrudder didn't know that. Tub rushed at Shad to repeat his earlier maneuver. This time Shad sidestepped and this time the grease worked against Tub. His slippery arms slid past his opponent.

Shad's fist pounded into Tub's kidney, and he tripped the big man, who stumbled and fell to his knees.

Shad's fist broke Tub's nose and spirit.

The next minute concluded with the decline and fall of Tub MacGrudder. In less than sixty seconds Shad Parker visited revenge upon the brute on behalf of all those in the valley who had suffered abuse and broken bones. Jim and Loretta Riggins led the cheering, and unknowingly, Shad by thus beating MacGrudder, probably saved the giant from subsequently being shot in broad daylight by Loretta Riggins.

The broken hulk declined to continue combat.

Goose Dunker had no choice but to proclaim Shad Parker "champeen"—permanent possessor of the ten-dollar prize and temporary possessor—at least until next Fourth of July—of the Little Green Jug.

But Shad Parker wasn't thinking about the ten-dollar prize money, or the Little Green Jug, or the whiskey in it, or the title of champeen. He was thinking only of that sublime face, those lustrous green eyes, and the blazing red hair. As soon as it was over, he turned and looked for her, but her face was hidden, now behind both hands, and it appeared that she had seen little, maybe nothing of Shad Parker's astounding recovery and triumph.

After being duly congratulated, cleaning himself up, and putting on his shirt, Shad grabbed hold of his best friend and didn't let go until Ben Warren told him everything he knew about a certain spectator.

Ben knew her name was Molly O'Connell. She and her sister Esmeralda recently had arrived from Ireland, and their uncle Patrick Vincent had procured them positions as teachers at the school in Cross Keys where he was an alderman. Ben happened to meet the ladies a couple of days ago while doing some business with Alderman Vincent in Cross Keys. Also Ben had happened to take a fancy to one of the ladies. Happily for all concerned, Ben's fancy fell upon Esmeralda, who was two years older than her sister, a bit taller, and a bit thinner. Esmeralda's eyes were more blue than green, her hair more brown than yellow, and her eyebrows glided straight across instead of arching as did Molly's. She was less fiery in appearance and in temperament, but undeniably a comely young lady. Ben led Shad, who had the Little Green Jug in hand, toward the sisters. After properly greeting Esmeralda, he introduced his best friend to his fancy's sister.

"Miss Molly O'Connell, may I present my friend, Shad Parker."

"Mr. Parker." Even with just the two words there was

a trace of that Irish cadence, and the lilt in her voice was the perfect complement to that perfect face.

"Molly O." That was as much as Shad Parker could vocalize. He said nothing more. He just stood and stared into those pastoral Irish green eyes and said nothing more.

Ben Warren broke the silence by pointing to the Little Green Jug in Shad's hand.

"Miss Molly, did you enjoy the rasslin' contest?"

"No," she replied quickly and honestly.

"Why not?" Ben asked just as quickly. "Surely you weren't rootin' for that son of . . . for that no-good MacGrudder."

"I wasn't rooting for anybody."

"Well, then, what is it?"

"It's just that I've seen enough of violence and brutality in the old country, and I sure as hell didn't come all this way to see more."

Shad Parker had never seen nor heard a woman with such beauty and spirit and honesty. Somehow his grip on the Little Green Jug loosened, it fell, hit a rock, and smashed to pieces, releasing the sour mash.

It was the best thing that could have happened. Molly O laughed as only the Irish can laugh, even though some of the whiskey splashed onto her skirt and shoes. Then Esmeralda laughed, and Ben and finally Shad.

That was the beginning of a summer of laughter and a lifetime of love. But they were not long, the summers of laughter. And Molly O's lifetime was much too short.

And while it lasted there was no question of the depth and unity of their love. Shad was a good man, but he became even better. And because of him, much of the sorrow and tragedy Molly O had borne in the old country was abraded.

Shad, Molly O, Ben, and Esmeralda were together as much as it was possible . . . and respectable. Rides, picnics, and dances. For almost a year while Shad worked his land and improved the house near Port Republic, Molly O taught school in Cross Keys.

It was on Christmas Eve that he had asked her.

"Molly O, will you marry me?"

"Shad, you know I love you, but there's something that separates us."

"Nothing can separate us, not while we're alive."

"Well, then, it's something that we have to live with, and I don't know if we can, if *you* can."

"I can live with anything so long as it's with you . . ."

"But, Shad, I'm Catholic and you're not."

"Molly O, Molly O, you're *you*. That's all I care about . . ."

"The children . . ."

"The children will be ours, and if they turn out like you, that's good enough for me and better than I deserve. Molly O, will you marry me?"

"I will."

And she did.

As a wedding present, besides promising never to wrestle again, Shad gave her the most beautiful young mare in the valley, with a coat as scarlet as Molly O's own hair. They named her Ruby, and Molly O rode her like a flaming lance across the countryside. Shad and Molly O rode together and he taught her how to swim, which was one of the few things she couldn't do when they first met. Life in the Shenandoah Valley was paradise and so was their marriage bed. Molly O had come to him in innocence, but quickly there flared within her a passion and a need to please and be pleased, to gratify and to be gratified, to love and be loved.

And now as he lay there in his bunk that cold December night staring at the dark corner of the ceiling, Shad Parker tried not to think of that marriage bed and their children . . . and of the three children in the cold hollow of the hillside cave.

Austin, Peg, and Davy lay bundled together in the darkness. After Shad left them they relit the fire and it burned for a time while they slept and tried to keep warm. Then the fire darkled and died.

Chapter 12

Deputy Homer Keeler finished up a hearty breakfast at the New Heidelberg. While he was washing it down with his fourth cup of strong black coffee, young Ralph Sweissgood returned from the jail, where he had delivered a not-so-hearty breakfast for the two prisoners who were waiting to be delivered to the federal marshal. As he entered, Ralph held the door open for the three Keeshaw brothers, who were coming in right behind him.

"Morning, Deputy," Deek greeted Homer.

"Morning, gentlemen."

"Where's the sheriff?" Deek inquired.

"'Cross the street in the office with the prisoners. Why? Is there anything you fellas need?"

"Just breakfast." Deek grinned and pointed to Homer's empty plate. "What do you recommend?"

"Ham, eggs, potatoes, muffins, and coffee is what I had."

"Sounds good." Deek looked toward the kitchen. "Smells good, too. My brothers and me have got some travelin' to do today, so we might as well load up our innards."

"Uh-huh." Homer headed for the door.

"Deputy."

"Yeah."

"Give our regards to the sheriff."

"I'll do that." Homer walked out the door and closed it behind him.

Lately Homer Keeler had been giving more thought to his future. He was torn between continuing his career as a lawman, like the man he admired most in the world, Sheriff Elwood Hinge, or spending all his savings and plunging into a mortgage for a spread not far from Gilead and settling down with Kathy Lewis, whom he had been sparking for a few months, and go to raising a family. He and Kathy made plenty of sparks, all right, but she wasn't keen on marrying a star packer. She said she preferred a quiet life, except in bed. Kathy's father and mother were becoming somewhat suspicious of Homer's intentions. Homer knew that they knew what was going on between their daughter and him, but looked the other way in hopes of marrying her off. There was a noticeable shortage of male eligibles due to the ravages of the recent war. But Homer also knew that they weren't going to look the other way much longer, particularly if Kathy showed signs of motherhood without benefit of a certain ceremony.

Besides, so long as Elwood Hinge remained sheriff there was no prospect of promotion for Homer unless he got an offer from another town. That wasn't likely. He knew that there were a lot more efficient and experienced lawmen available than young deputy Homer Keeler.

"Morning, Elwood."

"Morning, Homer."

"Everything peaceful?"

"Yep. Homer, pick up your shotgun and come on back here with me." Hinge led the way back toward the cells.

"What's the matter, Elwood?"

"Nothing's the matter." The sheriff stopped in front of the two cells where Charlie Reno and Red Borden lay in their bunks digesting their breakfasts. "You see those two prisoners layin' there peaceful and quiet?"

"Sure, I see them."

"Well, don't let all that peace and quiet fool you."

"What do you mean?"

"I mean Charlie and Red and I had a little talk last night, didn't we, boys?"

Both prisoners smiled and said nothing.

"They might look peaceful and quiet, but they be a couple of desperate men. Right, boys?"

No answer.

"You see, Homer, they told me that they got nothing to lose. They said that they just might try to bust outta here like they and them two corpses busted outta Fort Smith. Right, boys?"

No answer.

"Now, Homer, these are my instructions. If either one, or both, of these two desperados blink the wrong way or twitch in the wrong direction, use that shotgun and blow their heads off. I give you, and them, my word that I'll sign a piece of paper swearing that they were trying to escape, not that anybody will give a damn. You got that, Homer?"

"Yes, sir. I got it."

"Good." The sheriff looked from Charlie to Red. "I hope you boys got it, too. Now, I'm going to go get me some breakfast."

"Oh, Sheriff. Them three strangers who come to town, them brothers . . ."

"What about 'em?"

"Ran into them over at the Heidelberg."

"And?"

"And they said to give you their regards."

"That was friendly. See you later, Homer."

Sheriff Hinge turned his collar up against the cold and started toward the New Heidelberg across the street.

"Sheriff!" Reverend Groves called out. "Sheriff Hinge. Good morning."

"Morning, Reverend." Hinge waited on the walkway as Reverend Groves approached from the direction of Inghram's General Store.

"Well, sir," Reverend Groves said as he arrived, smiled, and looked around at the early activity on the street. "It appears people hereabouts are getting into the holiday spirit."

"It appears so."

"Yes, it does."

"Anything I can do for you, Reverend?"

"Well, Sheriff, Mrs. Groves and I are still looking forward to seeing you at services sometime soon. Mrs. Groves is over at Inghram's putting in an order and visiting with Mrs. Inghram. Are we apt to see you soon? Maybe at the Christmas service? Mrs. Groves is a mighty fine organist and we'd admire to have you join us, Sheriff."

"Well, I don't know, Reverend." Hinge glanced back toward his office. "I've got some people staying with me."

"Oh, yes, I know. That's another thing. I've brought along my Bible and while Mrs. Groves is waiting for the order and visiting with Mrs. Inghram, I thought it might be a good time to stop by and try to be of some comfort to those two souls."

"By 'those two souls' you mean Charlie Reno and Red Borden?"

"I believe that's what they're called. Thought I might read to 'em from the book of Matthew." Reverend Groves held up his Bible. "Start off with the Sermon on the Mount: 'And He opened His mouth, and taught them, saying, Blessed are the poor in spirit, for theirs is the kingdom of heaven. Blessed are they that mourn, for they shall be comforted . . .' and so on."

"Yes . . . 'Blessed are the meek, for they shall inherit the earth.'"

"Why, that's right, Sheriff, you do know your Bible. Well, what do you think?"

"I think that I appreciate your concern for those two souls, and I'll convey the message. But right now I'm not allowing those two souls any visitors. Particularly when I'm not around, and right now I'm going to go over and have some breakfast."

"How come?"

"Because I'm hungry."

"No, sir, I mean how come no visitors?"

"No visitors, no distractions. No distractions, less chance of an escape attempt."

"Escape? You mean . . ."

"I mean, suppose you got too close while you were doing that sermon, and suppose one of 'em grabbed you, choked you, or used you for a shield or hostage? Deputy Keeler would have to do what I told him—blow both their heads off, and, Reverend, your head might just get in the way. You see what I mean? I mean, we wouldn't want that to happen, would we? And neither would Mrs. Groves, would she?"

"Well, yes." Reverend Groves put the Bible into his pocket. "I see what you mean."

"Merry Christmas, Reverend." Sheriff Hinge headed toward the New Heidelberg Restaurant.

"Merry Christmas, Sheriff." Reverend Groves headed back toward Inghram's General Store.

Chapter 13

Shad Parker had been up since just before Reb's daily salutation. He had had breakfast, collected the eggs, saw to the hogs, and went to work with the pick and shovel.

Not once during the morning had he so much as glanced up toward the hillside cave. Nor did he intend to. He had hoped that they were gone.

But they weren't gone.

Austin, Peg, and Davy watched from above while the three of them waited for Austin to decide what they were going to do.

The Keeshaws were on horseback and had been for nearly half an hour. When Sheriff Elwood Hinge had entered the New Heidelberg Restaurant, Deek was inclined to engage the lawman in conversation to find out what more he could about the sheriff's watchdog habits where his prisoners were concerned, and when those prisoners would be turned over to the proper authorities for proper punishment.

Deek figured after the prisoners were disposed of the sheriff would ease up on his vigilance around the jail and more importantly, the bank. But it was obvious from the sheriff's attitude when he entered the restaurant that he was disinclined to engage in conversation with the Keeshaws or anybody else. He walked swiftly past the table where the Keeshaws sat and went directly to the last stool at the counter, the stool closest to the kitchen, where Erika Sweissgood was already pouring a mug of coffee for him.

Hinge nodded at Mrs. Sweissgood and gulped down close to half of the coffee in the mug before setting it back down on the counter, where she was waiting to fill it back up again. The sheriff turned his face away from the Keeshaws and the other customers until his breakfast came just a couple of minutes later.

Evidently, Deek reasoned, the Sweissgoods had spotted Hinge leaving his office and commenced preparing his breakfast, which must have been the same every morning because Hinge hadn't ordered anything or said a word since he entered. Deek waited for Hinge to look in their direction so he could at least nod a greeting or get a chance to approach the lawman, but Hinge wasn't having any of it. He just went about consuming his steak, eggs, and potatoes along with several mugs of coffee.

Deek decided that it would be wise to postpone any exploratory conversation with the sheriff until another time. The Keeshaws paid their bill, picked up their animals from the stable, and rode west.

As they approached a fork in the road, Deek reined up. So did Tom and Bart. Bart had been mumbling through his missing teeth for the last few minutes. As they stopped he checked his timepiece and wound it tight, as he had done first thing in the morning and last thing the previous night.

Deek pulled out of his pocket the map that Amos Bush had drawn and unfolded it while Deek continued to talk to himself.

"Bart," Deek said, looking up from the map, "if you got somethin' to say just flat out say it and I'll listen, but you keep mumbling like you have been for some miles back and I swear, I'll knock out the rest of your teeth, you hear?"

"I hear." Bart nodded and put the watch back into his pocket.

"Well, then, what is it?"

"Hell, Deek, I'll tell you what is it . . . it's searchin' out them sodbusters . . . Waste of time, I call it."

"You do."

"Well, ain't it?"

"It is . . . and it ain't."

"I can reason how it is—but I can't reason how it ain't." Bart looked from Deek to Tom and back to Deek again. "You know we're not gonna buy no farm."

"I know that, and you know that, and so does Tom," Deek explained as would a patient teacher to a pupil, "but we don't want Amos Bush to know."

"How's he gonna find out?"

"I'll tell you how he might. What if one of these dirt-movers," Deek pointed to the map, "pays Amos Bush a visit at the bank . . . and what if we haven't paid that dirt-mover a visit after all the trouble Bush went to . . . drawing the map and all. Might'n banker Bush start getting suspicious, maybe even pass on those suspicions to his next-door neighbor, the sheriff? You ever think of that?"

"No, I didn't," Bart admitted.

"Deek's right," Tom said. "We got to go through the motions. Deek's right."

"What about that shotgun sheriff?" Bart asked.

"What about him?"

"You seen him. Him and that deputy, one or both of them's always there. For all we know they sleep there, right next to that bank."

"That's what we're gonna find out."

"When?"

"I've been studying on that. Just as soon as we can without him getting suspicious, either. I think he's a pretty wise ol' party, that sheriff. I'll know the proper time to talk to him." Deek folded the map and returned it to his pocket. "In the meantime I'll say this—Amos Bush might be a good banker, but he's an almighty poor mapmaker."

Deek spurred his horse and headed west. The brothers Tom and Bart followed.

Austin, Peg, and Davy, still on the craggy ledge of the cave, continued to look down at Shad Parker as he worked on still another rock with the pickax. The sun was now well above the rim of the hill and the day was about as warm and bright as it was going to get. But the outlook for the children seemed neither warm nor bright.

"I'm hungry," Davy said.

Peg took hold of his hand.

"So am I," Austin said. "And so is Peg. You've been a real good boy, Davy. We'll get somethin'."

"What?"

"I don't know, but somethin'."

"Remember what an egg tastes like?" Davy smacked his lips. "Could you get us an egg, Austin? Boy, I could eat a hundred eggs. That man down there, all them chickens, all them eggs. He might give us one or two. What do you think, Austin?"

"Let's go down and ask him," Peg said. "He just might."

"I know his kind. Won't do any good. You saw the way he acted last night."

"He smelled of whiskey," Peg reasoned. "Maybe he'll look at it different this morning. Maybe we could help him do some chores. Want me to go down and ask him, Austin? . . . Austin?"

"Hey, look!" Austin pointed east.

Three riders turned off the road and approached the man working in the yard.

Shad had been aware of their approach. He took a couple of steps toward a large rock where his rifle leaned. He recognized the men as the Keeshaws. Shad stopped, still holding the pickax. The Keeshaws pulled up to within speaking distance.

"Howdy," Deek greeted.

There was no response.

"Nice little spread you got here."

Silence.

"We're the Keeshaws, remember? We're looking to buy a place around here ourselves. Talked to the banker in town about it, Amos Bush. He said the Davis place might be for sale. Drew up a map." Deek took the map from his pocket. "You happen to know where the Davis place is from here?"

"No," Shad said finally.

"Ever hear of . . ." Deek looked at the map . . . "something called Squaw Rock?"

Shad pointed toward a gnarled formation on a nearby hill, but didn't speak.

"Davis place supposed to be just to the north. That'ud be over that way," Deek did point north, "wouldn't it?"

Shad didn't so much as nod.

"Uh-huh." Deek smiled. "You know, we're liable to end up being neighbors. Wouldn't that be something?"

"Yeah," Bart mumbled. "Somethin'."

"Say," Deek did not give up smiling, "we need to water our animals. Mind if we use your well?"

"There's a creek half mile to the north," Shad said.

"Oh, there is, huh?" There wasn't much left of Deek's smile. "Well, much obliged, neighbor."

Deek nodded toward his brothers, moved his horse back toward the road. As always Tom and Bart followed.

Shad looked after them a moment then went back to work.

"Well, Austin," Peg said, "we just can't stay up here like this all day."

Austin continued to watch the man working and said nothing.

"We got to do something."

"I'm really hungry," Davy said once again.

"I'm going to go down there." Peg took a step forward.

"No."

"What, then? Austin, you think he knows we're still up here?"

"He knows, all right."

"He hasn't even looked up this way once, not all morning."

"He knows."

"I'll bet," Davy looked at Austin, "he ate that hen for breakfast."

"Austin," Peg took another step, "I'm going down."

"No, you're not, not alone. Come on," Austin moved ahead, "we'll go down together."

"You ever seen a white man," Tom said after the Keeshaws rounded a bend far enough away so there was no possibility of Shad Parker hearing the comment, "mean as that son of a bitch in all your life?"

"Can't say I have," Deek noted.

"Must be part Injun," Tom added.

"Part rattler, I'd say," Bart said.

"Least a rattler makes noise before he hits," Tom continued. "With one like that, you can't tell."

"You see that roll of bills he peeled off from, back there in that saloon the other day?" Bart commented. "He sure as hell ain't as poor as he looks. Deek, how much money you reckon he carries?"

"Don't know."

"Well, if he carries that much," Tom reasoned, "he's likely got a lot more salted somewhere in that cabin. Either that or he's got it over at that bank in town, in which case, he's gonna be mad as hell when we lift it. If we ever do."

"We'll lift it, all right, when the time comes," Deek assured. "But he don't look to me like the kind who puts his faith in banks . . . or his money."

"Why don't you ask him, Tom?" Bart grinned. "Next time we see him?"

"I'm not anxious to see him, or talk to him, or winter with him."

"Don't have to," Deek said, "Well, let's get to that crick, then find the Davis place."

"Wonder," Tom mused, "if that Davis fella's anything like his neighbor back there?"

"Don't matter." Deek nudged his horse on. "Don't have to winter with him, either."

Chapter 14

Shad Parker looked up and saw the three of them making their way down the hill and toward him. He had thought that the encounter last night would have been enough to discourage the young ones from further encroachment on his property or privacy but evidently they were not discouraged, at least not enough.

First the three Keeshaws had come poking around and now these three. Shad rested the head of the pickax on the ground and held on to the handle as Austin, Peg, and Davy approached.

They stopped about ten feet away and stood in straight formation. The older boy's eyes were just as unfriendly and challenging as Shad's.

Silence.

Peg looked from Austin to the man with the pickax and decided that she was going to have to initiate the conversation if there was going to be one.

"Hello, mister."

Shad didn't speak.

"My name's Peg, Peg Coats, and this is Davy, and . . . Austin."

Shad neither introduced himself, nor broke his silence.

"We don't mean to bother you none . . ."

Shad looked up toward the cave, then back to Peg.

". . . we just wanted a place to stay the night and, well, Austin spotted the cave up there yesterday and so we just . . ."

"Look here." Shad pointed to the hill. "That might not be my cave, but this sure as hell is my land. Any of you read?"

"Yes, sir. Austin and I both read."

"Well, then read that sign, it says 'No Trespassing' and that's what you're doing. So just turn your-selves around and find someplace else to squat. There's a town not far from here in that direction." Shad pointed east. "You can find yourselves plenty of people to pester. You'll be a lot better off than sticking around here and squatting in that cave and so will I."

Shad Parker hadn't put together so many words out loud since coming to Texas, but he hoped the speech, logical as it was, would convince the minor intruders to leave once and for all.

But now it was their choice to be silent, and they were. It was Shad who spoke again.

"Well? What's wrong with that?"

"Just one thing, mister," Peg said.

"What?"

"Well, sir, you see, we tried that before in other towns and they always want to send us back."

"Back?"

"Yes, sir, to old Miss Stritch."

"Miss Stritch?"

"Yes, sir. She's in charge of the Faith, Hope, and Charity Orphanage over at Palestine . . ."

By that point Shad felt himself falling into a snare he had sought to, and succeeded in, avoiding since returning to and leaving the Shenandoah Valley. It was his intention to avoid as much contact and especially involvement with any and all form of humans or even animals to which he might in any way become attracted or attached. Shad Parker did not want to care about anybody or anything. It was his further intention to put a stop to this conversation.

"Never mind! I don't want to hear about who you are, or where you come from, or where you're going. Just get out of here." Shad took up the pickax and slashed it into the ground near the rock where he had been working.

"Mister." Davy spoke for the first time. "Whatcha gonna do with all them rocks?"

"I'm gonna build a wall, so people like you," Shad kept working and pointed in the direction the Keeshaws left, "and them can't get over it."

"Around this whole place?" Davy's gaze circled the area. "That's gonna take a lot of rocks."

"Shush, Davy." Peg put her hand on the little boy's shoulder. "Mister, we're sorry Austin stole your chicken."

"All right, you're sorry. Now, git."

"Come on, Peg," Austin finally spoke. "I told you . . ."

"Mister, we thought . . ." Peg persisted, ". . . maybe

if we did some chores . . . you might let us have some eggs."

"I'm hungry," Davy said.

"If you're hungry, go back to Miss Stitch, or whatever her name is, because you're not getting anything from me." He dug the pickax into the earth again. "You've wasted enough of my time. I got work to do."

Austin, Peg, and even Davy knew that it was hopeless. There was nothing they could say or do that would reach this man. He was as hard as the rocks he dug out of the ground and as cold and uncaring as the earth in which he dug. The man had made it clear that from him they would get nothing, not an egg to eat, nor even water to drink.

The man on the mule was right. The sign meant what it said: NO TRESPASSING. Not on his property. And there seemed to be another sign, unseen, but there around his body and soul that meant the same thing.

NO TRESPASSING
Private – Do Not Enter
BEWARE! DANGER!

And still, Peg seemed to notice something in his eyes, a look that reminded her of their father and the way he looked at his young children, a warmth and gentleness, but in this man buried like the rocks on his property, hidden by a sign that proclaimed NO TRESPASSING.

Further still, Peg noted somehow that his mouth was severe, but not fierce, his eyes cold but not cruel, his face more tragic than savage.

In their short span of living Peg, Austin, and Davy

had suffered misfortune, tragedy. This man had lived much longer and from the look of him had been wracked and battered, pummeled by an avalanche of adversity, but stood alone wanting no one and nothing near him.

Austin took Peg's hand, then Davy's. He knew if he were to find food or help of any kind that day it would not be here, not from this man. Austin started to lead his brother and sister back toward the hill and the cave.

Shad Parker had succeeded in dislodging another sizable stone. He grasped it with both his hands and started to roll it over.

It was a terrifying noise, then noises. Frenzied, shrill, skirling, a shattering cacophony. It came from the chicken coop. But even the hogs from the nearby pen scurried and snorted.

The three children shuddered and stopped in their tracks, paralyzed at the sight and sounds. But Shad Parker was racing for the rock where his rifle rested. He grabbed up the Winchester and ran toward the attacker.

The cougar sprang out from the flutter of feathers and fowl, and as the chickens scrambled and screeched in the coop, the animal with a fat hen in his jaws vaulted over the fence and raced away with leaping, supple strides.

Shad Parker swung the Winchester to his shoulder and fired once, twice, three times.

The second and third shots found their mark. The cougar pitched, then dropped. It quivered as it lay until Shad fired again, then it lay motionless.

After the sound of the last shot and at the sight

of the lifeless but still bleeding cougar with the mangled chicken just out of its gaping jaw, Davy began to tremble, then sob. He buried his head against Peg's small belly. Her hands stroked the back of his neck and she swayed slightly in an attempt to soothe and reassure him.

"Don't cry, Davy. It's all right. It's all over. Nothing going to hurt you. Davy . . ."

Shad Parker lowered the rifle. In St. Louis he had made the right choice picking the new Winchester '66 as the weapon he would take to Texas. Until then he had favored the seven-shot Spencer. The Spencer was larger in caliber—.50 against the Winchester's .44—but it had a lower velocity and a shorter range. The rifle he now held in his hand was the first true Winchester, trim, easily carried, and accurate. And the Winchester held seventeen cartridges. This was the most cartridges Shad had spent except in target practice after he first bought the weapon. He doubted that the Spencer would have done this job.

Still carrying the rifle, Shad walked toward the chicken coop and stopped just outside the fence. Austin watched for a moment, then came up and stopped a short distance away from Shad's right side. Peg and Davy followed.

"Damn," said Shad as he surveyed the destruction. Half a dozen chickens lay dead, in addition to the one the cougar left with. At least Rebel was still alive, although less proud and arrogant than he had previously appeared. Shad turned and looked at the three children. Davy's eyes were wet but he had stopped sobbing.

"You're a good shot, mister," Austin said.

Shad said nothing.

"Mister, you can't eat all them chickens." Austin pointed to the carnage. "We'll clean up the place if you give us one."

Without answering, Shad turned and walked toward the cabin. The three children watched as he opened the door and went inside, leaving the door open.

"What's he gonna do?" Peg wondered.

"No tellin'." Austin shrugged.

"Peg," Davy said. "I'm scared. I think we ought to leave. Austin, let's go."

"I thought you were hungry."

"I *am*, but I'm scared, too."

"Be quiet a minute, Davy."

"Austin?" Peg asked. "You think we should start cleaning things up?"

Austin shrugged again and kept looking toward the cabin. It wasn't long before Shad came out, still carrying the rifle, but with the other hand holding a long, sharp flensing knife.

The three children looked at one another uneasily. Davy looked the uneasiest of the three as Shad came closer.

"Mister," Austin took a step forward, "what you gonna do?"

"I'm gonna skin that cougar."

The answer came as a relief to Austin, Peg, and Davy.

"Can we take a chicken?" Austin asked. "If we clean the place up?"

"You can take one," Shad answered sharply, "if you just get the hell out of here, and stay out." He walked toward the carcass.

"Can I watch?" Davy hollered after him.

"No!"

Shad came to a stop close to the dead animal, hoisted its forepaw with the tip of his boot, then allowed the paw to fall to the ground with a finality.

This cougar was about as big as they got, close to eight feet long, but obviously undernourished. The cougar, also known in various regions as mountain lion, catamount, and panther, usually favored the high country and generally preyed on deer, horses, and cattle. And usually he was a night creature except when he got hungry enough. The skin was reddish-brown with lighter underparts. Shad set the Winchester down nearby and went about the bloody work.

Austin watched for a couple of minutes, so did Davy, but Peg turned her eyes away as Shad's knife sliced the skin of the predator. Shad never looked up from his labor.

"I'll fetch the fattest one and we'll get outta here." Austin started for the chicken coop.

"Austin." Peg touched his arm.

"What?"

"I think we ought to help clean things up."

Austin paused, looked at the chicken coop, then back at his sister.

"Austin? Don't you think we should?"

"Godalmighty," Tom said as the Keeshaws stopped at Dirty Creek on their way back from the Davis farm, "if that don't beat all!"

"If *what* don't beat all?" Deek's animal lapped at the cold, dirty water from the creek.

"That sodbuster back there, Davis."

"What about him?"

"Six kids, and it looked to me like the missus had one in the oven, either that or she's gone to fat."

"So?"

"So the whole herd of 'em in that two-room shack, and him callin' it their 'home' and sayin' that they'd decided to stay and make their future here in this part of the world."

"So?"

"So, some future. Hell, I thought we was bad off before the war back in Clay County, but those damn fools don't have no more chance than a quail with one wing."

"Looked to me," Bart grinned, "like she was a good-lookin' woman about three kids back. She's gone to pot, all right. The whole lot of 'em is pathetic."

"Well," Deek said, "that's their lookout. Good thing they didn't want to sell. Saves us the trouble of dickering about the price."

"Yeah." Bart checked his timepiece. "Imagine us livin' on that patch of hell."

"Boys, all we got to imagine is those good times and señoritas waiting down south."

"Suppose one of them other sodbusters *is* anxious to sell out?" Tom grinned. "Then what do we do?"

"Let me worry about that."

"Deek, do we have to see any more of those people on that map today?" Bart put the watch back into his pocket.

"Hell, no. Save some for tomorrow. I think we've done an honest day's work, don't you, boys?"

"Yeahbo," Bart agreed. "'Sides, I'm close to four bucks ahead on that poker game."

"Yeah, well, first we'll pay Mr. Bush a visit and let him know about our talk with his friend Davis . . ."

"Say, Deek," Bart poked his tongue through the gap between his teeth and licked his lips, "you think you're ever gonna catch up with that there Yellow Rose?"

"Oh, I'll catch up with her, all right, and when I do, I'll give her somethin' to remember me by. Let's go."

They moved their horses out of the shallow stream and headed east.

"I'm getting pretty damn hungry." Tom said.

"Me, too." Bart patted his gut. "We got to pass by ol' Mr. No Trespassin'—maybe he'll invite us in for a bite to eat."

"Not likely," Deek said.

Shad Parker paid no attention to what the children were doing. He had finished skinning the cougar; its pelt was stretched out to dry.

He had vowed to kill nothing unless it was absolutely unavoidable. Maybe he could have avoided killing the cougar, but if the animal got away with preying on Shad Parker's possessions once, then he'd be back. Firing a couple of shots past the predator might discourage him for a time, but when he got hungry enough, he'd muster up his courage and come back for more. This way he'd never come back.

Shad thought of all those he had killed during the war, Bluebellies, his comrades called them then, and worse. They, too, were looked upon as predators who came to kill and destroy. Shad never owned a slave, nor cared to. Neither had his father and grandfather before him. The Parkers had always done their own work, or hired others to help them, but always paid top wages and expected fair measure in return.

Still, when the war began, it was impossible to remain neutral and subscribe to the policy of whichever side won—particularly in the Shenandoah Valley. It was one thing to live in the West, hundreds, even thousands of miles away from the clashing armies and await the outcome, it was another matter in the Shenandoah Valley. The valley was a battlefield and no one stayed neutral in a battlefield.

To the armies of both North and South the Shenandoah was a strategic position, a vital link that meant conquest or defeat, a position that had to be taken and held, even if it meant destroying it in the taking and keeping. The fact that it had been haven and home to hundreds, thousands, for generations was inconsequential. The farms, orchards, homes, and the families who worked and lived there were expendable. If it had been expedient for the Southern forces to destroy it, they would have done so. The Shenandoah would have been just another Confederate casualty in the "cause" as had been the city of Atlanta. Both sides contributed to the destruction of that site. There, railroads and factories were dynamited by Hood's troops as they withdrew from their positions so they would not fall to the advancing Union armies and be used to help that advance. And Sherman's hordes utterly destroyed what was left.

There were no factories and railroad networks in the Shenandoah. There, it was the possession of the land itself that was vital as a strategic passageway.

Both sides fought for that possession, but it was the Northerners, the Bluebellies, who were the predators. It was they who had to be stopped and turned away.

And Shad Parker had no choice, except to try to stop them. At first it seemed that might be possible, and if any one man could convert that possibility to reality, that man was Jubal Anderson Early. But if any one man could prevent him from doing so, that man was Philip Henry Sheridan. And unfortunately for the South, Sheridan made the ride that would be talked about, then written about, so long as classes in warfare were studied and taught. Shad Parker was there when it happened.

Phil Sheridan with forty-five thousand men had invaded the Shenandoah Valley with orders from U. S. Grant to follow Jubal Early and his army to the death and to peel the land.

The surprise attack succeeded in driving back and disorganizing the Union troops. When word of the rout reached Sheridan he sprang on his strong, coal-black horse, Rienzi, and rode full speed into the center of his disorderly, retreating forces. Astride his tired and lathered horse he drew his sword from its scabbard.

"Goddamn you!" he shouted, and waved his sword, "turn and fight! Follow me!"

The retreat stopped dead. The men began to chant "Sheridan! Sheridan! Sheridan!" Caps were thrown to the tops of the scattering oaks.

"Don't cheer me! Goddamn you! Fight! We'll lick them out of their boots!"

And lick them the Bluebellies did. And Shad Parker was one of those who had been licked. But he lived.

By then Shad Parker had a bellyful of killing, and what he had known in his heart from the beginning was confirmed. The Confederacy was doomed. Still he kept on fighting and killing, haunted by the ghost battalions that had fallen on both sides, until the bitter end. But never did Shad Parker think that the end would be as bitter as it turned out.

He piled more dirt on the mound and patted it with the shovel.

"Why you doing that?"

Shad snapped up from his work and memories, turned, and faced the smallest of the three children who stood nearby watching him. He went back to patting the mound.

"Why did you bury it?" Davy pointed to the heap of earth.

Shad Parker had forgotten about the young squatters.

"Huh?" Davy persisted.

"Don't want buzzards hanging around," Shad replied after a pause, "or anybody else, either."

"I know that people get buried when they die."

Shad gave no response.

"My mommy and daddy are buried."

The man with the shovel wanted to hear no more about it. He wiped the cold sweat from his brow and whacked the spade against the cougar's grave.

"They got the fever and . . ."

"Quit yapping!"

That startled the boy into silence. Shad slammed

down the shovel, picked up the Winchester, and walked away, leaving Davy by the gravesite.

He moved in the direction of the cabin, but stopped and looked toward the chicken coop, where Austin and Peg were still cleaning things up. Shad noted that neither sister nor brother was afraid of work, nor were they squeamish in handling the ravaged poultry. They had retrieved the stray chickens, set the six that were dead in a straight line against the fence, repaired the area, and generally set things right—better than before. It was almost as if they were working in their own backyard.

Shad Parker didn't want them to get any such notion. He didn't want them to take advantage of the cougar's attack by using it as a way to ease themselves onto his property or his privacy. The youngest one had left the mound where the cougar lay buried, walked over to the chicken coop, and looked at Shad while his brother and sister continued working.

"All right, you three," Shad hollered out, "that's enough."

"We'll be through in just a few minutes." Peg looked up but her brother kept working.

"You're through now."

"But, mister, what do you want us to do with . . ." But Peg saw that the man was neither watching nor listening to her. He had turned and was facing the three riders. Deek Keeshaw waved as they pulled up.

"Hello again."

Shad Parker did not wave back nor speak.

"On our way back to town."

Still nothing.

"We found the place, all right. Had a nice visit.

Mr. Davis got himself quite a family." By now it was evident that this was going to be a one-sided conversation. Deek glanced from Shad Parker over to the three children by the chicken coop, who looked very much at home. "Fine-looking family *you* got there."

The Keeshaws rode on toward Gilead.

Deek's last remark had been too much for Shad Parker to endure. When the riders were out of earshot Shad looked directly at Austin.

"Take your damned chicken and get outta here!" He turned and walked into the cabin, this time slamming the door behind him.

Chapter 15

Amos Bush's chair was vacant.

Deek Keeshaw was the first to enter the bank, followed by his brothers, as usual, in the order of their births. Bart closed the door.

Deek ambled a few steps toward the big desk then looked back, past the teller's cage toward the rear of the room.

"Can I help you, gentlemen?" The teller spoke with an important voice that denoted he was the more regnant of the two employees present. The clerk who had often been reminded of that fact during President Bush's absence didn't bother to look up from his bookkeeping.

"We're the Keeshaws." Deek smiled amiably. "Stopped by to see Amos yesterday, remember?"

"Yes, of course." The teller seemed somewhat offended at the notion that he wouldn't remember. "I'm Raymond Osgood, Mr. Bush's—associate."

Deek knew damn well that the little man was just an ordinary teller, but if the little man wanted to bestow a title on himself during Amos Bush's absence

Deek figured there'd be no harm, and maybe even some advantage, in going along with the affectation.

"What can I do for you, gentlemen?"

Deek noted that Raymond Osgood seemed to be doing an imitation of Amos Bush's voice and manner. He half expected Raymond to step over and sit in Amos Bush's chair. But Osgood stayed in his cage.

"Oh, nothing special, just wanted to report to Amos on our progress, that's all. Will he be back later?"

"Oh, I'm afraid not. Amo . . . uh, Mr. Bush has a meeting with a depositor away from the office."

The clerk side-glimpsed with a flicker then went on balancing the accounts.

"Be in tomorrow?" Deek pulled the pipe out of his pocket.

"Oh, yes. First thing in the morning."

"Well, like I said, nothing special. We'll catch up to him."

"Very good." The teller cleared his throat as if he might say something important. "Good day, gentlemen."

"Good day, Mr. . . . . Osgood."

All the Keeshaws cast a farewell glance at the safe, then left the premises.

Raymond Osgood knew, but didn't mention to the Keeshaws, that Amos Bush's "meeting" with the depositor would last through most of the night as it had, once a week, every week for nearly two years. The meeting took place between Bush and a young eye-filling widow named Hannah Brown. And it was Bush who made the deposits.

There were others in Gilead who also knew, including Bush's wife, Laureen, but nobody ever talked about it, except in whispers, for three reasons. Out of respect and affection for Laureen Bush, who was crippled and confined to a wheelchair and bed. Because Hannah Brown was not a bad woman. She had suffered the loss of a husband during the war and was attempting to prevent suffering the loss of her home, on which Amos Bush held a considerable mortgage. The third reason was that almost everybody in town had to do business with Amos Bush. He was not a man to cross—a few had tried and borne the consequences.

Outside, Deek Keeshaw stepped from the wind into the doorway of the sheriff's office and lit his pipe. As he did he looked inside and saw that Deputy Keeler was passing the time playing solitaire. Elwood Hinge was nowhere in sight.

As Keeler glanced up, Deek waved. The deputy waved back with a ten of diamonds and went on with his game.

"I'm hungry enough to eat a horse, hair and all," Tom said. "Let's go over to the restaurant."

"I'm going over to the barbershop, get a shave."

"Hell, Deek, you just got a shave yesterday. You're gonna wear the hide right off your jaw, ain't he, Bart?"

"I think he's thinkin' about wearin' the hide offa Yellow Rose, that's what I'm thinkin'."

"I think you better shut up, Bart, and let me do the thinking. Now, you can go eat, or you can go up to the room and wait for me."

"We'll go up to the room and wait. That okay with you, Bart?"

Bart shrugged.

Tom and Bart headed across to the Eden, and

Deek took a puff from his pipe and sauntered toward Tony's Barber Shop.

It was not yet dark when Homer Keeler looked up in response to a rap on the window of the door. Kathy Lewis knocked again and turned the knob. The door opened. Homer hadn't locked up for the night. He was waiting for the sheriff to return.

Homer Keeler placed a queen on a queen and rose to meet her. Kathy Lewis was eighteen, leaned a little toward plumpness, but had an attractive, deep-dimpled, heart-shaped face and plenty of soft brown hair. Her eyes were doleful and fawnlike. Tonight they were particularly doleful. A long, knitted shawl covered most of her upper body.

"Kathy, sure didn't expect to see you. What're you doing in town?"

"Ma and Pa are over at Inghram's picking up some goods. Told them I was going to stop by for a minute."

"Good." Homer glanced out of the window, then took her in his arms and kissed her.

Kathy Lewis trembled. She was crying.

"Kathy, honey. What's the matter? Something happen? Somebody hurt?"

She sobbed even more.

"Kathy . . ."

"Oh, Homer, I'm in trouble . . . bad trouble. I . . . I guess we both are." She stepped away from him and opened the shawl with both hands. "Homer, what am I going to do? Pretty soon it'll start to show . . . I didn't want to tell you, but . . ."

"My God! Are you sure?"

She nodded.

"My God!" he repeated.

"I think it was that night after the dance, remember? I told you . . ."

"I remember . . . Does anybody know? Did you see a doctor?"

"I'm afraid to."

"Damn!"

"I'm sorry, Homer, I swear I didn't mean for it to happen like this. What's going to happen when they find out?"

"Damn!" he repeated.

"I knew you'd be mad, Homer. I didn't mean . . ."

"Kathy, stop saying that! I'm not mad . . ."

"You're not?"

"Well, I . . . I don't know what I am. I just wasn't ready for anything like this."

"You think I was?"

"No, that's not what I mean."

"What do you mean?"

"I just don't know what I mean. I've got to think on it."

"What's there to think about? I'm going to have a baby . . ."

"Shhh, not so loud." He looked toward the cells. "There's a couple of prisoners back there." He wiped the tears from her eyes, but the tears kept coming. "Kathy, quit crying. Just let me think about it, and I'll . . ."

"You'll *what*, Homer? Will you marry me?"

"I guess . . . if I have to . . ."

"Well, what else is there?"

"I don't know. I guess there's nothing else. Now,

look. First off stop crying. I'll see you tomorrow, or soon as I can. Don't say anything to anybody. I'm not going to leave you. I'll be here with you."

"But will you *marry* me?"

"Kathy, please. Elwood might be back anytime. I'll come see you tomorrow. I promise."

"Promise."

"I swear."

"Homer, do you love me?"

He looked into her fawnlike eyes, then nodded.

"Say it, Homer."

"I love you, Kathy."

The moon continued its upward arch across the dark, seamless canvas of sky.

Shad Parker had eaten as much of the chicken as he was going to, at least this night, and was going up against the bottle. The boy had been right when he said "you can't eat all them chickens." Shad ate only one, and only part of that one. The other four he plucked and hung in the smokehouse. He wondered how the three youngsters were going to prepare the bird they took up to the cave with them. He doubted if they had a pan or kettle, but he wasn't going to think about it, or them, if he could help it.

They had introduced themselves by name, but Shad purposely didn't pay attention to the girl as she told him who they were. Shad didn't want to know their names or anything about them. Better they remain nameless, faceless, and better still if they got out of the cave and out of his life. But he couldn't help thinking about them, particularly the girl. And he did remember that her name was Peg. Her eyes were twin pits of tragedy, but somehow there was still an aspect of strength, even dignity, about her little face and frame. It was apparent that she was mother as well as sister to the smaller boy. As for the older one, it was apparent that he sought no pity, nor even quarter. He would be a fighter when he grew up, if he grew up—if any of them grew up. But then Shad's children never grew up. One of them didn't even get born.

Chapter 16

There was nothing left of the chicken except bony remains, and Austin leaned against the wall of the cave and gnawed on the last of the chicken leg.

They had plucked the bird and used Austin's pocket-knife to cut it up, and somehow Peg had managed to fry the parts on the sharp ends of sticks. A couple of times the sticks burned through and fell into the fire along with the chicken parts, but Peg succeeded in retrieving most of the parts and all three of them succeeded in eating the cooked meat, including some of the ashes from the fire that the parts had fallen into.

Peg emerged from out of the shadows, walked close to Austin, and sat near him.

"He's already asleep."

"Sure ate his share of that bird," Austin said.

They were no longer hungry. But they were tired. More than tired. Weary. Almost worn out. They sat in silence for a moment, looking at the dwindling fire.

Austin placed another branch on it from the fallen tree and sat back close to Peg again.

"You're a good cook, Peg."

"When I got something to cook." She tried to smile.

"I know."

They sat, wordless shadows for a few moments.

"Austin."

He looked at her.

"What we gonna do?"

He ran his dirty fingers through his hair and wiped at his mouth.

"Austin?"

"I don't know." He tossed the bone into the fire. "You want to go back to . . . that place?"

Peg didn't answer. She just stared into the fire.

"You want to go back to old Miss Stench? She'd really have it in for us now. I can't abide the way that she treats you," Austin pointed at a dark corner, "and little Davy, whacking him like she does."

"I know . . . maybe . . ."

"Maybe what?"

"Maybe this time somebody'll come along who'd take all three of us."

"Who? Who needs three more mouths to feed in times like these? 'Sides, there's no new people coming into Palestine. People are leaving, going west or north and they ain't taking no extra baggage with them. No, Peg, if we go back, it's to stay—at least till I can get out and find someplace for all three of us."

"I know. But, poor Davy, I just don't know how much more of this he can take, either."

Silent shadows again.

"Austin."

"What?"

"That man down there in the cabin . . ."

"What about him?"

"I don't think he's as mean as he lets on."

"I do."

"He gave us that chicken, didn't he?"

"We're just lucky that cougar came along when he did, otherwise we wouldn't've got nothing from him, and don't expect to get anything more."

"I guess you're right."

"Peg, you know those men we saw today? Those three of 'em?"

"Yes."

"Well, they said they was coming from a place near here. Said there was a family there, the Davises. Isn't that what they said?"

Peg nodded.

"Well, tomorrow, you and Davy stay here. I'll go find the Davis place. See what they're like. Maybe I can find some work there. Don't you think that's a good idea?"

"I guess so." Peg yawned, tired and sleepy.

"Get some rest, Peg."

"I will." She touched his hand. "Austin, things'll come right."

He nodded and did his best to smile.

Naked, she lay on the canopied bed. Uncovered. Unashamed. Only a part of him was covered with a towel.

At the Appaloosa or on the street, he, like all the others, called her Yellow Rose. But here, in her room, in her bed, she was Rosalind. His body hard and strong, though past the mid-fifties mark, Elwood Hinge kissed the lips of Rosalind DuPree, an after-passion kiss. She smiled and did not move. Then the smile faded.

"El . . . I've got to leave."

"You going to the Appaloosa tonight?"

"That's not what I mean."

He rose, leaned on one elbow, and looked at her.

"What *do* you mean?"

"I'm leaving Gilead."

"Rosalind . . ."

"It's no use, El. It'll soon be Christmas, then New Year. I'm not going to spend another year here. There's nothing for me here."

"Nothing?"

"Except you, El."

"But that's not enough. What about your half of the Appaloosa?"

"Hooter said he'd buy me out. Not for what it's worth, but that's all right. I'll just consider it a business loss. I've lost before."

"Where you going?"

"Not sure. Someplace different. Anyplace. Maybe San Francisco."

"Well, San Francisco is different, all right."

"What's the matter, El?" She smiled. "Don't you think that I can compete with the girls in San Francisco?"

"Rosalind, far as I'm concerned you haven't got any competition with anybody, anyplace. And you haven't got any business . . ."

"Now, El, don't get maudlin, please. Don't even get

ordinary. That's one of the things I liked about you right from the start. You weren't ordinary, like the rest of them."

"Neither are you, Rosalind."

"All right, so we're a couple of extra-ordinary people. We met. We . . . well, here we are." Rosalind patted the bed. "We had something. Something good. But how long can it stay good? No, El, it's time for me to move on again."

"You mean to run away again? Like you been running since New Orleans?"

"What's the alternative? The Appaloosa . . . and you?"

"Does it have to be both of us, the Appaloosa *and* me? Isn't one enough?"

"Which one?" She smiled again.

"Cut it out, Rosalind. You know what I'm talking about."

"No, I don't think it is enough, El. Not because I don't love you, because I guess I do, at least as close as I'm able to come to love. I just don't think it's right and after a while you wouldn't, either. Somebody would say something, somebody I knew once at the Appaloosa or one of the other places, and you, dear El, would have to defend my . . . honor."

"We could go someplace else, Wyoming, the Oregon Territory. Look, Rosalind, I'm not much, not educated like you. Hell, I was the oldest soldier in our outfit, and I'm pretty damn old to be a lawman, most of 'em don't last this long, but I've got some money coming and . . ."

"El, not only are you not ordinary, you're noble.

And I appreciate it, with all my heart. But it wouldn't work. There are too many ghosts. Living ghosts. Now, you'd better get back to your duties. You've been here a lot longer than usual."

"Rosalind."

"No, El. We'll talk another time."

"All right. Are you going to . . . the Appaloosa tonight?"

"No. Not tonight."

Deek Keeshaw had been shaved again by Tony and had gotten doused again with lilac toilet water. He had stopped by the Eden, met up with his brothers, proceeded with them to the New Heidelberg, and eaten a steak.

He had made it a point to look into the sheriff's office to see if Hinge had returned. He hadn't. So the Keeshaws then proceeded to the Appaloosa, had a few drinks, and sat in on a poker game.

But once again Deek Keeshaw's mind was not set on poker. Once again Yellow Rose had failed to appear and once again Deek's game suffered for it. Once again the shave and lilac toilet water had gone for naught. He sure as hell wasn't going to waste it and the money on Francine or that bag of bones, Stella Bright. So Deek played poker and kept one eye on the saloon door for Yellow Rose and the other eye across the street for the sheriff. While doing so he lost six dollars and twenty-five cents.

Yellow Rose never did appear. After about an hour Deek quit playing poker and stood by the window. It wasn't too long before he spotted the sheriff across the street. Damn, if he wasn't coming from the direction of the Eden.

Deek intended to go over and talk to Hinge, find out what he could about the disposition of the prisoners, but thought it best to wait until the deputy left.

As the door opened Homer Keeler looked up with a start. His head had been burrowed into both palms.

"What's the matter, Homer? You sick?"

"No, sir, not exactly?"

"Not exactly? What's that mean?"

"Well, sir . . . it's just that I've got a . . . There's a situation . . ."

"Has it got anything to do with them prisoners back there?"

"Uh, no, sir."

"Well, then, I guess it's none of my business—and will you quit *sir'n'* me like that!"

"Yes, sir, I mean . . . Well, Elwood, you know I got a lot of respect for you and I was wonderin', can I ask you for some advice?"

"You can if you get up and let me sit in my chair."

Homer bolted up from the chair and the sheriff sat in front of the rolltop.

"What is it, Homer?"

"Well, you know I haven't got any kin, leastwise around here, so you're about the closest . . ."

"What *is* it, Homer?" Hinge repeated.

"Kathy Lewis."

"What about her?"

"She . . . That is, she and I . . ."

"Are you gonna have a baby?"

"How'd you know?!" Homer seemed startled.

"Oh, just a wild guess. That and the way you're stuttering and stammering and look like you're gonna wet your pants. So what are you gonna do?"

"Well, she wants us to get married."

"That's not unusual."

"I know . . . but I'm not sure I'm geared to gettin' married."

"Homer, you should've thought of that before you put your poker in the fire. Look, Homer, there's worse things than getting married. Sometimes I wish I would've got married myself."

"You do?"

"Sure I do. Kathy's a nice girl. She'll make a nice wife, particularly since she's already on her way to being a mother. You've got a job. You make enough money."

"But she don't like me being a lawman."

"Well, that's too bad because you're both gonna have to do a little compromising."

"I guess so."

"Well, then, you tell her so. And, 'sides, I won't be around forever. You'll be steppin' up in the law business, maybe sooner than you think."

"You make it sound smooth and easy."

"No, Homer, it ain't all that smooth, nor all that easy—nothing is. You'll have your share of lumps and bumps but you've both got a lot going for you. You're young and healthy and . . . well, I was going to say 'bright,' but make that reasonably bright. So you'll be all right. And I'll toss in a share of that reward as a wedding present. Now, go home."

"Yes, sir, thank you. Good night, Elwood."

As Homer Keeler left, Elwood Hinge reflected on the irony of their situations, his and Homer's. Kathy Lewis wanted to get married and Homer didn't. At least he said he wasn't geared for it. Elwood Hinge had proposed to Rosalind DuPree and she sure as hell didn't say yes.

From inside the window of the Appaloosa Deek watched as Homer came out the office door, closed it behind him, looked up at the blue ball of the moon, pulled up his collar, and walked away. Deek turned toward Tom and Bart, who were still sitting in the poker game.

"All right, Bart, Tom, that's enough for tonight. Let's turn in."

"Hold on," Bart said, looking at his hand. "I got a . . ."

"I said, that's enough. Play your hand and cash in."

"Cash in is right," Chris Perkins said, not in good humor. "I'm out twenty. What's the big rush to cut out all of a sudden?"

"Got to get going." Deek tried out his charm.

"What's the matter? They afraid of the dark?" Chris said. His humor hadn't improved any. "I'll walk 'em home, when I get some of my money back."

"You'll get it back tomorrow." Deek smiled. "We got to get an early start. Business."

"Two pair!" Chris slammed his cards on the table, spilling the small stack of chips in front of him. "Kings over."

"Beats me," Tom said.

"Me, too." Bart threw in his cards.

"You see, Chris," Deek pointed at the pot, "you got some of it back already. You'll get the rest tomorrow."

Chris Perkins raked in his pot with both gnarly hands.

"I had him beat, you know," Bart said as the brothers walked across the street. "Three deuces."

"I know." Deek nodded. "You used your head . . . for once."

Elwood Hinge was trying to pry off a boot as the door opened. At the sound the sheriff instantly unbent and reached toward the shotgun.

"Take her easy, Sheriff." Deek smiled as they entered.

"What do you want?" The sheriff did not smile.

"Just a little information if you don't mind. Bart, give the sheriff a hand with his boots."

"Sure. Glad to." Bart walked over to the sheriff, who held up his right leg. Bart straddled it as Hinge shoved Bart in the butt with his left boot.

"Told you the other day we're looking to settle around here, buy ourselves a spread . . ."

"So you said."

"Well, Amos Bush, seems like a nice fellow, Mr. Bush, he gave us the names of some people who might be interested in selling. Drew us a map. Rode out to see Mr. Davis today but he's not selling . . ."

The sheriff's right boot came loose from his foot. Bart dropped the boot and assumed the position again in order to remove the other boot.

". . . we're riding out to talk to Sam Allen in the morning." Deek withdrew the map from his pocket.

"Now, this map Amos drawed us—once we get off the road here, I don't recollect what he said—turn to the left or to the right?"

Off came the second boot. Bart dropped it on the floor next to the first one.

"To the right."

"Uh-huh, much obliged." Deek looked around. "Say, Sheriff, you sleep here?"

"Just when the county's got guests. Part of our hospitality."

"Yes, we heard about them. What're they wanted for?"

"Busted out of jail back in Arkansas. Murder and robbery, to boot. This is as far as they got."

"What's going to happen to 'em?"

"Marshal be by to pick 'em up before Christmas. Thought he'd be here by now."

"See, there's a reward." Deek pointed to the dodgers.

"Yep."

"Congratulations. From what we heard you earned it."

"That's my job."

"From what we've *seen* and heard, you're good at it. Right, boys?"

Tom and Bart both nodded.

"Well, thanks and good night, Sheriff." Deek started for the door. Tom and Bart followed. Deek opened the door.

"You boys . . ."

Deek and the others paused and looked back.

". . . ever been to Arkansas?"

"Never have."

The door closed behind them.

* * *

Amos Bush sat on the edge of the bed, lacing up his shoes, with his back to Hannah Brown, who still lay on the bed covered only by a thin sheet that failed to disguise the attractive mold of her outstretched body. She faced the ceiling but her eyes were closed. The bedroom was lit by a single kerosene lamp on the dresser.

"Hannah."

"Yes?"

"I'm going to ask you to do something."

"What is it?" Hannah's eyes opened slowly but she did not look at him.

"That picture." Amos Bush pointed to a large photograph that hung on the wall. It was of a handsome young man in a Confederate uniform. The handsome young man held a rifle with a bayonet attached, pointing straight ahead.

The photographer had shot the picture so that no matter where the viewer stood or sat or lay looking at the picture the sharp point of the bayonet followed the viewer.

"What about it?" Hannah said.

"I'm going to ask you to take it down."

"Why?"

"You know why. I don't want to come here again and have him . . . well, I just don't. You can understand that."

"Yes, I can."

"Good." Bush had finished with both shoes. He leaned across the bed and kissed Hannah Brown. She did not respond.

"Mr. Bush, we made an agreement, you and I.

I intend to live up to it. There was nothing in that agreement about the picture. The picture stays. If you want to break the agreement, Mr. Bush, then that's up to you."

"Will you stop calling me 'Mr. Bush.' And don't tell me there was an agreement about that, either!" He rose and picked up his jacket from a chair. "Hannah . . ."

"Yes, Mr. Bush."

"Never mind." Amos Bush walked to the bedroom door, stopped, and looked back. "I'll see you next week."

Chapter 17

The frosted dew, scented with the mysterious fragrances of dawn, clung failingly to the field, rocks, and hillside around the cabin until the sun reached over the eastern rim, then surrendered.

Shad Parker felt no better, no worse, than after most of the other nights he had lived through since coming to Texas. He ate the same morning meal, drank the same number of cups of coffee, and went about the same chores with the horses, hogs, and hens, although this morning there were fewer hens to feed than yesterday and fewer eggs to pick up.

All of his life he had been either a farmer or a soldier and both endeavors entailed getting up early, except being a soldier sometimes meant getting no sleep at all while wondering through the night if the next day sleep would be eternal.

Shad Parker looked up from his chores. There was movement near the opening of the small cave. The older boy was taking leave of his sister and brother. His silhouette, backlit against the sun, made its way along the crest of the hill. Satisfied that the silhouette wasn't coming down in his direction, Shad glanced toward the sister and brother standing near the cave. He doubted that from this distance she had caught his glance but she did wave at him. Once, then again.

Shad went back to his work without acknowledgment. He had no intention of encouraging any further encounter or even communication with the pint-sized intruders. He was content to spend the day in the society of the horses, hogs, and hens.

Even after he turned away the little girl waved again. Then she put her arm around the small boy's shoulder and they went back into the cave.

They had not shared a marriage bed since the accident. Still, every morning, with the help of her housekeeper, Candida Guzman, Laureen would come to the breakfast table in the wheelchair while Amos Bush ate, drank his coffee, then left for the bank.

Her seraphic face was magnolia pink and delicately structured, much more delicately than her body had been structured before the accident. Since the fall, Laureen had lost weight, her former well-knit figure now a minimal framework for a wasteyard body, sustained mostly by soup and tea.

The conversation, sparse but civilized, was always even sparser on the morning after his weekly visit to Hannah Brown. Laureen always brought her Bible to the table. But this was one of the few times during the day or during the night when she wasn't asleep, that she did not open it.

Located on the southeastern outskirts of town, the Bush house—the townspeople called it the Bush Mansion—was the biggest and best dwelling in or around Gilead. It was two full stories, three-quarters surrounded by a filigreed porch wide enough to accommodate a two-up horse and carriage. Amos Bush had it built for his bride from Louisville a dozen years ago, half a dozen years before the start of the War for the Confederacy.

They had shared the huge master bedroom upstairs until the accident in the winter of '63. After that the drawing room on the first floor was converted into a sleeping room, a room in which Amos Bush had never spent a night with his wife.

Those who saw her astride the stallion that night said she was galloping as if riding into hell—or away from it. There was frost on the ground. The stallion slipped, fell, and broke its leg. Laureen broke her back. The stallion was, of course, shot and put out of its suffering.

A doctor from Dallas said an operation by a specialist in Chicago might enable Laureen to walk again, but Laureen never went to see the specialist, never left the house. There was a war going on, and after the war Laureen never mentioned Chicago or the specialist. She seemed resigned to her fate: the house, the husband, and the Bible.

There were some who said, again in whispers only, that Laureen and Amos's troubles began when they quarreled because she felt that his sympathies and financial resources were not as strong for the cause as they should have been. There were rumors that

Amos Bush had personally invested his money in enterprises that supplied the needs of the Northern armies.

The rumors were never substantiated, but Bush was one of the few in Texas whose funds flourished in the battlefield of Southern defeat.

There were other rumors, in even more subdued whispers, that Laureen was not a "warm" woman. But, of course, Amos Bush did not know that before the marriage. What he did know, was that she came from a rich Southern family and that she also came with a considerable dowry, money Bush needed to infuse into the lifeblood of his hemorrhaging bank.

That was why he had gone to Louisville, to secure a loan from Claude Kingsly, president of the Louisville Trust. Bush succeeded in procuring the loan as well as a bride, who happened to be Kingsly's daughter, and the dowry, to boot. Ironically the Louisville Trust went bust during the war. Kingsly inserted the barrel of a shotgun into his mouth and proceeded to blow his brains out against the back of his banker's chair.

"Did you enjoy your . . . breakfast this morning, Amos?" Laureen asked while she sipped her tea.

"Yes, thank you, Laureen. Just as I do every morning."

"One morning a week more than the others, I dare say."

"Laureen, please . . ."

"Oh, it's all right, Amos. I'm quite past caring."

"It seems you were past caring a long time ago."

"Since I discovered that we had a different set of values about several things."

"All right, Laureen, since you see fit to bring up the subject from time to time . . ."

"I think you know the times, and somehow you didn't manage to slip out early today . . ."

"Nor do I intend to slip out early ever again. Let's talk about the value you put on being a wife," he pointed to the book on her lap, "in the biblical sense." The grip of her left hand tightened on the Bible as he spoke. "The Bible, which you read and study and sleep with. 'And Ruth said, "Entreat me not to leave thee, or to return from following after thee, for whither thou goest I will go; and where thou lodgest, I will lodge . . ."' For how long did you place a value on being a wife, if ever? From that first time in our marriage bed did you ever try to be a wife? Was I that repugnant to you, Laureen?"

"Not you, Amos. It. The act. The act itself. Unclean. Debasing. I tried . . ."

"Did you? So did I, Laureen, as gently and patiently as any man ever tried."

"As you do with your whore?"

"She's not that . . ."

"Then, what is she? Do you love her, Amos?"

"I need her. Or someone. Every man does. And so should every woman. Every woman but you, Laureen. I'm sorry. The accident, if that's what it was, is just an excuse, a convenience, so now you don't have to turn away from me. That's why you won't consider that operation, because now you're afraid—not afraid that you might die, or that it might fail—you're afraid it might succeed. That wheelchair is your escape—from me, from life. You can change that anytime you want,

Laureen, but you won't. So, I'll keep going to her as long as she'll let me."

Amos Bush rose and left his wife in the wheelchair with the Bible still gripped in her hand.

Raymond Osgood had been instructed by Amos Bush to be in front of the bank every workday at 9:25 A.M. If Bush hadn't arrived by precisely 9:30 A.M. Osgood was to use his own key, let himself and the clerk Henry Wordsly into the bank, and open for business.

That's exactly what Raymond Osgood did that morning. While Osgood had told everyone in Gilead that he had a key to the bank, he didn't tell anyone that he did not have the combination to the safe.

Only Amos Bush and the company in Chicago had that.

Since Bush had not arrived by precisely 9:30 A.M. Raymond Osgood looked around and with as much ceremony as possible withdrew his key chain from a pocket after returning his silver watch into another pocket and carried out instructions while Henry Wordsly didn't even try not to look bored even before the business day began.

Osgood and Wordsly could accomplish only a restricted amount of business until the safe was opened, but it didn't matter much because nobody came in to do any business.

Only the Keeshaws came in, and when they were told by Osgood that Mr. Bush had been unavoidably detained that morning, the Keeshaws, actually Deek, made a point of letting Raymond Osgood know that they were on their way to see Sam Allen, using the map that Amos Bush had so kindly drawn for them.

Elwood Hinge and Homer Keeler were both at the sheriff's headquarters. They had verified the fact that both Charlie Reno and Red Borden were both still alive and still incarcerated.

When Hinge went to make the daily pot of coffee he discovered that their supply of ground beans was dangerously low.

"Use what's left of them beans and brew up some tar, Homer. I'll go over to Inghram's and have Pete grind us up some more."

"Sure thing, Elwood."

"Homer."

"Yes, sir."

"Don't give them two back there any hot coffee till I get back."

"Yes, sir."

"As a matter of fact don't even go back there till I get back."

"All right, Sheriff. But . . ."

"But what?"

"Suppose there's some kind of emergency?"

"Like what?"

"Oh, I don't know . . . Suppose one of 'em manages to hang himself or something . . ."

"Let him hang."

"Sure thing."

"If you have to go back for some reason, take that scattergun with you but don't get too close."

"I understand."

Hinge put on his jacket and started out but stopped at the door. Keeler had started to make the coffee.

"Oh, Homer."

"Yes, sir."

"Have you had that talk with Kathy Lewis yet?"

"No, sir, not yet."

"I told you to quit that sir'n'. Well, talk to her today. You'll both feel better."

"Yes . . . I will, Elwood."

"Five hundred."

"What?"

"That's your share when we get the reward, five hundred."

"Thank you."

As Elwood Hinge, without his shotgun, walked along the boardwalk toward Inghram's General Store he was "merry Christmas'd" by close to a dozen of the citizens of Gilead, and the sheriff responded sometimes vocally, sometimes with a nod.

He paused on the corner and looked up at the second story of the Eden Hotel. He didn't really expect that Rosalind DuPree would be looking out of her window, and she wasn't. Elwood Hinge figured if he was lucky and didn't lean into a bullet, he had another dozen or so years left of reasonably good health. The time was close by—maybe he was already stepping on it—when he'd have to decide how, where, and with whom he was going to spend those years. The pause was barely perceptible, then Elwood Hinge walked on, across the street.

* * *

The wagon came in from the east.

The driver, a painfully thin man whose left arm had been amputated above the elbow—with him a comely woman and two children, boys, ages seven and four—also aboard were the worldly possessions of the family.

The wagon stopped in front of Inghram's General Store. The livery was still closed.

With some difficulty, the thin man got off the wagon then reached up to help his wife debark.

"You boys can stretch your legs, but don't stray." Both boys eagerly jumped off.

Sheriff Hinge passed by the group and entered the store.

Pete Inghram sat at the rolltop desk working on the books. He looked up at the sheriff, then got up.

"Morning, Elwood. What can I do you for?"

"Outta coffee. Will you grind me up three, four pounds?"

"Martha." Mrs. Inghram was already coming through the curtains from the back room.

"Morning, Sheriff."

"Morning."

"Martha, will you grind up . . ."

"I heard him, Pete." Martha Inghram went about the business of grinding up the coffee. Pete Inghram pointed the stub of a pencil toward a cigar box on the counter.

"Sheriff, care for a fine ceegar while you wait?"

"Thanks, no." The sheriff pointed toward a jar of candy not far from the cigar box. "But I do have that powerful sweet tooth."

"Hep 'self."

The sheriff did.

"Hummm . . . horehound."

The thin man and comely woman had entered and closed the door behind them. Pete Inghram came forward a couple of steps and greeted his new customers.

"Howdy . . . and merry Christmas."

"Hello," the man replied.

"Merry Christmas." The comely woman smiled.

"Strangers, aren't you?" Inghram, of course, knew that they were.

"Around here." The man also smiled. "But not in Virginia. Ben Warren . . . my wife, Esmeralda."

"Virginia! You come a distance. Pete Inghram . . . wife, Martha. And this here's our sheriff, Elwood Hinge."

Elwood Hinge nodded and helped himself to another piece of horehound.

"Settling here?" Pete asked.

"Passing through," Ben Warren answered. "Friend of ours settled here. Thought we'd stop by and see him. Shad Parker."

"He trades with us." Pete glanced toward the sheriff. "Friend, huh?"

"Best friend a man ever had. We were neighbors— until the war."

"He seems sorta . . . private." Pete Inghram figured he was being diplomatic.

"That man's been through hell, Mr. Inghram," Ben said.

"Shad lost his wife," Esmeralda explained, "two boys, his home . . . everything."

"Lost?"

"Burned in the war." Ben looked from Esmeralda to Inghram.

"Sherman?" Pete asked.

"Sheridan." Ben Warren bit into the word.

"That explains a lot," Pete observed after a pause.

"What do you mean?"

"Oh . . . about his being so . . . private. He don't talk much. Keeps to himself . . ."

"Yeah, I guess he would. Can you tell us where to find him?"

"Be glad to. Say, what part of Virginia you people from?"

"Most beautiful valley in the world. Used to be. Shenandoah."

Chapter 18

The Warren wagon rolled along the russet Texas countryside. Ben and Esmeralda had said next to nothing since getting directions at the store, but both were churning with memories, bittersweet.

Tradition dictated in Irish families that the elder of two daughters was the first to be married. And so it was with Esmeralda and Molly. First Esmeralda and Ben were married, then ten minutes later, Molly and Shad, at the same church by the same priest. It wasn't much of a ceremony, or ceremonies, because both were what the church termed "mixed marriages" and frowned upon. Many of the older priests refused to conduct such a service, but young Father Courtney didn't frown much and agreed to say the necessary words so long as both bridegrooms agreed that all of the children would be baptized and reared properly. Both Ben and Shad signed the appropriate articles and Father Courtney conducted the "off the altar" ceremonies at tiny St. Brendan's in Port Republic. The entire congregation didn't consist of more than three score parishioners, including men, women, and mostly children. Father John Courtney reasoned that with each addition to the Warren and Parker families his parish would probably exceed or at least keep pace with the mortality rate of his congregation.

Both Ben and Shad did their best not to disappoint Father Courtney. The Parkers were the first to bear and baptize. Sean Parker became part of St. Brendan's congregation in March of the following year. Others followed with galloping regularity. All boys. Shad Parker kept hoping and trying for a girl.

The Parkers and the Warrens were virtually one happy family as well as neighbors. The crops were abundant and so were the joys of life.

"Shad, my friend," Ben once said, and then repeated many times, "you and I are two of the luckiest buckos in God's sweet world. We have our women and our work. Can't wait to go out in the morning, can't wait to come home at night. What did we ever do to deserve such good fortune?"

"Well," Shad Parker responded the first time Ben put forth the question, "to begin with, we licked Tub MacGrudder, that was the day it all started . . ."

"Right you are," Ben pounded on his friend's back, "beat him to a fare-thee-well, we did! If we hadn't, I would have been reluctant to introduce you to the O'Connell clan!"

It seemed too good to last and it lasted until a tall shadow fell across the Shenandoah as well as the rest of the South, with the election of Abraham Lincoln in 1860.

Then, at Harper's Ferry, the clash of ideas became the clash of arms. Both Shad Parker and Ben Warren resisted the call to arms but only as long as their love of family, home, and the Shenandoah Valley would permit. They both knew they had to answer that call and they answered it together.

Both Shad Parker and Ben Warren joined General Thomas Jonathan Jackson's brigade to defend the valley against, and defeat, the invaders.

Defend and defeat they did, Parker and Warren together with Jackson at the First Battle of Bull Run and at Front Royal and Winchester, then later at the Second Battle of Bull Run and finally at Chancellorsville, where Stonewall Jackson died.

After that both Shad and Ben managed to return home for a short time before being reassigned, this time to different outfits and campaigns. And during that short time at home, both of their homes had still so far been spared—Molly and Esmeralda became enceinte.

Major Shad Parker joined up with General Jubal Early and Captain Ben Warren marched and fought with General Joseph E. Johnston at Manassas, Seven Pines, and finally with him against Sherman when Johnston was forced out of Dalton to Resaca, to Cassville and to Allatoona where a minié ball shattered Ben's left arm and ended the war for him and him for the war.

The last time Ben and Esmeralda had seen Shad Parker was at the gravesites of Molly and the two children after the war. He was a different man, in some ways not a man at all. A silent, brooding, bitter thing who stood staring at the stone that Ben had secured to mark their burial place.

The next day Shad Parker left the valley without a word, a letter, or a look back.

* * *

"Sorry, boy," Webb Davis said. "Got five sons of my own," and added with less approbation, "and a daughter, to boot." Davis stood on the porch of the ramshackle two-room farmhouse and looked at Austin Coats, who stood a few feet away. "Don't need help. Need a son-in-law and you're a few years short."

Austin nodded, turned, and started to walk away.

"Just a minute, boy."

Austin turned back.

"Where you headed?"

Austin shrugged.

"Don't know, huh. Well, where'd you come from? Must know that."

Austin said nothing.

"You're right, boy. It's none of my business . . ."

"Webb." Mrs. Davis appeared at the doorway. "Food's on the table. We're waitin'."

Webb Davis nodded at his wife.

"Maybe," Mrs. Davis said, "the boy's hungry."

"Ever know a boy who wasn't?" Davis smiled. "Hey, boy . . . come eat."

"Would I consider sellin'?" Sam Allen chewed on the words and the tobacco, then spit. "What'd you say your names was?"

"Keeshaw, Deek, and my brothers, Tom and Bart. Mr. Bush allowed as how you might consider sellin' . . ."

"Why? Because I'm gettin' old?"

"Well, no, Mr. Bush didn't say that, he . . ."

"That's what he meant. Well, Mr. Bush don't know wormwood from sarsaparilla. He's just lookin' for me to sell so's he could slap a mortgage on this spread like he's got on most every stick and stone in the county. But this one's free and clear, tall and uncut, just like me and that's the way it's gonna stay."

"No mortgage involved, Mr. Allen. We'd pay cash money."

"You ain't Texacans." The way he said it was an accusation.

"No, we ain't, but we're lookin' to be."

"Why?" Sam Allen spit again.

"Oh, I don't know, just because it suits us, I guess."

"Well, Mr. Heeshaw, the . . ."

"Keeshaw."

". . . the question ain't whether Texas suits you. It's whether you suit Texas."

"I see what you mean."

"No, you don't. You're just sayin' that 'cause you think I'm old like Amos Bush. Well, he couldn't find his ass with a funnel." Another spit.

"Well, we're sorry, Mr. Allen, we didn't mean to . . ."

"There you go again, bein' too polite just because I'm old or you think so, like that Amos Bushwhacker. Where you from?"

"Uh, Louisiana."

"Well, this here's Texas, belongs to Texacans, and always has ever since we took it from the Mexicans so you might just as well head back east to Louisiana."

"Sorry to have troubled you and sorry if we was too polite. Didn't mean to be."

"Hold on, you seem like good honest folk even if you ain't Texacans. When I do get old come back and see me and we might do business. I'm a fair judge of character, you can bet on that, and bring cash."

"You can bet we will, Mr. Allen . . ."

"Sam."

"You can bet we will, Sam."

"We was related you know."

"Who was?"

"Why me and Sam Houston, of course. I was with him at San Jacinto, used to bounce Temple on this knee."

"Temple?"

"Sam's son, Temple, fine fella even if he growed to be a lawyer." Allen spit again.

"Merry Christmas . . . Sam."

"That was funny." Tom said after they rode away.

"What was?" Deek asked.

"Couldn't find his ass with a funnel."

Chapter 19

Shad Parker finished pouring water from the bucket into the trough of the hog pen. As he turned and took a step he saw the wagon.

At first uncertain, and then less so, not wanting it to be, then knowing it was, a part of his past, a part he had been trying to bury in the deep unremembered recesses of his body and soul, not wanting it to be exhumed.

But there it was.

Shad put down the bucket and stood unmoving as the creaking wagon drew closer.

Ben Warren smiled. Esmeralda waved. Shad stood silent, but screaming inside, trying to wipe out the words to the song they had sung together so many times—Ben, Esmeralda, Shad . . . and Molly O.

Shenandoah, I hear you calling,
Calling me across the wide Missouri.
Oh, Shenandoah, I'm going to leave you.
Away, you rolling river.

Oh, Shenandoah, I'm going to leave you
Away I'm bound
Across the wide Missouri.

The wagon groaned to a stop. This time it was Esmeralda who jumped off first, without assistance. She ran to Shad and embraced him, not trying to stanch her tears. The bonnet fell from her head as she placed her face against Shad's shoulder.

"Shad. Dear Shad. It's so good to see you."

He did not respond. His body remained rigid, ungiving. Ben was off the wagon, approaching. The boys followed after him. Esmeralda let go of Shad and moved a step to the side.

Ben looked at Shad for a moment, then extended his hand. After too long a pause Shad put forth his hand. As they shook, Ben nodded to the two boys.

"Benjie, Todd, say hello to your uncle Shad."

Benjie and Todd nodded back uncertainly at the strange man whose expression remained stolid. Shad let loose of Ben's hand.

"They hardly remember," Esmeralda said as she picked up the fallen bonnet. "So much has happened . . ." She paused awkwardly. "You look well, Shad."

"Why? Why did you come here?" Those were Shad Parker's first words to them. "What do you want?"

Ben and Esmeralda were deeply hurt. She tried to think of something to say, something to soothe the pain, but Ben spoke first, to Esmeralda and the boys as he turned toward the wagon.

"Get back up there!"

Benjie and Todd started to follow their father's

command, but Esmeralda did not move and Ben stopped as she spoke.

"We're on our way to Yuma. We just wanted to see you. Maybe stay the night. Wish you a . . . well, it's near Christmas." Her eyes moistened again. "That's all, Shad."

"Es!" Ben motioned toward the wagon.

"Hold on," Shad said hoarsely, and bit his lip. "Ben . . . Es . . . stay the night."

Esmeralda looked at her husband. A look that pleaded. Ben's face was a battlefield of hurt and pride and there was no denying the emotion.

Finally he nodded and smiled.

A small, dirty pair of hands thrust out, but the sage hen escaped. Austin's hands landed on the nest and one of the three eggs broke under the impact of the boy's palm.

Austin carefully picked up the two unbroken eggs. He would be back to the cave before dark.

But back to what? How long could he expect Peg and Davy and even himself to go on running? They were tired and hungry and cold, but in spite of all that, in some ways they were lucky. None of them had gotten hurt or sick as had their mother and father.

Alvin and Sara Coats had fled from bleeding Kansas south through the Oklahoma Indian Territory, across the Arkansas River, and farther south into Texas. They settled near Palestine with their young son and daughter, and eked out a meager existence and Davy was born. They held on, thinking that things would be better after the war ended. But the great blizzard of '66 with high wind, driving snow, and freezing temperature made things even worse. Alvin tried to repair what was left of the homestead. First he fell with the fever, then as she tried to minister to him so did Sara, and became even worse. They died within hours of each other, Sarah then Alvin.

Austin left Peg and little Davy with the bodies and walked seven miles to Palestine. There was no sense in bringing a doctor, so the undertaker came back in his wagon with Austin and took the bodies and the children back to Palestine, buried the bodies, then delivered the children to the Faith, Hope, and Charity Orphanage and Miss Stritch.

The major inheritance Alvin and Sara left their children was having taught the older two to read and write. What little else was left went to pay debts and funeral expenses.

In the cabin Ben Warren sat in a chair near the table and awkwardly went about filling his pipe with tobacco from a pouch, then lighting it.

Shad looked back at Ben then removed a liquor bottle from the cabinet. Esmeralda cooked supper while the two boys set the table.

Shad picked up a couple of glasses, walked over to where Ben sat, and poured stiff shots into the glasses. He lifted one of the glasses and handed it to Ben. But Ben had the pipe in his mouth and had to take it out and balance it on the table before accepting the drink.

"Thanks, Shad." He smiled.

Shad nodded.

"Remember what we used to say?" Ben held out the glass toward Shad. "How many times have we said it? A thousand? Ten thousand? Maybe more. But who kept count? Well, Shad, it's good to see you. And one more time, 'confusion to the enemy.'"

They touched glasses and both drank about half the whiskey in each glass. Neither man spoke for the moment. Each drank more whiskey but just a sip the second time.

"This stuff's been keeping good company, and speaking of good company . . ."

Shad poured more whiskey from the bottle into the glasses.

"Supper'll be ready in just a few minutes," Esmeralda said from the stove. "It sure will seem good eating with a roof over our heads again. And cooking on a real stove! I almost forgot what it's like to sit around a dinner table with the fam . . . Todd, put the salt and pepper on the table. Benjie, fetch me the parcel."

Benjie and Todd both "yes, ma'am'd" their mother. Todd took the salt and pepper shakers from the stove and brought them over to the table. Benjie walked toward a pile of items the Warrens had carried into the house from the wagon before Shad had unhitched the team, led the animals into the barn, and fed them.

Shad glanced at both of the youngsters. Benjie was born less than a month before Shad and Molly O's second son, Shannon. Todd was the same age as the unborn son or daughter who died with Molly O.

"It's a nice place you have here, Shad." Ben sipped his whiskey.

Shad thought to himself that if he had passed Ben Warren on the street he might not have recognized the boy and man he grew up with. While Ben hadn't been as tall and powerfully proportioned as Shad, he had always been the more energetic and carefree of the two. He was one for mischief and laughter, the instigator and troublemaker of the two. Not conceited, but confident, even more confident when Shad Parker was around to back his play. Not that Ben Warren wouldn't tweak the devil's nose on his own, but it just seemed to happen more often when Shad was there. But now Ben was almost skeletal and it even seemed a task for him to breathe.

"It's just a place," Shad finally responded to Ben's remark.

"Shad, my friend, we've come nigh a thousand miles, I guess. Across half a dozen states, hills and streams, rivers, valleys and fields. Never saw anything or anyplace to compare to the Shenandoah."

Shad stiffened at the word. He had neither heard the sound of it, nor mentioned it since the day he left there.

"Sheridan!" Ben Warren bit into the name again. "If I could get my . . ." he looked at the pinned-up left sleeve then held out his right arm, ". . . my hand on him . . ."

Benjie had brought his mother a package. She began to untie the string attached to the plain wrapping paper.

"Ben," she said, "you can't blame General Sheridan. He was a soldier. He . . ."

"He laid waste to the most beautiful valley on God's earth to where it'll never be the same—he scorched the land and everything on it—and may he rot in hell forever. He . . ."

Ben stopped when he looked at Shad's face. Shad Parker stared at the unwrapped object in Esmeralda's hands as if he had been struck a knife blow.

He was looking at a shawl.

"Where'd you get that?"

"Molly loaned it to me when I was carrying Todd. Never did give it back to her. I thought you'd like to have . . ."

Shad's eyes were on fire. He rose and whirled to the door, opened it, and bolted into the darkness.

Esmeralda went to the door he had left unclosed and looked out after him. Ben was on his feet. He went and stood next to his wife.

"What happened, Mom?" Benjie asked. "What's wrong with him?"

Nobody answered the boy.

"I better go after him," Ben said. "He's liable to . . ."

"He went into the barn."

"Is he sick?" Todd tugged at his mother's dress.

Ben took a step toward the door, but Esmeralda stopped him.

"Ben," she said softly, "I'll go." She handed her husband the shawl.

Chapter 20

The shadowy form of Shad Parker leaned with both forearms and elbows against a stall, his head buried in his arms.

Oh, Shenandoah, I hear you calling . . .

The words burned in his brain along with the image of Molly O and Sean and Shannon when he left them for the last time. Jubal Early's brigade was already on the march. He held her closer than he had ever held her before.

"You'll miss your brigade . . ."
"I'll only miss you, Molly O."
"Come back to us, Shad."
"You be here, Molly O, and I'll come back."

* * *

He came back to their graves.

The fields, the orchards, the barns, the house, and every living thing in them. Gone.

All the others had left that part of the valley early that day. Molly had promised Esmeralda that she would leave the next day. Shannon had taken sick and needed rest before he could travel. The boy was weak and delirious.

The Yankees thought that the entire valley had been evacuated. That night they swept south, a burning swath of hellfire and devastation. It was reported that when they heard the screams from inside the house the soldiers tried to enter. But it was too late.

Esmeralda, carrying a lantern, came in through the open barn door. The animals reacted to the light. One of the horses nickered.

Shad turned toward the light from the lantern, which cast a wavering amber pall. Through the quavering haze Esmeralda appeared like a ghost. Her resemblance to Molly O startled Shad, but within that same moment he regained much of his composure.

"Shad. It doesn't do any good to go on torturing yourself."

Silence.

"I know how you feel. When . . ."

"Do you?"

"Some. Molly was my sister. Shad, you were away. There was nothing you could have done, but I was there. How many times, day and night, since then have I blamed, no cursed, myself for not *making* her leave? But she was afraid to move Shannon, and nobody knew how fast the Yankees were moving, how close they were. But I've lived with that, too. I loved her."

He wiped at his eyes but said nothing.

"Shad, you can't run away from what happened."

"Is that what you think I'm doing, running away?"

"That's what you're *trying* to do—by leaving the Shenandoah—us—everything and everybody you've ever loved. But, Shad, it won't work. It can't. Keep the memories, treasure them—but that's what they are—memories . . . You've got to start again."

"Why?"

"Because you've still got a life ahead of you . . ."

"What kind of life?"

"You'll find someone . . . There's got to be something . . ."

"*Something!* Can't you understand? I don't want to find anybody or anything. I don't want to feel anything. I don't even want a pet hound. Nothing! Not ever again!"

He turned away. Esmeralda moved closer.

"Shad, the only time you stop feeling anything is when you're dead."

"I am dead. I want to stay dead."

"Can't anything touch you?"

"I won't let it."

"What happened was the will of God . . ."

He turned again, now facing her, a fierce anger in his face, but his voice a hoarse whisper.

"Don't talk to me about God. Just don't."

"Shad, when Ben lost . . ."

"And I don't want to hear about what Ben lost. What did Ben lose? His arm? What's an arm or a leg

or his damn Shenandoah Valley? What's anything?
He's got you. He's got his kids."

"Yes, he has . . . for a little while."

"What's that mean?"

"Why do you think we're going to Yuma? Can't you
tell by looking at him, your best friend? Don't you
see? The doctor said . . . in a dry climate Ben might
last a year . . . maybe two. He can't help thinking
about that every time he looks at us."

"Es . . ."

"And that's why he wanted to come by and see you,
for the last time." She held back the tears. "Please . . .
come inside."

Shad nodded.

Esmeralda set the lantern on a box and walked to
the door. She paused there, framed in the moonlight.

"And, Shad . . . don't let on to Ben that I told you."

As Shad and Esmeralda walked into the wind-
brushed night, from the barn toward the house,
there was a muffled cry from the hillside. Esmeralda
did not react because she did not hear. Her thoughts
at that moment were filled with pleasure, because
Shad walked beside her and for that night at least,
what was left of the two families from the Shenandoah would be together.

But Shad Parker heard and reacted. Cougar, coyote,
or wolf? Shad could not tell. The sound came again,
and fought the wind, it did not sail with it.

Cougar? Coyote? Wolf? Shad tried, but could not

define it. But something was up there, and not far from the cave. Nor far enough.

Shad glanced back and upward.

There was a faint circular glow from the hillside. The trespassers were still there.

Peg poured water out of the tin can Austin had found and she had used to boil the two eggs. The can had cooled enough for her to hold it by the lid still hinged on top.

There were two thick slices of hard bread on a stone, and Austin was cutting an apple in half with his pocketknife while Davy sat watching and shivering a little.

"I'm cold."

"Take my coat," Austin said. "Have a piece of this bread."

Davy took the coat and the bread.

"You ought to eat something, too." Peg cracked the shells of the eggs and started to peel them.

"Stuffed myself at the Davises. Sure wish I coulda taken more'n a couple slices of bread and that there apple. But there was so many of 'em and someone kep' watching me all the time."

"This'll do fine, Austin."

"Well, it looks like we made it through one more day."

"Thanks to you."

"Yeah, but tomorrow we got to start all over again. I can't go back to the Davises."

"Don't think about it tonight. Are you . . ." All three

heard the animal sound. "There it is again. What do you think it is, Austin?"

"Don't know."

"Remember Soldado? How he used to howl sometimes at night?"

"Yeah, but he didn't sound like that. Pa said he thought Soldado was part wolf . . ."

"Tell me about Soldado," Davy said as he bit into the egg.

"I told you before."

"Tell me again, Austin. I'm tired of hearing them stories about knights and dragons, tell me about Soldado, about how you and Pa went hunting that day and . . ."

"Look here, Davy, you want to tell it?" Austin winked at Peg. "Or you want me to tell it?"

"You tell it, Austin, go ahead."

"Well, I wasn't too much older'n you are right this minute. It was in the fall, sometime before Thanksgiving, don't remember exactly. Pa had his rifle and took me along, course I didn't have no rifle. We was going out to hunt quail and Pa spotted some birds, but they weren't quail, no, sir. Even from that distance I could see they was way too big to be quail or ordinary birds."

"Buzzards is what they were, right, Austin?"

"That's right. Buzzards, circling and waiting to pounce on something dead and eat it. But they was circling and waiting 'cause there was something else out there that wasn't dead . . ."

"Soldado, right?"

"You might as well go ahead and finish up the story, Davy."

"No, I don't remember it all. Go ahead and tell it, Austin, it's way better'n them knights and dragons and besides it's true."

"All right. Well, Pa and I went to the spot where the buzzards was flying over and laying there was a dead ol' dog and standing right beside her was another dog, a big ol' brute he was, looking up at them buzzards and growling to keep 'em away. He seen us coming, looked like he was making up his mind whether to run away or stand his ground.

"Well he didn't run. Pa smiled at that dog, then he lifted his rifle and shot up at the buzzards. They scattered into the clouds and Pa shot once again to keep 'em going. That dog barked at them buzzards till they was outta sight.

"Pa pulled out his hunting knife and I asked him what he intended to do. He said he was gonna dig a hole and bury that dog so he wouldn't get eaten . . ."

"Just like the man did with the cougar," Davy couldn't help interrupting.

"Not exactly. Pa didn't skin the dead dog. Well, he dug a hole with his knife while the other dog and I watched. That dog seemed to know what Pa was doing and why. He just stood there and watched. Pa talked to him some, called him Soldado, told me that meant 'soldier' in Spanish—'cause that dog had been standing guard like a soldier.

"When the burying was done, Pa piled on some rocks and we left Soldado there and went about hunting us some quail. Got some, too. Pa was a good shot.

"Next morning right outside the door to our house, there stood Soldado. Guess he'd followed us at some distance 'cause neither Pa nor I had spotted him. Came up close to the house but never came inside.

"All through that fall and winter he'd show up. Pa wouldn't let us put out food for him. Said that Soldado had to stay independent. If he started to get fed he might start relying on it and he'd lose his hunting ability. But I don't think that Soldado wanted or expected to be fed. I don't know, I guess he just craved company of some kind on account of he lost his wife. Sometimes at night we could hear him howling out there. It went on like that through the winter and into the spring.

"And then one morning Soldado was gone. For days, I guess weeks, I waited for him to come back, even cried some 'cause I was still little. But he never did come back. Pa said it was all right. Soldado probably found himself another wife and he was out there where he belonged and we should be glad for him . . ."

"You think so?" Davy asked.

"What do you mean?"

"You think he found another wife?"

"Well, Davy, every story's got to have an ending. Might as well be a happy ending. Sure, I do."

"That was a lot better story than knights and dragons."

"Well, don't expect me to tell it to you every night."

"I won't. Just once 'n a while."

Peg smiled at Austin. She had enjoyed the story as much as Davy and probably needed it more.

"I wish we had some more chicken," Davy said as he finished off the egg.

"Yesterday you was wailing for an egg." Austin shook his head.

"That's before I tasted that chicken."

"You're getting spoiled." Austin smiled.

"Davy," Peg said, "be grateful for what we've got."

Shad and the Warren family sat around the dinner table. The Warrens' heads were all bowed, but not Shad's as Ben said the words.

"Lord, we thank Thee for the food before us—and for bringing us safe this far. We thank Thee for guiding us to our friend Shad Parker . . ."

Shad Parker was staring at the shawl neatly folded on the ledge of the fireplace.

". . . look upon us all with grace and goodness and bless this house. Merry Christmas. Amen."

In the cave Austin, Peg, and Davy had already finished their meal and were getting ready to go to sleep.

Chapter 21

At the Lewis house Homer Keeler and Kathy Lewis had been talking for the better part of the night. Homer had ridden out after he left the sheriff's office and Mr. and Mrs. Lewis had asked him to stay for supper. Hardly anything was said after the prayer and during the time they ate.

When they finished the missus suggested that Kathy and Homer might want to go into the front room and "talk a spell" while she and the mister cleaned things up in the kitchen.

The "spell" had lasted over an hour and the conversation finally was winding down.

"Homer, you know I don't believe in violence . . ."

"Neither do I, Kathy. But I believe in working and earning a living. I'm good at this job. Elwood said so. We've got to have food to eat and a place to live. Maybe it wouldn't be much of a place at first . . ."

"We could live here. There's plenty of room and you could work with Pa. He could use some help and there's . . ."

"Kathy. I'm not going to sit at somebody else's

table and sleep with my wife on somebody else's bed. Whatever we eat and wherever we sleep is going to be ours, yours and mine . . . and the baby's. That's got to be the way it is if we're going to be together . . ."

"But what about when we're not together? What about when I'm alone with the baby and wondering if you'll be coming home at night or if you're out there between two people who want to kill each other and one of them kills you instead? Or if you get shot for no good reason of your own and end up crippled?"

"I could get crippled falling off a horse."

"Not as likely, isn't that right?"

"Sure it is. But I can't be living off your father just because I . . ."

"Just because you what? Got his daughter in trouble and married her out of pity?"

"It's not pity, Kathy. I said I loved you and I meant it. But don't try to bend me too much. I ain't geared to too much bending. Let me be myself, at least till I find out a few things. We'll see how it works out. Elwood said we'd both have to do some compromising . . ."

"Who am I marrying? You or Elwood? Is that why you're here? Because Elwood told you to come?"

"I wouldn't be here if I didn't want to, no matter what anybody told me. Kathy, please let's try. Elwood . . ."

"There you go again with Elwood . . ."

"Listen! I'll be getting five hundred when we turn over those two to the federal marshal, thanks to Elwood. Five hundred. That'll more than get us started. I've got some saved. And it'll be you and me . . . and the baby together, not beholden to your pa or anybody. Kathy, will you do it? Will you marry me?"

"And that badge?"

"That might not be permanent. But you and I will be, Kathy."

"I guess . . . you'd better ask Pa for permission." Kathy Lewis smiled.

Homer Keeler kissed her and they called in Mr. and Mrs. Lewis, who happened to be standing just outside the door.

Deek Keeshaw, smelling again of lilac toilet water, figured that this was his lucky night, and not at cards, although he had been sitting in at the poker game with indifferent luck since after supper at the New Heidelberg.

There was the usual gathering at the Appaloosa with the usual card games and smoke and Francine Needle and Stella Bright had made about the usual amount of ascents and descents up and down on the stairway to the second floor. But Deek Keeshaw figured that the change of luck on his part occurred when he saw Yellow Rose enter the Appaloosa less than a half hour ago.

She had walked, and Deek couldn't help but react to the way she walked, over to Hooter at the end of the bar and engaged in solid conversation since then.

Goshin, the other bartender who filled in part-time, was seeing to the needs of the customers who weren't interested in being served by Francine and Stella.

Deek was slightly disappointed in the way Yellow

Rose was dressed that night. Her outfit was obviously more subdued and considerably less revealing than the garments she usually wore. But Deek wasn't nearly as interested in how Yellow Rose looked dressed as how she'd look upstairs.

He played the game and bided his time until she'd be finished talking to Hooter, then he'd make the play he'd been waiting for since he first laid covetous eyes on her. More than once he had to be reminded by Chris, Tom, Bart, or one of the other two games-men at the table that it was up to him to "bet 'em or fold 'em." No matter which Deek did, it was wrong.

Finally it appeared to Deek Keeshaw that the conversation between Hooter and Yellow Rose was close to the curtain. Hooter poured each of them a cup from the top shelf and they seemed to be drinking to something or other. Deek was pretty close to being in the drink himself.

"Well, Rose, we both know that your share of the Appaloosa is worth more than that but on the other hand the reason it is, is because of you in the first place."

"It's all right, Hooter."

"No, ma'am, without you around business'll peter down to next to nothing."

"You'll do all right, Hooter."

"What about you, Rose? That thousand won't take you very far."

"That depends on which direction I go."

"You said something about San Francisco."

"Did I?"

"Seems to me you did, more'n once."

"A lady can change her mind . . ."

"Sure you won't change it? About leaving, I mean. Tomorrow you might see things different. If you do . . ."

"I won't. Not about this. The Appaloosa's all yours, Hooter, and welcome to it."

"Not yet, it ain't. I still got to float a loan with Amos Bush."

"That's his business, floating." She smiled.

"Yeah, even if he has to sink other people to do it."

"You won't sink, Hooter. You're too damn buoyant."

"Well, I been called a lot of things before but never that. How about one for the road?"

"No thanks, Hooter, and I'll tell you something else. That might've been my last drink."

"Next thing you'll be singing in Reverend Groves's choir."

"You never can tell, but not around here."

"When'll you leave?"

"No hurry. Next year, but the first part of next year. So long, stranger."

"So long, Rose."

Deek Keeshaw was up and waiting as Yellow Rose moved away from the bar.

"Miss Rose."

"Yes."

"I'm Deek Keeshaw." He even bowed slightly, courtly as a chevalier.

"Yes, I know."

"Oh, you do." He seemed surprised and pleased.

"Part of my business at the Appaloosa."

"I see. Well, that's what I wanted to discuss with you . . . upstairs," he oozed.

"Well, Mr. Keeshaw, you're a little late."

"What do you mean?"

"I mean . . . I'm out of business."

Elwood Hinge had been looking through the office window across at the Appaloosa ever since he saw Yellow Rose walk in nearly an hour ago. He had risen in his stocking feet from the chair in front of the rolltop and started for the cot when he glanced out and caught sight of her.

Instead of continuing to the cot he went back to the desk, picked up one of the "fine ceegars" Pete Inghram had proffered a few days ago, and lit up.

He had no halter around Rosalind DuPree and certainly not around Yellow Rose, but he had hoped that she would have continued to absent herself from the place as she had done the previous two nights. But he did notice even at the distance and through the darkness that there was something different-looking about Yellow Rose that night.

He wasn't eager for sleep anyhow so he lit up and leaned on the edge of the rolltop and blew out a few sets of smoke rings. Hinge could hear one of the two prisoners snoring in his cell. He knew it was Red Borden. Borden had snored every night since he took up lodging at the county facility. Slept like he didn't have a worry in the world. He soon wouldn't, at least not in this world.

Hinge was getting close to the butt end of the "fine ceegar" and was about to douse it and hit the cot when he saw Yellow Rose coming out of the Appaloosa. He thought that she paused and glanced toward the sheriff's office before she walked on to the

Eden, but he couldn't be sure. He had a notion to go out and talk to her, just a notion. He knew he wasn't going to do it. He wasn't going to leave Charlie Reno and Red Borden even though they were both securely locked up and Borden was sawing away on his cot.

But Elwood Hinge was pleased that Yellow Rose had not stayed the night at the Appaloosa. He had been thinking about a lot of things and wanted to talk about some of those things to Rosalind DuPree.

As he took what he intended to be the last puff from the "fine ceegar" he heard the whispered voice.

"Sheriff, hey, Sheriff . . . come back here a minute."

Elwood Hinge left the shotgun where it leaned, but was still wearing his .44 when he walked back close to the cell. Borden went on with his snoring.

"What do . . ."

"Shhhh . . . shhh."

"What is it, Charlie?" Hinge whispered. "You got a secret you don't want to let Red in on?"

"That's right." Charlie paused while he made sure that Borden was still snoring.

He was.

"How'd you like to make some real money, Sheriff?" Charlie breathed. "Sheriff?"

"Already have." Hinge breathed back. "Thanks to you boys. Two thousand."

"You can more than double it."

"How?"

"Easy. Real easy." Charlie continued to whisper while Borden continued to snore. "We got nearly *six* thousand stashed from that bank job in Garden City. It's stashed outside of town, close by."

"How close?"

"Close enough."

"Go on."

"One of us escapes, me. You come along, we split the six thousand, and nobody's the wiser."

"What about him?"

"He stays and you collect on him anyhow."

"Suppose he don't want to stay?"

"That's easy, too. Kill him."

"*You son of a bitch!*" Red Borden roared and jumped up from his cot, springing toward Charlie Reno, who jumped back in his cell four feet. "I'll kill you, you son of a bitch, if it's the last thing I do!"

"I hope it is, Red," said Elwood Hinge as he walked away. "I sure as hell hope it is."

Chapter 22

Ben extended his hand. This time Shad took it without hesitating, but still he did not smile. Esmeralda stood nearby. The boys were already on the loaded wagon in front of Shad's cabin.

Early that morning Esmeralda had fixed a hearty breakfast of fresh eggs, smoked ham, potatoes, and warm bread, with a pot of coffee for the men and plenty of milk for the boys. The conversation had been pleasant but guarded, with Ben and Es careful not to mention Molly O or the Shenandoah and Shad avoiding any reference to Ben's health.

Since the days were short this time of year Ben said he wanted to get an early start and cover as many miles as possible during the daylight hours. Shad agreed that that was a good idea.

As Shad and Ben shook hands, each man knew that this would be the last time they would see each other, but each man did his best to act as if he didn't know.

"So long, Shad."

"Ben."

"Confusion to the enemy." Ben managed a smile. Shad nodded.

Ben turned and went to the wagon. Esmeralda came to Shad. She kissed his face. He stood motionless.

"I'll write when we get settled. Thanks, Shad . . . and God bless you."

His left hand moved only slightly, but he pressed some folded money into her palm and closed her fingers around it. Esmeralda started to protest, but before she got started his eyes stopped her. For just that moment they were the eyes of Shad Parker of the Shenandoah Valley.

She smiled, turned away quickly, and went to the wagon. Benjie extended his hand and helped her up.

The wagon started to move west. Both boys waved back toward their uncle, then Esmeralda waved. There were tears in her eyes.

"Mom, what's wrong? Why're you crying?"

"Nothing's wrong, Benjie." Esmeralda turned away. "Nothing. Everything's just fine."

From above, at the entrance to the cave, Austin, Peg, and Davy watched the wagon pull away, then saw the man turn and walk slowly to the cabin.

"Austin, who do you suppose those people were?"

"I haven't any notion, Peg."

"Well, whoever they were, he let them stay the night."

"That he did, but it looks like they're on their way to somewhere, with everything they own."

"Did you see the man?" Davy said. "He only had one arm."

"Yes, Davy," Peg answered. "We saw."

"Wonder how he got it cut off? Do you think it was in that war everybody's always talking about, Austin?"

"Probably."

"Maybe Indians chopped it off."

"I don't think so, Davy, probably the war."

"I don't ever want to go to war," Davy grabbed ahold of his left arm, "and get my arm chopped off."

"Talk about something else, Davy," Peg said.

"I'm hungry."

"Sheriff! Sheriff! Come on back here!" Charlie Reno hollered. "I got to talk to you!"

Elwood Hinge made his way back toward the twin cells.

"Sheriff!"

"What is it?"

"You got to get me outta here, *now*!"

"What do you propose I do, Charlie? Book you into the Eden Hotel?"

"I don't care what you do so long as you get me outta here. He kept me up all night." Reno pointed at Red Borden, who stood in his cell glowering at Charlie, who stood bleary-eyed as far away as possible from his fellow inmate.

"I didn't hear anything." The sheriff looked from Charlie to Red.

"Whisperin' . . ."

"What?"

"Kept whisperin' all night long that he was gonna kill me . . . all night long . . . over and over again . . .

wouldn't stop all night long. Like to drive me crazy. Tell him to stop it."

"Red," Elwood said nicely, "stop it."

"I will when I kill him."

"He seems determined, Charlie."

"This ain't funny, Sheriff."

"That depends on where you're standing. Out here I can see some humor in the situation."

"It's your job to protect me."

"It is?"

"Well, isn't it?"

"Yes, it is . . . and it isn't."

"What the hell does that mean? He's threatenin' to kill me."

"It means I'm obliged to use my best effort . . . do what I can."

"Well?"

"It doesn't mean I have the right to gag him so long as he acts in a quiet and orderly manner. Now, Red, I'm warning you officially, if you persist in threatening your compadre, do it in a quiet and orderly manner so as not to disturb the peace of this here community, particularly these immediate environs. Otherwise I'll knock your teeth out. There, that's my best effort." The sheriff turned away.

"I'm gonna kill the son of a bitch," Red Borden said in a barely audible voice.

"See you boys later."

As Elwood reached his desk, Homer Keeler came into the office.

"Morning, Sheriff."

"Morning, Homer. How's the weather out there?"

"Nice. Everything quiet last night?"

"Might say that. Boys back there had a little falling-out. Charlie tried to bribe me into killing Red, then splitting the loot from Garden City and letting him escape, but Red overheard the plot and now he's set on killing Charlie, so keep an eye on 'em. Other than that, everything's quiet."

"Are you serious, Elwood?"

"Yep." Hinge nodded. "So's Red."

"Jesus Christ!"

"No need to blaspheme, Homer. Just keep an eye on 'em."

"Yes, sir."

"Did you have that talk with Kathy Lewis?"

"Yes, sir."

"And?"

"Well, the situation is all straightened out. Just like you said, we're both gonna do some compromising. We're gonna get married and I'm gonna stay in the law business, so I asked her daddy's permission for her hand in marriage."

"And?"

"He agreed."

"Good."

"And suggested that under the circumstances, New Year's Day would be a good time to do it."

Hooter had just settled into the chair near Amos Bush's desk while Bush went about the business of lighting up a six-and-one-half-inch stogie. Somehow Amos succeeded in making a near ritual out of the procedure, drawing the match flame, slowly, ever closer to the cigar, but never quite touching it. He revolved the cigar grandiloquently in his fingers and mouth until the yellow flame ignited the far end, then savored the smoke against his tongue and through his teeth before exhaling a blue spume across his desk and toward the man in the chair.

While Hooter, himself, was not a smoker, he was used to smoke, cigarettes, pipe, and cigar, although the cigar smoke he was used to came from far less expensive brands than Bush blew out.

"Well, Mr. Hooten, what was it you wanted to see me about?" Bush's voice and manner assumed a completely businesslike thrust.

Gerald Hooten couldn't remember the last time he had been called anything except Hooter, but he cleared his throat and attempted to match Bush's business demeanor while being subjected to another outflow of premium vapor.

"Well, Mr. Bush, as you probably know I have a partner in the ownership of the Appaloosa . . ." Hooter reached for a businesslike term ". . . enterprise. This, uh, particular party is interested in . . . as a matter of fact . . . is anxious to sell out . . . for I might add a very reasonable amount—one thousand dollars, to be precise—and I wanted to talk to you about a . . ."

Hooter never quite got the word "loan" out of his mouth. Amos Bush cleared his throat, looked over toward Raymond Osgood and Henry Wordsly, rose from his chair, and pointed toward the entrance. For the moment, Hooter thought he was going to be dismissed and the business transaction was going to be terminated. Not so.

"Mr. Hooten, I just recalled that there is a matter of some urgency that I need to attend to." Bush was already taking his topcoat from the nearby clothes tree. "Would you mind walking with me outside while we continue this discussion?"

"Why, no, I guess not. Sure. Sure thing, Mr. Bush."

"Good. Very good. After you, sir." Bush ushered Hooter toward the door. "I'll be back shortly, Raymond. Take care of things."

"Yes, sir." Raymond Osgood nodded from behind his cage. "Don't worry about a thing." He was already in command of the exchequer.

"Which way are we going?" Hooter asked when Bush closed the door behind them on the street.

"Doesn't matter, Mr. Hooten. Let's just walk and talk. This way, please." Bush indicated toward the west.

Hooter walked alongside as Amos Bush's voice lost some of its businesslike edge and assumed a more friendly aspect.

"One thousand dollars." Bush smiled.

"That's right."

"And what percentage does . . . your partner own?"

"Fifty percent. Fifty-fifty."

"I see. Well, Mr. Hooten, I have a proposition that should be of interest. I might say of great interest to you."

"That so?"

"Yes. Now you must understand that this has nothing to do with the bank. This is strictly between you and me. Man to man. You do understand that?"

"Just so I get the thousand."

"You'll get more than that. Let's say fifteen hundred."

"Fifteen hundred?"

"For twenty-five percent of the profits. I'll be what is known as a 'silent partner.' Very silent. You run the business. You keep the books. At the end of each month we split the profits, seventy-five percent to you, twenty-five percent to me. The fifteen hundred is yours to keep and you own seventy-five percent of the business instead of the fifty percent you now have. How does that strike you?"

"Well . . . I didn't expect . . ."

"No, of course not. I'm sure it's *more* than you expected. As a businessman, one to another, I don't see how you can refuse. It's a risk-free deal. You make a tidy profit going in and end up with more than you now have and a silent partner who will give you absolutely no interference in running the enterprise."

"Well, that's something, all right. Of course it's not like having Yellow . . . Miss DuPree. She's quite an attraction."

"Yes, well, I'm sure that you can import another attraction, attractions . . . younger, even more attractive, from other places and without giving up ownership. You know, sort of upgrade the enterprise. Of course, that's strictly up to you. You're in charge. But since I'll have a vested interest, I'll do everything I can to help, from a distance of course. It would not be seemly for, let's say a man of my position to be in any way connected or associated. As far as the community is concerned you are the sole owner and operator of the Appaloosa. Incidentally, as you know, I do own the building and I'll reduce the rent, let's say ten percent. Well, Mr. Hooten, yes or no?"

"Well, since you put it that way . . ."

"That's the way I put it. The answer I presume is yes."

"Yes."

"Good." Bush looked up and down the street. "You'll excuse me if we don't shake hands, but we have a deal. Come in a half hour after the bank closes. I'll have the necessary papers for you to sign and of course the fifteen hundred in cash. Good day, partner." Bush started to walk back toward the bank.

"Good day . . . partner," Hooter mumbled, and scratched behind his ear. He couldn't help wondering in how many other enterprises Amos Bush was a "silent partner."

Yellow Rose, née Rosalind DuPree, lay naked where she had passed the night alone, atop her oversized canopied bed with the open book at her side. She picked up the volume and looked again at the words she knew so well.

> *I traveld thro' a Land of Men*
> *A Land of Men & Women too*
> *And heard & saw such dreadful things*
> *As cold Earth wanderers never knew*

Rosalind DuPree set the book aside, rose, and went to the large oval dressing mirror that stood near a wall. She tilted the mirror slightly to get a full view of her face and body. Unlike that day in Paris when she looked for any sign of her African heritage, this time she sought the telltale signs of her profession. Eyes, mouth, the entire assembly of face and body, of Yellow Rose. Whore.

But that was not what she saw. That was not what was in the mirror.

Rosalind DuPree looked back at her, and at the world. Away from the Appaloosa, away from Gilead, away from Texas, she could walk and be welcomed anywhere as a lady. In Europe she might even pass for royalty. There, there were scores of titled men, older men who might share the family title for the favor of sharing the family bed with a woman like Rosalind DuPree. If not the family title, then the family fortune, or a goodly part of it, if Rosalind DuPree were so inclined, or reclined.

But Rosalind DuPree was not disposed toward Europe. Europe was the east, the past. The future lay west. Yes, west. Probably San Francisco.

San Francisco, the Athens of America, a sobriquet used frequently by the citizens of that city, those citizens who knew there was an Athens.

Rosalind DuPree had read and consumed much about the city that had been proclaimed a possession of the United States by Commander John Montgomery when he landed in the largest natural harbor in the world in 1846 from the U.S. naval vessel *Portsmouth*. The few hundred Spaniards who had been in possession of the territory since Captain Juan Bautista de Anza brought a boatload of settlers there in 1776 were in no position to decline the honor.

In 1847 the town council officially named the village of 450 persons San Francisco. Shortly after that James Marshall found a glittering substance at Sutter's Mill and unleashed a stampede of "forty-niners" who swelled the city to 25,000 seekers of fortune.

Women were scarce, and the all-night variety were remunerated four to six hundred dollars for their time and effort, depending on their wares.

The rich rose to the top of Nob Hill. Crocker, Huntington, Stanford, Hopkins, Towne, Tobin, Flood, Haggin, and the others looked down from their magnificent mansions on the masses who literally lived below them. But even below, the landscape was awash with opportunity, particularly for someone with the beauty, charm, grace, and ability of Rosalind DuPree.

She continued to look at her naked self in the mirror. Yes. It would not be a severe task to find one of the pillars of the community, or even a son of one of the pillars, to set her up in a much more ornamental style than the citizens of Gilead, Texas.

But when was a whore not a whore? When she was a mistress?

Yellow Rose had allowed her body, if not her soul, to be used by hundreds of men thousands of times in the last ten years. Two of those men she had shot with a derringer for trying to abuse her. Both survived, but only because Yellow Rose knew where she was aiming.

In San Francisco she would be used by only one man, once she had selected the right one. But she would still be in the same business, only on a more exclusive basis. But it would have to be soon. She was not yet thirty. The sooner, the richer the fatted calf, the better the bounty. By the time she was forty she could retire in splendor without obligation. Without belonging to anybody but herself.

The alternative? Maybe a legitimate business. A shoppe. She had fifteen hundred dollars in an account at Amos Bush's bank. Another thousand, ten one-hundred-dollar bills, secreted among the pages of the *Collected Works of Shakespeare*. And there was the thousand she'd get from Hooter for her share of the Appaloosa.

Thirty-five hundred dollars from the rental of her body for the past ten years. In San Francisco she could lease instead of rent her body. Or she could open a shoppe and wait for the customers, many of whom might be in the business she was thinking of getting out of.

There was still another alternative. But she didn't want to think about it. Not now.

"Sheriff! Sheriff! Elwood!" Deputy Homer Keeler had risen from the chair outside of the sheriff's office, held on to the sawed-off shotgun with one hand, and was knocking on the window with the other.

Keeler had been sitting there daydreaming for a couple of hours after making sure the two inmates ate breakfast without doing bodily damage by hurling tin plates and cups at each other from the New Heidelberg settings used exclusively in serving prisoners. No knives or forks were permitted. The inmates had to make do with a spoon apiece. But that was no great hardship since the breakfast consisted of coffee, toast, and mush. Red Borden persisted in muttering through his mush about killing Charlie Reno. Reno cowered on the corner of his bunk as far away from Red as the geography of the two cells would permit.

Red's nocturnal mutterings were taking a visible toll on Charlie, whose eyes had become a couple of baggy slits from lack of sleep. He complained to both Elwood Hinge and Homer Keeler that his head "ached and buzzed" and that he was in dire need of medication or doctor's attention, or change of venue, but his complaints fell on an unsympathetic audience.

"Eat your mush and shut up," the sheriff responded.

"Don't want mush. I need medicine."

"I'll eat his mush," Red Borden growled. "Then I'll kill the son of a bitch." He appeared to have suffered no ill effects from staying up and torturing Charlie.

"Make him stop! Make him stop!" Charlie pleaded. "He's making me crazy."

Elwood Hinge instructed Homer to collect the tin plates and cups then take his post outdoors. The sheriff returned to his desk and resumed his Christmas tree carving.

Since then the deputy had been sitting in front of the office thinking about how it would be to be married to Kathy Lewis and spend the night—nights—with her in a real bed instead of making love to her in makeshift surroundings.

Just about everybody who passed by "good morning'd" or "merry Christmas'd" Homer, who just nodded and went back to the vision of him and Kathy in a bed of their own. Until he heard the sound.

The stagecoach clattered into town and made for the front of the livery, which also served as the depot. The livery had been reopened that morning by Dutch and Bub, who both showed visible effects of their previous encounter with Shad Parker. Dutch's son also had returned to his post outside of Inghram's.

"Sheriff!" Homer repeated as he knocked again on the window.

Elwood Hinge came out with his shotgun in one hand and brushing off wood carvings with the other.

"I saw it." The sheriff nodded toward his deputy, who went back to the chair.

Elwood Hinge proceeded across the street toward the stagecoach, where several passengers already were debarking. Curious citizens of Gilead from every direction also converged toward the coach.

Hinge watched as a woman with two young children stepped off. One of the children, about seven years of age, was crying, holding himself below the belly, and proclaiming, "I gotta go to the toilet! I gotta go to the toilet!"

"Well, Teddy," the weary woman said, "go behind the livery and pee."

"I don't gotta pee . . . I gotta go to the toilet!" Teddy replied through his tears.

A tall man whom Hinge recognized as a drummer who had called on the community many times before jumped off the stage and headed for the Appaloosa, followed by a middle-aged man and woman who were strangers to the sheriff.

The driver, a crusty sort, named Shorty for obvious reason, unloaded baggage and was being assisted by the Shotgun.

"Morning, Shorty."

"Hello, Sheriff." Shorty tossed down a suitcase that landed hard not far from Hinge's feet.

"Shorty, you got a U.S. Marshal aboard?"

"Nope." Another suitcase crashed on top of the previous luggage and bounced off.

"You sure?"

"Not unless he's in one of them suitcases."

Elwood Hinge knew from prior encounters that the driver was not much given to small talk. Those who had ridden beside Shorty on his runs had remarked that one sentence per hundred miles was about average for Shorty, as far as conversation was concerned.

The sheriff was disappointed that he would not be relieved of Charlie and Red for the present and would have to countenance more threats and possibly an attempt or attempts on the safety and well-being of the surviving Reno brother. But that was part of his job. Besides, he was thinking of the six thousand stashed somewhere nearby. The bank at Garden City would provide a reward for the return of the stolen money. Hinge wouldn't mind adding that to his account.

Hinge started to take a step back toward his office.

"Elwood."

The sheriff stopped and looked back at Shorty as the last piece of luggage met the ground rudely. Shorty reached inside of his jacket and removed a sheaf.

"What is it, Shorty?"

"Packet of dodgers for you." Shorty tossed the dodgers, which were folded once and tied together by heavy string, at Hinge, who caught them before they hit the ground.

"Much obliged, Shorty." But by this time Shorty

had disappeared off the top of the stagecoach to the opposite side.

"Sheriff." A different voice called out to Hinge, and Dutch appeared from around the stagecoach. He limped, obviously ached when he moved, and instead of a hat he wore a bandage around his head. One eye was blue and swollen shut. He looked more like Halloween than Christmas. Elwood Hinge didn't bother asking him how he felt.

"Has that son of a bitch come back into town?"

"Which son of a bitch is that, Dutch?"

"You know who I mean, that crazy bastard who was pesterin' my boy. The one who sucker punched me when I wasn't lookin . . ."

"Oh, *that* son of a bitch."

"Yeah."

"Well, Dutch, in the first place I'm not so sure he's any son of a bitch and I wouldn't call him on it even if I was. In the second place, for your own health and safety, I hope you and Bub, who I guess he also sucker punched, aren't thinking of pursuing your conversation with him about this or that."

"I'm thinking about filin' charges."

"What charges?"

"Well, you seen it, you name it. Assault with a deadly weapon. Intent to kill . . ."

"What I 'seen' was that he intended to mind his own business . . . morose though he was . . . until the two of you made the mistake of taking on more than you could haul. Was I you, I wouldn't make any further mistakes far as he's concerned . . ."

"What kind of law we got around here?"

"It's the law according to Sheriff Elwood Hinge. You want to file a complaint against that, too?"

"Maybe I do."

"Then exercise your right to vote next election. In the meanwhile," Hinge looked at the young boy who stood a few feet behind his father and lowered his voice as he concluded, "you've already embarrassed your boy and damn near made him part orphan, so how about burying the matter and starting off the New Year right?"

"Well, I . . ."

"I thought you'd see it that way, Dutch. Merry Christmas." Hinge smiled at the young boy. "You, too, son." He turned, began to walk toward his office again, and saw the Keeshaws astride their horses coming back into Gilead.

Sheriff Elwood Hinge also had seen them ride out just over two hours ago. If it were true, as they made a big display advertising to anybody who'd listen, that they were scouting for a spread to buy, they were spending more time talking than scouting. There were a few things about the brothers Keeshaw that didn't sit right with the veteran lawman. They were brothers, all right, one look at the three of them was evidence enough, but beyond that Hinge had some doubts. He wasn't so sure that, as they claimed, they were from Louisiana. There were more than a few from all parts of that state that served alongside Hinge in the war and none of them sounded like the Keeshaws. The Keeshaws sounded more like Kansas or Missouri.

And the Keeshaws didn't look to Hinge as if they'd be content to live inside four walls made out of

Nebraska marble, as the sod huts were called, and sweat out a living on a piece of hardscrabble Texas dirt. Their eyes weren't made to look down a plow, more likely a barrel of a Winchester or Colt . . . or at least a deck of cards, a cold deck.

It was just a lawman's instinct, but it had kept that lawman alive. Hinge hadn't seen their likeness on any dodgers so far, but sometimes those dodgers were a year or so behind events and some of the worst hardcases never got celebrated on posters at all. But Elwood Hinge intended to go through the new edition of dodgers he held in his hand with an eye out for the three pilgrims who just rode in and whose leader was waving at him from horseback.

Hinge scarcely waved back, with the dodgers.

Deek reined in and so did Tom and Bart and watched as the sheriff walked with the shotgun in one hand and a packet of papers in the other, toward his deputy who sat cradling his own scattergun. The sky turned darker.

In the last twenty-four hours Tom and Bart had become even more edgy. Francine and Stella had quelled the edginess for a spell last night, but by noon this day both brothers were back to grumbling about the situation.

Once again they had taken Amos Bush's map and gone through the motions. This morning's sodbuster seemed willing to part with his spread at any price and throw his wife and twin daughters into the bargain. Deek promised that they'd be back . . . after the holidays.

Up to the moment that Deek spoke to Yellow Rose he had occupied his thoughts with time-consuming visions of the two of them together. But since the abrupt, nearly rude rejection, he, too, was getting anxious. There no longer was any point in visiting the barbershop for a shave and splashes of lilac toilet water. Tony didn't talk a hell of a lot for a barber. Maybe that was because besides barbering Tony also served as town photographer and undertaker. It appeared that he was more content to shave corpses than citizens.

Tony did tell Deek how he had shaved and photographed Frank Chase and Johnsy Reno after they became cadavers so the sheriff could prove their identify and collect the reward instead of turning the bodies over to the U.S. Marshal when he got to town. Bodies wouldn't keep too well for long stretches even in this kind of weather.

Deek Keeshaw had changed the cadaver subject just as soon as he deemed proper. He didn't relish hearing details about outlaw corpses. At that time the only body he wanted to think about was Yellow Rose's. He had tried to turn the conversation with Tony to Yellow Rose, but the barber didn't respond to that subject, so Keeshaw had closed his eyes and requested more lilac toilet water.

But since the rejection in the Appaloosa, Deek Keeshaw had only one object in mind, and the biggest hindrance to that object was carrying a shotgun and walking toward his office next to Amos Bush's bank.

"How much longer?" Tom grumbled.

"How much longer what?" Deek said even though he already knew what Tom was grumbling about.

"How much longer we gonna wait till we do what we come here to do?"

"I'll say it one more time, Tom, and you listen, too, Bart, 'cause I don't ever want to say it again. We wait till the marshal gets here and takes them two fugitives into custody and away from the sheriff and deputy and their shotguns. When Hinge and his man got no more reason to sleep in that office and sit in that chair next to that bank," Deek nodded toward the corner, "then, and not till then, do we do what we come here to do. Now, does that spell it out plain enough?"

"Yeah, well . . .

"Yeah, well *what*, Tom?"

"If that marshal don't get here pretty soon . . ."

"What?"

"Well, we're gonna end up saddle sore, that's what."

"That'd be too bad, Tom, because that's what you usually think with."

"Deek's right," Bart said. "No sense goin' up against them scatterguns."

"No sense at all," Deek confirmed. "We need all the odds we can get. We'll wait it out. Can't be more'n a day or two. Sheriff said the marshal'ud be here before Christmas. Meanwhile we'll . . ." he looked toward the saloon, ". . . hit *that*."

"Good idea," Tom said.

"That *is* a good idea," Bart concluded.

Elwood Hinge had reached the front of the sheriff's office, where Homer sat in the Douglas chair.

"No marshal?" Homer asked even though he knew the answer.

"Nope." The sheriff set his shotgun against the door, untied the packet of dodgers, unfolded, and started to riffle through them.

"Anything interesting?" The deputy nodded toward the dodgers in Hinge's hand.

"Yeah."

"What?"

"The railroad's still looking for Frank and Jesse."

"Well, I'm not," Homer said.

"Ben Thompson," Hinge continued looking through the posters, "Bill Longley, the Daltons . . ."

"Pass, pass, pass."

"Here's something different, but no reward."

"What?"

"Circular from some orphanage. Faith, Hope, and Charity over in Palestine . . . looking for three orphans."

"Escape, did they?" Homer smiled.

"I guess."

"Armed and dangerous?"

"Could be. Ages eleven, ten, and six."

"Some gang."

"Uh-huh."

"Elwood . . ."

"What?"

Homer looked upward at the suddenly deep, blue-black sky.

"I think it's fixin' to rain."

Several droplets splashed onto the circular in Hinge's hand.

"Fixin', hell," the sheriff said. "It's raining."

* * *

Austin, Peg, and Davy sat inside the cave and watched the midday turn near-black and the rain beat into the cold, solid ground and form rivulets all around and into their bunker.

With fury and the sound of a thousand drums, the wind drove from the north and whipped the rain through the opening.

"I never seen it rain so hard," Davy said, shivering and staring outside. "Have you, Austin?"

Austin said nothing.

"Austin?"

"What?"

"Have you ever seen it rain so hard?"

"Sure," Austin said but not too convincingly. "Lots of times."

"You have?"

"Yeah, but mostly in the summer, summer storms. Usually don't last long."

"Yeah, but this ain't summer."

"It'll be all right, Davy." Peg put her arm around him. "We'll just sit here and wait it out."

"Don't have much choice." Austin rose and made his way toward the entrance, getting wetter as he got closer, and looked out.

"What're you doing?" Peg asked.

"Just looking."

"For what?"

"I don't know. You know, he hasn't come out since those people left this morning."

"I know," Peg said.

"This is the first time he hasn't been out there digging since we got here."

"I know," she repeated. "Wonder what he's been doing in there all this time."

"Well, whatever it is"—Austin walked back toward his brother and sister—"he's better off than we are."

Chapter 23

Breakfast, with Ben, Esmeralda, and the two children, was the only meal that Shad Parker had eaten that day and night.

After they left he had come back inside and was still sitting in the same chair, staring at Molly O's shawl he had put on the table along with the small metal container holding her letters. His Colt was also on the table and a bottle of whiskey, now empty.

He did not know, nor care, how long he had sat there. He was vaguely aware that it had begun to rain sometime that afternoon and continued now well into the night.

All the memories he had tried to erase ever since leaving the Shenandoah, all the pain and suffering, all the ghosts, the haunting vision of three graves left behind, a thousand miles away, but buried in his brain, unearthed again by the visitors from the past, pounded into his every thought as the unceasing rain pounded from the black sky into the tough skin of Texas.

The unwelcomed memories flooded, then funneled

one by one, dripping to his whiskey-drenched senses . . . at first almost out of focus. Then sharper, much too sharp . . . at the rasslin' contest, the first sight of the most beautiful creature he had ever seen on the face of God's earth. Green eyes sparkling. Flowing red hair blazing in the sunlight. Full crimson lips . . . "Champeen" . . . Ben Warren introducing him to Molly O . . . the shattered Little Green Jug . . . picnics, dances . . . the Christmas Eve he asked Molly O to marry him . . . life and love with her in the paradise of the Shenandoah Valley . . . the babies, Sean and Shannon . . . a shadow across the land . . . Harper's Ferry . . . the first blood of battle, Stonewall Jackson . . . home again for just a little while . . .

"You'll miss your brigade" . . . "I'll only miss you, Molly O" . . . "Come back to us, Shad" . . . "You be here Molly O, and I'll come back" . . . "back" . . . "back" . . . "back" . . . but back to three graves . . . *Oh, Shenandoah. I hear you calling . . .*

Calling . . . Calling . . . Calling . . . the words and music . . . the song that had been their theme had become his curse . . . *Away, I'm bound away . . . across the wide Missouri . . . Oh, Shenandoah, I'm going to leave you . . .*

But Shad Parker had come over a thousand miles and still he had not left the Shenandoah and the Shenandoah had not left him . . . *Away, I'm bound away* . . . And the farther he had come, the closer seemed the memories . . . the closer the song, the song that had become a curse that would not, could not, be purged from his mind and body and soul . . . not as long as he lived.

As bad as it had been before they came, Ben and

Esmeralda and their children had made it even worse, harder to bear . . . Ben, his best friend, Ben, with his armless sleeve pinned to his coat, the hollow, dried-out remnant of his carefree comrade who was born with a gift of laughter and who would die in a year or two, a skeletal remnant of his former self . . . but at least Ben knew he had some time left with his family and could savor that time with Esmeralda and the two boys . . . He could put his arm around his wife and kiss her and tell her with his dying breath that he loved her and know that Es and the boys would survive.

If only Shad could have given his life in place of Molly O's and their children's . . . If they could have survived instead of him. Soldiers, at least some soldiers like Shad who had fought in battle after bloody battle, are apt to die; they know that when they advance with fixed bayonet, but they die for a cause and the women and children they leave behind . . . not the other way around.

And even though Esmeralda knew that she would soon be a widow, she had had time to prepare. Death would not strike their family in one swift, fiery blow as it had struck Shad Parker's family. Ben would leave Esmeralda more than memories. There were Benjie and Todd, who would live in their father's image and grow and help their mother.

Shad thought of them, out there in the cold, wet Texas night. But still alive, still together. No matter what might happen, this night they were together.

Shad Parker was alone.

Alone. Except for Molly O's shawl.

And the gun.

* * *

Austin stood looking out of the entrance of the cave as the rain lashed through the opening and onto his already wet face and soaked clothes. Jagged streaks of lightning and the sharp sound of thunder ripped through the black cloak of night.

But there was no shield. No comfort in the cave.

Austin turned and walked back toward Peggy and Davy, who had sought refuge on the elevation of a rock.

The mud in the cave was now ankle thick as it sucked at Austin's feet with every step he took. Water ran down the creviced walls and spilled onto the muddied bottom.

"No sign of it letting up." Austin wiped the rain from his eyes and face. "It just means to keep on coming down."

"I'm cold." Davy shivered.

"I know, Davy." Peg patted her brother's face. "Austin, we've got to do something."

Austin looked at his half-submerged feet, then back toward the entrance.

"Austin?"

"You're right, Peg. This place leaks like a sieve. It's turning into nothing but a mudhole."

"We just can't stay here."

"We're not going to." Austin motioned down toward the spread below. "We're going down there."

"To his place?"

Austin nodded.

"*He* won't take us in."

"He will if he doesn't know about it."

"What do you mean?"

"I mean the barn. That's what I mean. He's probably drunk asleep . . ."

"You think so?"

"Sure. The barn. I'll bet that's nice and dry with lots of warm hay in it. How does that sound?"

Davy shivered again. Peg looked at her little brother, then nodded to Austin.

"Let's go," Austin said.

"What if he wakes up?" Peg was also shivering. "And catches us?"

"What if he does? What's he gonna do? Kill us?"

Chapter 24

Everything was quiet except for the rain and the intermittent lightning and thunder.

At five minutes until midnight most of the inhabitants of Gilead already were asleep.

But not all.

Hooter had closed the Appaloosa early because the customers either didn't come in that night or went home sooner than usual. The rain had a dampening effect on business. Hooter sat alone at the bar, illuminated by only a single lamp, and thought about how things would be without Yellow Rose and with a new partner. A silent partner. His feelings about the situation were mixed. Yellow Rose had made up her mind to leave, and the Appaloosa, the town, and he, would miss her and the business she attracted. That was on one side of the mix. On the other was the fact that he was buying her out at a bargain price and as his silent partner had pointed out, Hooter would end up with a profit going in, a bigger percentage, and the benefit of a partnership with the town's leading citizen, who just happened to be his landlord anyhow and could jack up the rent out of spite if Hooter refused.

Hooter already had made up his mind to make it a clean sweep by getting rid of Francine Needle and Stella Bright in favor of younger, better-looking attractions. Yes, he'd miss Yellow Rose even though he had never touched her. She had made that part of the deal going in. "Strictly a business arrangement," she had said. "No personal involvement," she added. "Partners shouldn't sleep together unless they're married." Hooter reluctantly agreed and there were times when he wished he hadn't. But he did. That was another advantage—none of the new, younger, more attractive ladies would be partners.

After the bank closed Hooter had walked over in the rain, signed the papers without even reading them, picked up the fifteen hundred dollars in cash, and walked back into the new Appaloosa.

Yes, it was going to be a merry Christmas.

Rosalind DuPree lay in bed, wearing a nightgown, reading from Corinthians.

> *Behold, I show you a mystery: We shall not all sleep; but we shall all be changed—*
> *In a moment, in the twinkling of an eye, at the last trumpet. For the trumpet shall sound, and the dead shall be raised incorruptible, and we shall be changed.*

She still had not made up her mind about San Francisco and about other things, but one way or another there would be a change.

Yellow Rose had died when she crossed over and out of the doorway of the Appaloosa, but she was not sure that the corruptible had, or could, put on incorruption.

The trumpet had not sounded. The only sound was that of rain . . . but would, or could, the rain wash away the stain of corruption?

Deek Keeshaw stood by the window of their hotel room sucking his pipe while his two brothers slept. He looked across at the dark, wet window of the bank and then at the sheriff's office next to it.

He knew that there were three men inside. Two of them slated to hang. The other, Sheriff Elwood Hinge, guarding them until he could deliver them to their fate . . . and collect the reward.

If Deek Keeshaw had his way, both prisoners would try to escape and be shot dead in the effort. That night. Then there would be no need for Hinge to guard them or the bank, and the Keeshaws could go about their business and collect their reward.

But as Deek Keeshaw puffed on his pipe everything was quiet. Except for the sound of the rain.

"Sheriff! Sheriff!" Charlie Reno cried out. "Make him stop! He's making me crazy! Sheriff!"

"I'm gonna kill you, you son of a bitch," Red Borden whispered. "I'm gonna kill you just as sure as the turnin' of the earth."

Elwood Hinge stood in front of the cells in his stocking feet, but holding the shotgun.

"Sheriff!" Charlie repeated.

"Red," Hinge said in a soft but firm voice, "unless you shut up for the rest of the night, I'm not going to gag you, I'm going to hit you on the side of the skull so hard you won't wake up till the marshal gets here . . . or maybe never."

"Tell him, Sheriff," Charlie squealed.

"I already did. And I just might put you out for the duration, too, Charlie. Now, both of you, shut up for the rest of the night."

Elwood Hinge went back to his cot, set aside the shotgun, and lay down. He had been thinking about the fact that Homer Keeler would soon be married and be a father a little too soon after that. There would be those in Gilead who would keep track of the calendar. Hinge, like all men, had sometimes thought about being a father. But he was not especially enamored of the notion. His younger brother, Frank, had seen to it that there were sons to carry on the Hinge identity. Three sons whom Elwood had never seen. Nor had he seen Frank and his wife, Gloria, since they went to Chicago just before the war. Like Sam Houston, Frank believed in the preservation of the Union. While he didn't believe in it enough to enlist, he did go north to practice law. Frank Hinge had prospered there and after the cessation of hostilities sent Elwood a letter and pictures of his three nephews—inviting his older brother to come to Chicago and visit.

Elwood politely declined but wished all of the Hinges well in his letter of response.

If he and Rosalind did get married, would they

have children? Where would he and Rosalind live? What would the children look like?

Elwood Hinge noticed that there was a leak in the corner of the office, not a big leak, but enough to make a crooked streak from the ceiling down to the floor.

He would have to see that it got fixed. Or tell Deputy Homer Keeler to get it fixed, if Elwood left Gilead and Homer became sheriff.

In his bedroom at the Bush mansion, Amos Bush lay in his bed and thought about amending his agreement with Hannah Brown. He thought about approaching her with the proposal that he visit her twice a week instead of once. Of course, he would have to offer quid pro quo. Her mortgage would be paid off twice as fast, five years instead of ten, but for the next five years it would be worth it to him. After that, anything could happen. Maybe Laureen would have that operation and get well. Or maybe she would die.

In any case, for the next five years, Amos Bush would have twice as many visits and he might even get Hannah to quit calling him Mr. Bush.

In another bedroom Laureen Bush lay with a Bible in one hand and her father's loaded pistol in the other.

She had been reading from Deuteronomy.

Laureen Bush had a secret, a secret that only she and her housekeeper, Candida Guzman, knew. For the past two years Laureen, with the constant encouragement and aid of Candida Guzman, had been able to walk. At first a few steps, then across the room, until now, when she could make it to the top of the stairs holding on to the rail, then back to her bedroom.

It would not be too long before Laureen Bush would be able to climb the stairs and walk, gun in hand, into her husband's bedroom. In the meantime she held on to her father's loaded pistol and thought of the words from Deuteronomy—chapter 32, verse 35.

To me belongeth vengeance, and recompense;
Their foot shall slide in due time:
For the day of their calamity is at hand,
And the things that shall come upon them make
haste.

Everything was quiet except for the rain and intermittent lightning and thunder.

At midnight most of the inhabitants of Gilead were asleep.

But not all.

Chapter 25

Shad Parker had not moved.

He stared straight ahead at the table in front of him. The table with the shawl, the small metal box, the whiskey bottle, and the gun.

The midnight sky resounded with lightning, thunder, and the persistent tattoo of rain. His hand reached out across the table.

As he brought the bottle close, he realized that it was empty. He rose, almost knocking over the chair. It was evident that the whiskey had gotten to him, but he made his way to the cabinet. He opened the door, reached in, and pulled out one of the remaining bottles.

Shad Parker walked back to the table. He wrenched the cork out of the bottle and let it drop to the floor. He sat in the chair, took a long drink, looked at the shawl, then his gaze moved slowly, painfully toward the tin box.

He gradually reached out and touched the box.

* * *

They had slipped and slid down the muddy hillside across the flat bottomland and made it to the front of the barn in the downpour.

Austin's hand unlatched and opened the barn door. Peg and Davy, drenched, stood beside him. Austin took a step inside and waved for his sister and brother to follow. They did.

Shad Parker's hand was still touching the tin box, but his eyes were fixed on the Colt. Then he looked at the shawl and lifted the lid of the box. *Oh, Shenandoah, I hear you calling.*

Gently, he removed one of the letters, brittle and yellowed. He held it carefully and heard the voice of Molly O.

My dearest darling,

I pray this letter finds you safe. The children and I are well and think of you every moment.

It is still impossible for me to understand and countenance the madness that has torn you— and the other men of our valley—away from us.

You who never raised a hand in anger—so gentle and compassionate—whose heart and mind recoiled at the very thought of slavery—turned into a machine of war.

And why? Because we are Virginians. Because other men—farmers like yourself who love the soil of their Ohio or Massachusetts—would devastate our valley.

If only our Blue Mountains were walls to shut them out and let us live in peace.

But the war draws closer to us. You can sense it in the air. Even the doves have left the valley.

And now, as the time we celebrate our Savior's birth is near, I feel another life stirring within me, too. I know you want a daughter—and may it be God's will to grant her to us.

I pray that next Christmas we will be at peace, together, our family . . .

Shad Parker could bear no more. He placed the letter on the table beside the shawl. He looked at the bottle, then the gun. His hand moved, but was stopped by a sound.

Once, twice, and then again. A slamming thud from outside.

He rose and walked toward the door. The slamming continued. He opened the door and looked through the driving rain.

The barn door, whipped by rain and wind, slammed against the front, hinged closed, then blew open again.

He took the jacket that hung from a nail near the entrance and started to put it on.

Austin, Peg, and Davy huddled in the warm, dry hayloft. A couple of the horses neighed as the barn door slapped shut again then flew open, allowing another tide of rain to sweep into the barn.

"Austin!"

"I know, Peg."

"You think he heard?"

"If he didn't, he will. I better get down there and latch up that door."

"Be careful."

"I will."

"Austin . . ."

"What?"

"Put on your shoes so you don't step on some nail or something."

"Okay . . . damn."

"What's wrong?"

"Can't find the other shoe."

"Here it is."

"Thanks."

"I'll be right back. Davy, okay?"

"He's sleeping."

"Be right back."

Shad Parker came out of the door of the cabin and staggered against the wind and rain. He slipped and nearly fell but walked on. A skirl of lightning ripped the hillside and was followed by a bellow of thunder that reverberated and echoed across the night.

He stopped and stood defiant. His face turned upward toward the churning heavens with a million needles of water whipping against him, bleached again by lightning and pounded by the blast of thunder.

The night had become his Armageddon, and Shad Parker flung up both arms and screamed a challenge with all the screams that were pent up inside of him.

"I'm here! Go ahead!"

He swayed against the elements, his hands still uplifted, and cried out.

"Strike me down! Damn you! 'Cast forth the lightning! Shoot out thine arrows and destroy!' Here! I'm here!"

Austin had seen nothing like it before. The boy stood watching from the doorway of the barn, paralyzed at the terrifying tableau out of a Walpurgis Night.

Shad Parker's eyes boiled, imploring, daring to be struck down. A ghastly figure framed against the graveyard darkness. Then he twisted suddenly as a burning, blinding branch of lightning split a wheelbarrow just beside him, scorching his body and knocking him face-first into the swamp of mud.

Austin shuddered.

A deafening roar of thunder followed after the bolt of lightning. He waited through the terrible echo, thinking that he, too, would be struck down by the next inevitable blow. How long he stood and waited he did not know.

But it did not come.

Shad Parker lay motionless, a twisted, unconscious pattern, half his face sunk in a muddy puddle. The rain continued to pour into the puddle and the inert figure sank deeper, and closer to death.

Still trembling, Austin came out of the doorway, through the rain and mud, toward the fallen man. The first thing he had to do was to get the man's face from beneath the surface of the dirty puddle or it would be too late to do anything. Maybe it already was. Maybe the man was already dead from the lightning bolt, or had already drowned.

The boy reached down, took the man by both shoulders of his coat, and managed to roll him faceup. Water eddied out of the man's mouth and nostrils, his eyes were closed but he still breathed. Austin tried to pull him out of the puddle, but the man's weight and the gluey mud were too much for him.

Austin, with all his strength, shook the man fiercely, trying to revive him. The man coughed and vomited but remained unconscious. It took all of Austin's strength to roll him just out of the puddle and on to his side so he wouldn't choke in his own vomit.

"Austin! Austin!" Peg's voice came from the doorway of the barn. "Are you all right? What happened?"

Austin hurried as fast as he could through the rain and mud back to the barn. When he got there, Davy was standing next to Peg.

"What happened, Austin?"

"I think he got hit by lightning. Fell into that puddle, but he's alive . . . so far."

"We can't leave him out there . . ."

"We're not going to."

"Austin, we can't lift him. We just can't, not even the three of us."

"No, but we can move him." Austin looked around the barn and settled on a canvas tarp folded on the bed of the wagon. "Both of you've got to help. Come on!"

He grabbed the tarp and ran outside. Peg and Davy followed.

Austin dropped the canvas next to the man and started to unwrap it. Peg and Davy stood watching.

"What're you doing, Austin?"

"Help me get this tarp unfolded. Spread it out close to him. Try to get some of it underneath."

The three of them spread the already soaked canvas onto the ground close to the man's body.

"That's it," Austin said. "That's good. Now, come on, roll him over onto the tarp."

They were on their knees in the mud, reaching, grabbing, pulling at the dead weight of the man until they finally managed to maneuver him onto the layer of canvas.

"Okay," Austin gasped, "I'll take the front end, you two on each side. Keep him on the canvas." Austin pointed to the door of the cabin, which was level to the ground. "Pull!"

Another crack of lightning split and lit up the sky, but farther away this time, still illuminating the three children and the man on the canvas for just a moment, and then the drumbeat of distant thunder.

They strained against the mud and rain, pulling the canvas sled across the sucking mire, tugging with all of their cumulative effort, themselves slipping and falling into the muck, then rising again, but slowly, inch by inch, foot by foot, edging the water-soaked load closer to the cabin.

Chapter 26

There was some slight movement of his head, then his eyes opened, but they were dull and unfocused.

Shad Parker lay on the kitchen floor, covered by a blanket, his face illuminated by the morning sunlight, head resting on a rolled-up shawl.

Davy sat on a chair nearby, biting into an apple and watching him. The man breathed heavily and then groaned with pain at the breath. His eyes closed then opened slowly, trying to focus toward the corner of the ceiling. It seemed that he tried to move his arms but for the moment could not. His body relaxed and sought to gather strength as well as consciousness.

"Peg! Peg!" Davy jumped from the chair and pointed with the apple toward the man. "He's comin' round!"

Peg was at the stove, frying eggs and bacon. She moved the skillet off to the side.

"All right, Davy. I see." She left the stove, taking a

kitchen towel with her, crossed to the rear door, opened it, and called out, "Austin!"

Austin was feeding the chickens and clucking back at them. The morning was cool, but clean, bright, and beautiful.

"Austin," Peg called again from the doorway. "Come inside."

"Breakfast ready?"

"Just about, but he's coming to."

"I'll be right there." He flung out the remainder of the chicken feed, set down the pan, and walked toward the cabin, "How is he?"

"I don't know. He's just coming to."

"Well," Austin walked past Peg and into the cabin, "let's find out."

Peg closed the door and followed her brother.

Shad Parker, dazed, hurt, and confused, managed with a mighty effort to prop himself up on one elbow and look around, then up toward the three children who stood close to him. His body ached and he wiped at his mouth, swallowed the sour taste there, and finally managed to speak.

"How . . . how'd I get in here?"

"We brought you," Austin said simply.

"Just you . . . kids?"

Austin nodded. So did Davy.

"I . . ." As Shad Parker tried to sit up the blanket fell from his upper body and revealed that much of his left side, including his shoulder and arm, was scorched, blackened, and covered with a greasy patina.

He looked at the injured arm for a moment and touched his upper left arm with his right hand.

"Lightning burned you," Austin said. "We put some lard on it after we brought you in."

The enormity of their endeavor sank into Shad Parker's still-dazed brain. He recalled the whiskey, the letter, the noise from outside. The rain, lightning, and thunder. His curse and challenge to be struck down. Then a blinding flash. Instinctively turning away. A burning bolt through his body and soul. Then sinking. The sensation of sinking into a wet, black, bottomless pit. And relief. Relief that it was over at last. But it wasn't over. They had saved him even though he didn't want to be saved.

They had reached into his welcomed grave and raised him up and out. Somehow three children, from God knew where, appeared through the stormy night and brought him back to life.

If they expected thanks, none would be forthcoming. Not from him.

But they didn't seem to expect anything. They just stood there, the three of them, until the girl moved to the table, which was as he left it.

She picked up the letter near the metal box to clear some space.

"Put that down!" Shad Parker said. Not loud. But hard. "Put it down."

She dropped the letter and took a step back, away from the table and him.

Silence.

"We was just fixing some breakfast," Austin said after a moment. "That's all."

With a major effort, Shad Parker managed to rise some more, propping himself up with his right hand.

As he did, he noticed Molly O's shawl, which they had placed under his head.

"Mister . . ." Austin said, "you better . . ."

But the man turned abruptly and looked at the boy, who changed his mind about offering any further advice.

Silence again.

"Are we gonna stay here?" Davy, still holding the core of the apple, finally asked. "Are we?"

For a moment there was only the scent and sizzle of the bacon.

"Eat your breakfast," Shad Parker said. "And get out."

Chapter 27

Charlie Reno hadn't slept all night. Red Borden had seen to that. But Charlie was sleeping this morning, as if he had been drugged. He lay facedown on his bunk, exhausted, breathing heavy, dull breaths.

When Elwood Hinge came back to check on his prisoners, Borden whispered that he had something important to tell the sheriff. It was about the six thousand from the Garden City Bank, but he wanted to go out front and talk to the sheriff where his erstwhile partner couldn't hear.

"Just let me come out for a couple of minutes, Sheriff. You won't be sorry," Red muttered.

"No, I won't," the sheriff said. "But even look sideways and you will."

Elwood Hinge had gone back to his office for the key and his shotgun, returned to the cell, opened it, and nodded to Red.

Charlie Reno continued to sleep.

"What're you doin', Sheriff?" a startled Deputy Homer Keeler inquired as he entered from the street and saw Elwood Hinge and the prisoner come from the cell into the office.

"Take 'er easy, Homer." The sheriff smiled. "Everything's in order. It's just that Red here's got something he wants to talk about, away from his ol' pal. Right, Red?"

"That depends."

"Don't depend on anything, Red. Either you talk and talk now or you're going right back there." Hinge pointed to the cells with his weapon.

"Maybe we can make a deal . . ."

"I don't believe so."

"All I want is a little . . . consideration."

"For what?"

"For tellin' where the six thousand is hid. Don't you think that's worth somethin'?"

"Sure . . ."

"Good."

"If you tell us, maybe they'll hang Charlie first and let you watch."

There was no denying the disappointment in Red Borden's face.

"On the other hand, if you *don't* tell us I got a feeling that Charlie will, and he'll get to watch you do the strangulation jig. Take your choice."

"Not much of a choice."

"Tell you what, Red. You draw us a map to where the money's stashed and I'll write a letter to the judge back at Fort Smith, praising your cooperation, give it to the federal marshal when he picks you up. You get a good lawyer and maybe they won't hang you. Maybe they'll settle for a couple of corpses and Charlie.

Maybe you'll get off with life and maybe you can bust out again. Maybe."

"Yeah." Red Borden nodded.

"It beats letting Charlie tell us and you swinging for sure."

"Goddamn, I'll do it!"

"Where's the money?"

"There's an old abandoned mill of some sort less than a dozen miles to the east . . ."

"I know the place." Homer nodded.

"I'll draw you a map to right where the money's buried, still in the sack from the bank . . ."

"That's smart," the sheriff commented.

"Well, we didn't expect to get caught," Red said in defense.

"We took some of it to have a good time in town, then we was goin' back for the rest of it . . ."

"Yeah. Well, the best-laid plans of mice and men . . ."

"What's mice got to do with it?"

"Nothing, Red. You draw the map and I'll write the letter." Hinge handed Borden paper and pencil and pointed to the chair near his desk. "Homer, when he's done, you ride out and pick it up."

"Sure thing, Elwood."

"Charlie shouldn'a tried to double-cross me, not after all we been through together."

"Yeah, but this way it just might work out to your benefit, Red," the sheriff observed as Borden drew on the paper.

"I guess so," Red Borden said, "but I just might kill the son of a bitch anyhow."

* * *

"Seven. Eight. Nine. Ten." Hooter counted out and placed ten one-hundred-dollar bills on the table in Rosalind DuPree's room. "One thousand dollars."

"So Amos Bush did come through." Rosalind DuPree smiled.

"Well, in a manner of speaking."

"What does that mean, Hooter?"

"Well, it means . . . I'm not supposed to tell anybody, but, hell, Rose, I never had no secrets from you and I know you won't say anything to anybody . . . ol' banker Bush bought into the Appaloosa, a silent partner. You know he owns the building anyhow."

"Yes, I know."

"What do you think, Rose?"

"Hooter, I'm through thinking about the Appaloosa and anything to do with it."

"Yeah, I reckon so. Oh," Hooter removed a piece of paper from inside his coat pocket, "Rose, would you mind signing this, just to make things . . . official?"

"Did Amos Bush draw it up?"

Hooter, half-embarrassed, half-sheepish, nodded.

"Sure, Hooter. I'll sign it . . . gladly."

"Thanks."

"And, Hooter . . ."

"Yes?"

"Nothing." Rosalind DuPree kissed her ex-partner on his left cheek. "You're a good man. Just take care of yourself."

She signed the paper.

* * *

Amos Bush walked toward Hannah Brown's buckboard in front of Inghram's General Store. The buckboard had already been loaded with supplies and Bush had watched and waited from the bank for his opportunity.

She walked out of the store with Pete Inghram and handed a few coins to the boy who helped load.

"Morning, Amos," Inghram said as Bush approached, then quickly went back into the store. Pete Inghram was not unaware of the relationship between Bush and the young widow. Besides, Bush owned that building, too.

"Good morning, Mrs. Brown."

The widow nodded.

"Quite a storm we had last night. But it looks like it's going to be a beautiful Christmas, doesn't it?"

"Yes," she said. "Under the circumstances."

Bush smiled pleasantly and looked both ways to make certain nobody could hear.

"May I help you aboard?"

"No, thank you. I can manage."

"Speaking of circumstances . . ."

"Yes, Mr. Bush?"

"Uh, there's a matter I'd like to discuss with you."

"Business?"

"Well, yes. You might say that . . ."

"Do you want me to come over to the bank?"

"No. That won't be necessary. I guess it can wait until . . . later."

"All right." She started to move to the wagon.

His right hand reached out and touched her, but withdrew quickly when she looked directly into his eyes.

"I just wanted to let you know that I believe we can . . . amend the . . . mortgage agreement . . . in your favor. So that it can be paid off sooner."

"And more often?" Her candidness startled the banker.

"I beg pardon . . ." Bush didn't know what else to say, under the circumstances.

"Are you saying that you want to collect more than once a week?" Her voice was not quite soft enough to suit Bush.

A couple of people passed by and Amos Bush was relieved that they apparently hadn't heard, or at least, reacted.

"Perhaps you're right, Mrs. Brown," Bush managed. "We can discuss this another time."

"Whenever you say, Mr. Bush."

"Good day." Bush tipped his hat.

"Good day." She mounted easily onto the buckboard. "Oh, and Mr. Bush . . ."

"Yes?"

"Thanks again for offering . . . to help. I'm always interested in listening to a favorable business proposition."

As the buckboard pulled away, Amos Bush tried but failed to repress a smile.

As Hannah Brown's buckboard rolled through the muddy main street of Gilead near the New Heidelberg, the Keeshaw brothers stepped out of the restaurant, first Deek, then Tom and Bart. Deek puffed on his pipe and Bart spiked a toothpick at what was left of his teeth.

Deek spotted Amos Bush standing in front of Inghram's looking toward the handsome woman as she moved past the brothers.

"There's Mr. Bush." Deek pointed with his pipe.

"So it is," Tom acknowledged.

"Let's pay our respects," Deek suggested, and moved. Tom and Bart followed.

Amos Bush still stood savoring his thoughts as the threesome approached.

"Morning, Mr. Bush," Deek greeted.

"Good morning, gentlemen," Bush responded, now smiling the smile he no longer needed to repress. "And a glorious morning it is."

"I'd say so," Deek said. "But that sure was a hell of a goose drowner we had last night."

"Ah, yes. But look at the results. Have you ever seen a sky so bright, a day so . . . stimulating?"

"No." Deek looked at his brothers. "I guess not, leastwise in December . . . not in Louisiana. Right, boys?"

The boys nodded agreement.

"Have you gentlemen found anything suitable?"

"How's that?" Deek asked.

"That spread you were looking for. Any prospects?"

"Well, yes, as a matter of fact. There just might be one or two."

"Going out again today? Certainly is a beautiful day to go out looking."

"Yeah, well, as a matter of fact," Deek repeated the phrase, "no, we're not."

"Oh."

"You see, Mr. Bush, Bart here's feeling poorly."

"Sorry to hear that."

"Yeah, it's his tooth. One of his back molars flared up on him. Right, Bart?"

"Uh, right."

"Well," Bush said, "that's nothing to fool around with. Ought to go see Tony."

"Tony the barber?" Deek asked.

"Yes. Besides barbering and a couple of other professions, Tony can pull a tooth, or teeth, if needs be."

"Yeah," Deek said. "Maybe we'll do that, uh, Bart?"

"Yeah, maybe. Unless it gets to feelin' better."

"Hope it does. Well, gentlemen," Bush continued to smile, "good day." He proceeded through the mud toward the bank.

"What's got into him?" Tom said as Bush moved out of earshot.

"Damned if I know," Deek replied. "Bart, you want to go see Tony?" he joshed, and puffed on his pipe.

"Hell, no!" Bart was indignant. "What's a matter with you, Deek? You know there's nothing wrong with my tooths."

"Then, would you rather go looking for a spread?"

"Hell, no. I'd rather go in there." Bart pointed at the Appaloosa.

"Well, let's go."

"I never seen a banker so happy," Bart noted as they walked toward the saloon.

"Yeah, well." Deek puffed and smiled even more. "We'll do something about that."

Chapter 28

The morning of Christmas Eve day Shad Parker had watched as the three children made their way up the mud-slick hillside after they gobbled their food in silence, following his telling them to "eat your breakfast and get out."

Peg had volunteered to wash the dishes, but their host said that wouldn't be necessary. She had placed a plate of scrambled eggs and several thick slices of bacon on the table for him, being careful not to disturb the letter, the tin box, or the gun. While they were there, Shad Parker did not touch the food.

It wasn't easy but he had managed to get to his feet as they ate. The children felt it advisable not to try to help him. He carefully folded the shawl and held it with both hands, leaning against the wall, until they finished eating. They finished as quickly as they could. It was then that Peg had mentioned washing the dishes.

They walked out as far away from him as possible while he braced his back against the wall and cradled the shawl.

"Hope you feel better, mister," Peg said as she walked by.

Shad Parker did not reply.

He waited just a couple of minutes then went to the open door and watched them as the older boy and the girl helped the youngest make the slippery ascent.

The older boy had seen to the needs of the animals as well as the chickens and, considering the deluge, the place was not in bad shape at all, except for the burned and shattered pieces of what used to be a wheelbarrow.

Shad Parker noticed something else that disturbed him, but for the time being he had to go inside and take it easy.

"What a mess!" Peg said from the threshold of the cave. The mud had even covered the area that they had used to build their fire.

"Mud must be a foot thick," Austin added.

"Well, what do you think, Austin? Should we try to clean it up, or go someplace else?"

"I'll go out and look after a while, but we'd better do what we can first, just in case we got to stay."

An hour later Austin and Peg were still on either end of a board that Austin had procured, using it as a blade to skim the mud off the floor of the cave.

Davy stood watching as the wave of mud came closer to him.

"Why are grown-ups always so mad?" he asked.

"Davy," Austin said, ignoring the question, "you're just getting in the way. Move over."

Davy moved.

"Just about everybody I can remember was always mad."

"That's not true." Peg looked up at him from the mud.

"Sure it is, like ol' Miss Stench. She was always mad, wasn't she?"

"Can't argue about that." Austin smiled. "But some others weren't, like that buffalo man—even that man on the mule. They weren't mad. They just got things on their mind. Things beside us."

"That man down there," Davy pointed below. "He's mad at us . . ."

"He's mad at everything," Austin said.

"Why?"

"I don't know, Davy . . . and I don't intend to ask him." Austin went back to work.

"Was our daddy and mommy always mad?"

"No, they weren't," Peg said. "They used to . . . laugh a lot. Didn't they, Austin?"

Austin just nodded.

"I wish I could remember them. I can't even hardly remember what they looked like."

"Well," Peg smiled, "you were pretty young."

"Are we ever gonna get another . . . a mom and . . ."

"Davy," Austin became exasperated, "quit asking so many questions. We're trying to work. Why don't you get outta here for a while? You're just in the way. Go on outside and play."

"By myself?"

"Yes, by yourself. Go on, but don't stray too far."

"All right." Davy shrugged and left.

Austin and Peg continued to work in silence for a few minutes.

"Austin?"

"What?"

"Why do you think he's so mad?"

"Huh?"

"That man."

Austin knew which man she was talking about.

"I haven't got any notion."

"Did you see the way he jumped when I took hold of that piece of paper?"

"Sure, I did."

"It was a letter. I could tell that much. And there were some other letters in that box . . . and the way he held on to that shawl . . . There's something sad about him . . . don't you think?"

"No, I don't. I don't think *anything* about him."

"Course you do. Austin . . . you think we saved his life? I mean, you think he woulda died out there last night?"

"Probably not. Too mean to die."

"He looked like he was drowning in that water when you got to him."

"I don't know. All I know is we're never gonna get this mud outta here if you keep on yapping."

Davy's brown eyes were wide open in astonishment. He leaned his head forward a little more, looking at a rabbit in the grass.

The rabbit looked right back at Davy. They both were frozen still for the moment. Then the rabbit scampered into a thicket. Davy didn't move his body but he turned his head back toward the cave.

"Austin! Peggy! Hey, Austin, come out here. Quick! Hurry up!"

Inside the cave they heard their brother's voice, dropped the board in the mud, and ran.

They stopped just outside of the entrance to determine from which direction Davy had called.

"Austin! Peggy!"

His voice came from their left and they both moved quickly.

"Come here, quick!"

The voice was closer as they ran.

"What is it?" Austin repeated as he caught sight of his brother.

"Come here! Come here!" Davy stood at the base of a rocky ledge and pointed toward the thicket just a few feet away. "There's a rabbit in there! Maybe we can catch him!"

At first Austin and Peg were both relieved that Davy was not hurt or in trouble. But the next instant Austin grabbed hold of his sister and stood aghast.

"Davy!" Austin exclaimed in a hard, frightened whisper.

"What's wrong?" Davy turned.

"Davy! Davy!" Austin implored. "Don't move!"

The cougar hunched above, on the rim of the ledge, poised within leaping distance of the little boy, who still did not see the open-jawed animal. But both Austin and Peg saw it, and stood terrified.

The cougar snarled and plunged out and downward toward the boy.

A rifle shot exploded.

The cougar twisted in midair, toppled, and dropped in a dead heap at the little boy's feet.

Together, Austin and Peg ran to their brother, who, crying and trembling, dropped to his knees.

Shad Parker with his Winchester took a couple of steps forward, stopped, then walked closer.

Peg cradled her brother in both arms and did her best to comfort him.

"It's all right, Davy. You're all right. Nothing's going to hurt you. Go ahead and cry, Davy, but it's all right . . ."

Austin looked over to the man with the rifle who stood looking down at the dead animal. The shot had entered from beneath the cougar's jaw and hit the brain.

"Was that . . . ?" Austin pointed at the cougar. "Was that . . . ?"

"Mate to the other one." Shad Parker nodded. "Caught a glimpse of her this morning."

The tip of his boot lifted the forepaw of the limp cat and let it drop. She was somewhat smaller than the mate Shad Parker had shot and skinned, about six feet long, tooth to tailbone, with a lighter, grayer color, but not less deadly and now no less dead.

"Gee, mister . . . I, well . . ."

"Never mind," Shad Parker said, still looking down at the cat.

The little boy turned from his sister and gazed across at the beast that had leapt toward him. He went from sobbing to a full burst of tears all over again.

Shad Parker looked from the little boy and girl to the older brother. He was through contemplating. He took hold of the older boy's arm.

"All right, you've had enough and so have I."

"What do you mean, mister?" The man's grip was tight on Austin's wrist.

"I mean, you're coming with me."

"Where?"

"Into town."

"What for?"

"Before you all get killed I'm turning you over to the authorities."

"We can take care of ourselves."

"Yeah," Shad Parker nodded toward the panther, "it looks like it."

"Well . . ."

"Well, what?"

"Can't you wait," Austin pointed to his little brother, "till he stops crying?"

"He can stop crying on the way."

Chapter 29

When the wagon stopped and the man stepped off, there was no doubt about it. The U.S. Marshal had come to town.

As he stood there in front of the livery, his shoulders spread more than a yard east and west and almost six feet off the ground. His massive head rose nearly another foot above the shoulders, rimmed by locks of long, bright yellow hair.

His outer garments were all of buckskin except for the black, wide-brimmed hat that was set squarely on his leonine head. The star was pinned close to the center of his buffalo chest. He wore two pearl-handled Colts, butts forward, out of twin black holsters attached to a black cartridge belt strapped high on his narrow hips. His eyes were slits of cobalt blue.

Just the sight of him reinforced any citizen's faith in law enforcement.

"Julius Trapp," he said to Dutch at the livery stable.

Dutch stared up at the man, who dwarfed even him, and nodded.

"U.S. Marshal. Picking up a couple of fugitives."

Dutch nodded again. By then several citizens had formed a semicircle and also stared at the buckskin giant who spoke with a voice so deep it rumbled.

Elwood Hinge, carrying his shotgun, stepped through the semicircle and approached the other lawman. The men Hinge walked by were the Keeshaw brothers.

"Elwood Hinge, Marshal." He put out his hand. "Pleased to meet you."

"And I you, sir." The two lawmen shook hands. "I've heard about you, and what you did. Congratulations. Good job. I'm Julius Trapp."

Elwood Hinge didn't know it, but there were very few men Julius Trapp addressed as "sir" since mustering out of the Confederate army.

"Would you excuse me for just a minute, sir, while I finish up with this gentleman?" Trapp nodded toward Dutch.

"Of course," Hinge responded.

"Oh, are the prisoners ready to travel?" he inquired of the sheriff.

"Two of them are."

"So I heard."

"You be leaving soon?"

"Yes, sir." Trapp turned to Dutch as several more curious men, women, and children joined the crowd. "I'll need fresh horses, a pair. Pick out the best team you have. I'll swap you and throw in a bonus. A reasonable bonus, paid in U.S. scrip. That satisfactory?"

Dutch nodded.

"Well, sir," Trapp turned back to Hinge, "lead the way."

The citizens opened a path as Elwood Hinge, flanked to the left by Julius Trapp, walked toward his office.

"Godalmighty," someone said out loud, "has somebody come to town!"

The Keeshaws headed back toward the Appaloosa, still looking at the two lawmen.

"Well, Deek," Tom whispered, "that's what we been waitin' for."

"Yep." Deek cast a glance toward the bank. "We don't have to wait much longer."

"I'm sure as hell glad," Bart mumbled, "that one didn't come after us."

Shad Parker's wagon was more than halfway to Gilead. Davy sat next to him up front. The little boy's eyes were still moist. Peg knelt behind them on the bed of the wagon, her eyes on the brink of tears. Austin sat staring at nothing.

"Please, mister," she pleaded, "don't let 'em send us back to that place. Please."

Shad said nothing.

"We'll leave the cave. You'll never see us again . . . we promise."

He didn't even look back at the girl.

"They'll split us up again. They'll put Austin to work on some farm, but nobody'll take Davy and me 'cause we're too small. Please, mister . . ." Now she was crying. "Please . . ."

"Quit it, Peg." Austin's voice was harsh. "He don't care."

From his expression, or lack of it, Shad Parker didn't.

Charlie Reno and Red Borden stood close together attached by a pair of handcuffs Julius Trapp had clapped on them tight as they would fit. As yet he hadn't spoken to either of the two prisoners.

Homer Keeler leaned against the office wall and watched as Hinge handed the marshal a couple of photographs.

"Here's pictures of the two deceased, identified as Frank Chase and Johnsy Reno, then buried."

"Good enough." Trapp took the photographs, folded them once, and put them inside his buckskin shirt.

"And here's the six thousand," Hinge pointed to his desk, "still in the sack from the Garden City Bank."

"That'll mean an additional reward for you, Sheriff. Fifteen percent of whatever is returned, and I'll see that it is. If that's satisfactory to you?"

"It is."

"Tell him what I done, Sheriff!" Red Borden blustered. "Give him the letter you wrote!"

"The money was recovered, by Deputy Keeler here, due to the cooperation of one of the prisoners as stated here in this document . . ."

"For which I was promised special consideration by the sheriff . . ."

"I didn't promise anything. Just wrote down what happened," Hinge said.

"Now, goddammit! Just a minute! I expect . . ."

Red Borden never finished.

Julius Trapp struck him a blow with his right fist on the side of the face that knocked both Red and Charlie off their feet.

The action took everyone, including Hinge and Keeler, by surprise, but Red Borden was the only one bleeding, from the ear.

"My name is Trapp. Julius Trapp. Does that mean anything to you?" He spoke to the men on the floor.

Red Borden shuddered, put his free hand up to his leaking ear, and managed to shake his head *no*.

"I volunteered for this assignment. My brother was Jonas Trapp. You killed him back at Fort Smith during your escape from justice. I'm here to see that justice is done."

"I didn't kill him!" Red cringed, still on the floor.

"He's dead. And as far as I'm concerned you killed him. All of you. It don't matter which one did it. You're both going to hang if you get there alive. If you don't hang, I'll kill you anyhow. Truth is, I'd rather. Now, get up."

Julius Trapp hadn't budged an inch from where he stood, all two hundred and forty-five pounds of him. Red Borden staggered to his feet, dragging Charlie Reno up with him.

Shad Parker's wagon approached the main street of Gilead.

The U.S. Marshal stood by the side of his wagon, which was hitched to a fresh pair of horses. With his left hand he held the sack of money from the Garden City Bank. In addition to the handcuffs his prisoners were further attached by a pair of leg irons.

A couple dozen townsfolk had gathered once more and watched as the marshal loaded the two manacled men on the flat bed of the cart. The Keeshaws were there again, and this time so was Amos Bush.

Pete Inghram had come out of the store, along with three customers and Mrs. Inghram. The marshal took no notice of anyone except his prisoners until he turned to Elwood Hinge and extended his hand. They shook.

"Have a good trip, Marshal."

"Better'n *they* will. I'll see to it that you get that reward, Sheriff."

"I'm much obliged, Marshal."

"So am I, sir. So am I." He looked at his prisoners, then climbed aboard.

They all stood watching. Elwood Hinge, Homer Keeler, the Keeshaws, Amos Bush, Pete and Martha Inghram, Dutch and his son, Bub and the others on the street, and from her second-story window at the Eden, Rosalind DuPree.

As the marshal and his prisoners rolled away, Elwood and Homer walked toward their office. Shad Parker's wagon came to a stop just in front of the office.

"Sheriff. Need to talk to you," Shad said.

"Sure," the sheriff replied. "What about?"

"Them." Shad Parker nodded toward the three children.

Chapter 30

Things had changed considerably in the sheriff's office. Instead of confronting a couple of desperate, killer fugitives, Elwood Hinge and Homer Keeler looked upon three mud-caked, ragtag children and the man who had herded them up and delivered the pathetic trio.

Shad Parker hadn't gone into detail, but he did mention that the littlest boy had had a close call with a panther and that the three kids couldn't go on living in a cave without food and proper clothes. He had said it in as few words as possible. The three kids, so far, had said nothing.

Elwood Hinge held a circular in his hand and glanced from Homer Keeler to the three children.

"Well, they fit the description, all right. You kids come from a place called . . ." he looked at the circular again ". . . Faith, Hope, and Charity Orphanage?"

"No, we don't *come* from there," Austin said.

"But you *did* run away from there."

"Yeah, and we'll run away again if you send us back."

"Got no choice, son." He looked back at Shad Parker. "Meantime, I sure hate to lock them up in jail. It's Christmas Eve, you know."

"Look, I don't give a damn what you do with 'em. Just keep 'em away from my place. I don't want them or anybody else hanging around."

"You've made that plain, Mr. Parker."

"Good. Then there's no more need my wasting any more time." He turned and started to leave.

"Mister." It was Peg's voice.

Shad Parker halfway turned back. She looked at Davy, then at the man.

"Merry Christmas."

He walked quickly out the door.

The sheriff dropped the circular on his desk and took a step toward the small boy.

"How you doing, son?"

Davy didn't answer. But Austin did.

"How do you think he's doing?"

"Yeah."

"Well," Austin said, "ain't you gonna lock us up?"

"I purely dislike doing that."

"Then just let us go." Austin spoke eagerly. "You won't ever see us again." It was hard for Austin to say the next word, but he did. "Please."

"Can't, son."

"Why not?"

"If something happened to you kids, I'd be responsible."

"Who'd care?"

"I would."

For a moment no one in the room said anything.

"Well," Austin broke the silence, "what *are* you gonna do?"

"Homer."

"Yes, sir."

"Go on over and find Reverend Groves. Tell him I want to see him right away."

"Yes, sir." The deputy smiled and left the office.

"Reverend Groves is a good man," the sheriff said to the children. "Maybe he'll put you up tonight till I . . ." Hinge looked down at the circular ". . . can make other arrangements."

Next to the circular on the desk there was the Christmas tree Elwood Hinge had been carving. He picked it up.

"You kids just sit down and take it easy till the reverend gets here. We'll fix you up with something to eat. How does that sound?"

"Thank you," Peg said.

"It's all right." The sheriff picked up the carved Christmas tree from the desk, walked closer to the little boy, and held it out. "Here, son . . . well . . . here."

Shad Parker was on the wagon going home. Dutch had watched from across the street as the man climbed aboard. Dutch's son had stood next to him, hoping that his father would do nothing. That's just what Dutch did. Nothing. Until Shad Parker's wagon pulled away, then Dutch walked back toward the livery.

* * *

It hadn't taken long for Homer Keeler to find and bring back the reverend. Hinge made the proper introductions and summed up the situation.

"You're right, Sheriff, and a good Christian. A jail is no place for three young children. Martha and I will be pleased to have them stay with us. We've got a spare room and I think we can find some clean clothes."

"That's very kind of you, Reverend. I was going to fix them up with something to eat first."

"Of course." Reverend Groves smiled at the three children. "But if you can hold off for just a little while, I'll promise you a first-class home-cooked meal. Mrs. Groves is a mighty fine cook, mighty fine. That be all right with you kids?"

The kids nodded.

"Good. Very good. Come along, then, and don't you worry about a thing, Sheriff. We're glad to have them with us."

After Reverend Groves left and took the three children with him, Davy, holding on to the carved Christmas tree, Homer closed the door and smiled back at Elwood Hinge.

"That was a decent thing for you to do, Elwood."

"Wish I could do more. I guess it'll be up to you to deliver them back to Palestine, Homer."

"Whatever you say."

"But in the meanwhile, at least they'll have a Christmas. Better than Charlie and Red," he added.

"You know, Elwood, I been thinkin'."

"About what?"

"After seeing that marshal, that Julius Trapp . . ."

"Yeah."

"The way he handled them two . . . I don't know if I'm really cut out to be a lawman. I sure ain't like him."

"Well, neither am I, Homer. But, then, they didn't kill my brother . . . or yours. Besides, it takes all kinds, and all sizes, to be a lawman. You'll do just fine, Homer, just fine."

"You think so?"

"I do."

When Shad Parker got home and put away the horses, he went straight for the bottle.

Chapter 31

The stars blinked down from the silent, black blanket of sky. The little town of Gilead was also, for the most part, silent.

The shops and stores and the bank, all closed, except for the Appaloosa. Almost all of the citizens had gone home, those who had a home. Those who didn't were at the homes of friends for dinner and drinks and the exchange of gifts. For most it had been a hard year. But the people of Texas were inured and used to hard years. Hard work, grit, and pride, the stuff of Texans, had tempered them against the odds of defeat. Some despaired, but there was no surrender. There was always hope, sometimes bitter and questioning, but still hope, for a better tomorrow.

Laureen Bush had taken an early dinner in her bed that night. Her husband had brought her his Christmas gift, a pearl necklace he had ordered from San Francisco. She shuddered slightly as he fastened it around her slender throat.

"I'm sorry I haven't anything for you, Amos."

"That's all right, dear, I understand."

"But I will have . . . soon." Underneath her blanket, her hand touched the pistol. It would have been a simple matter for Laureen Bush to pull out the gun and shoot her husband at close range as he stood hovering over her. But that was not how she wanted to do it. She wanted to walk into his room while he slept, dreaming of his whore, wake him, and watch the look on his face when he realized that she could walk, then squeeze the trigger before he could beg forgiveness and make his peace with God. *To me belongeth vengeance, and recompense.*

That was her plan, and Laureen Bush was in no hurry to execute it, or him. She would wait until the next time he went to his whore and came home with her scent still upon him, steeped in the sin of adultery, asleep in the comfort of his house and room and bed.

"Merry Christmas . . . and good night, Laureen. I think I'll read for a bit. It's early yet."

Laureen Bush only nodded and said nothing.

No, she thought as her husband left her alone in the room. *No, Amos, it's not early. It is much later than you know.* The pearls felt like ice about her throat. She thought of tearing them from her neck, but decided not to. They would soon grow warm from the heat of her body . . . and hate.

"Well, Homer," Sheriff Hinge said to his deputy, "I guess we can call it a night. Things seem to be about as quiet as they can get around here."

"About time. We've had more'n our share of excitement, considering there's no war going on."

"Homer, there's always a war going on, somewhere."

"I reckon so."

"Give my regards to the Lewises, specially to the bride-to-be."

"I will, sir. You sure you won't come over to dinner? They did ask me to ask you, you know."

"Yes, you told me. Appreciate it, and convey my thanks, but there's somebody I want to see and talk to about something."

"I understand."

"You do?" The sheriff smiled a curious smile.

"Well, I don't know . . . maybe I do and maybe I don't . . . but . . . well, Elwood," Homer Keeler extended his hand, "I just want to thank you and wish you a merry Christmas."

They shook.

"Thank you too, Homer, and merry Christmas."

Deek Keeshaw puffed on his pipe and watched from the window of the Appaloosa as first the deputy, then the sheriff, left their office and walked in different directions. His brother Tom stood next to him. Bart played solitaire at one of the tables. The smattering of customers hadn't been interested in starting up a poker game on Christmas Eve.

Hooter stood alone at the end of the bar, drinking from a bottle of his best whiskey, his and Amos Bush's, only nobody there but Hooter knew that.

"Well, Tom," Deek spoke softly, "looks like them two fellas are closing up shop like just about everybody else in town."

"Looks like." Tom grinned.

"Yeah, the sheriff can finally get a good night's sleep in his own bed and dream about that there reward."

"Yep."

"And while he's dreaming . . ." Deek Keeshaw blew forth a billow of smoke and smiled.

For the first time in days Shad Parker finally felt that he was the way he wanted to be since coming back from the war. Alone.

That was why he had left the Shenandoah and the graves. He did not want to inflict his suffering and pain on others. Nor did he wish to suffer the company of others, no matter how good or innocent their intentions. He was better off alone, and so were they. Whoever they were.

The people he had left behind. The people of Gilead, and lately the others, too many others. The strange man on the mule. The three Keeshaw brothers to whom he had taken an immediate dislike. Ben, Esmeralda, and their sons. And especially the three orphans. So sad. So brave. So bothersome.

He could have taken the rest, but there was something about them, the three of them. Of all the places in all of Texas, what brought them to this god-forsaken patch of damnation? Why not somewhere else? Somebody else. Instead of him, who wanted only to be left alone.

They had saved his life and he had saved one of theirs in return. They were even on that score. The difference was that he hadn't wanted his life saved. That night, like the other nights, he had wanted to die. But if he had died, the odds were that the little boy would be dead, too.

Now, on this Christmas Eve, he was alone. He didn't know, or care, where any of the others were. Shad Parker was alone on this Christmas Eve.

The trouble was that he couldn't help thinking of another Christmas Eve . . . and Molly O.

Shad Parker reached again for the bottle.

Chapter 32

It was a small tree—still, it was decorated—not for children, only for the Reverend Groves and his wife and whatever parishioners might drop by, but it was more of a tree than Austin, Peg, and Davy had hoped to see when they were clearing the mud out of their cave on that morning of 24 December.

And they were still together, and Davy was alive, due to a man who was always mad, but an accurate shot with a rifle.

Last year the tree at the Faith, Hope, and Charity Orphanage was much taller, and with many more decorations, and they were with children their own age, but they were also with ol' Miss Stench, who kept telling them how lucky they all were and led them in singing "God Rest Ye Merry, Gentlemen" and a dozen other carols without ever cracking a smile, but she did crack a couple of the kids, including Davy, with her stick for not sitting up straight while they sang.

Now Austin, Peg, and Davy sat in the Groveses' parlor on a davenport, hands folded in front of them. Davy held on to the small carved Christmas tree. For the first time since running away the three of them were scrubbed clean, their hair combed, and wearing clean clothes, albeit the clothes didn't exactly fit.

Still, they were together, warm and safe for the time being, and they could smell food cooking in the nearby kitchen.

Reverend Groves, smiling at the children, was taller than the tree he stood next to.

"I'm sorry those clothes don't fit any better than they do, but that's all I could gather up on such short notice. But you look fine, mighty fine . . ."

"Thank you, sir," Peg said.

"Yes, indeed, you certainly look different than you did a couple of hours ago. Supper'll be ready in just a few minutes. Mrs. Groves is a mighty fine cook, yes indeed, mighty fine."

"Thank you, sir, but . . ."

"Yes, Peggy, what is it?"

"Well, couldn't I help the missus in the kitchen? Or do something?"

"No, Peggy . . . Are you always called Peggy? Or sometimes Margaret?"

"No, sir, just Peggy."

"My mother's name was Margaret, may she rest in peace. No, Peggy, don't you worry about a thing. Everything's under control. You'll have a mighty fine supper and then a good night's sleep."

"Yes, sir."

"As I said, I'm afraid you'll have to share the same room. We only have one spare bedroom."

"That'll be fine, sir." Peg nodded.

"Tomorrow we'll all go to services. I've got quite a

good sermon prepared, different than last year's . . . and after that . . ."

"Edward!" Mrs. Groves called from the kitchen. "Can you come here a minute, please?"

"Yes, dear. Be right there." He smiled at the children. "Excuse me."

The children smiled back and nodded, unaccustomed as they were to such politeness from strangers, or any adults. The reverend started to leave but glanced back.

"I'm sorry we don't have any toys for you to play with."

"We're fine, sir," Peg said as the reverend left the room.

When Austin could hear the sound of voices from the kitchen he leaned closer to Peg and Austin, who both sat to his left.

"Eat all you can," he whispered, "'cause we're getting outta here tonight."

"But, Austin!" Peg was surprised.

"It'll be our last chance," Austin whispered more emphatically. "They'll send us back tomorrow, Christmas or no . . ."

"Maybe . . ." Peg started to reason, but Austin didn't let her go on.

"There's no 'maybes.' We're getting out tonight. That's it!"

"Edward," Martha Groves said, "they are such nice children."

"Yes, they are."

"But frightened."

"Well," the reverend lowered his voice, "from what

the sheriff said, they've been through a lot. Had more than their share of adversity, much more."

"It's a shame we . . ."

"What, Martha?"

"We can't find a home for them."

"I just don't know who'd take them . . ." the Reverend shook his head, ". . . times being what they are."

"I hate the thought of them going back to some orphanage."

"So do I, Martha. So do I."

"Couldn't we . . ."

"What?"

"Couldn't we keep them . . . ?"

"Martha."

"I mean, until we find someplace?"

"That's liable to be a long time."

"Edward, that's the only way in which the Lord hasn't blessed us. I've always wanted . . ."

"I know, dear. But we're getting a little old to start raising a family."

"May I wish you a merry Christmas, Miss DuPree?"

"You may, Mr. Hinge. Won't you step inside?"

Mr. Hinge stepped inside. He was not carrying a shotgun. In his hand he held a bottle of French wine. He had cleaned up and changed into his Sunday suit.

When she answered the knock on her door Rosalind DuPree was wearing her finest evening gown. She looked as if she were going to the theatre, maybe even playing the part of the leading lady. There certainly was no place in Gilead worthy of the way she dressed and looked.

"I was hoping you'd drop by." She smiled teasingly.

"Nothing short of a natural catastrophe could have prevented it, ma'am." He carried on the flirtatious charade. "May I dare to hope that you would share with me this miserably inadequate gift of outrageously expensive French booze?"

They both broke into laughter and she kissed him.

"Merry Christmas, El."

"Merry Christmas, Rosalind."

"You know, the truth is, I was thinking of giving up booze . . . along with a couple of other things."

"Present company excluded, I hope."

"Well." She arched an imperially slim eyebrow and looked from the bottle to him. "I just might have one last fling at both."

"That's what I want to talk to you about, Rosalind." He turned serious.

"Now, El, I thought we were just going to have a party tonight. Save the talk for another time."

"It might be a better party if we talked now."

"Or it might be a worse party. Did you think of that?"

"I did."

"And?"

"I'll take my chances, if you will."

"Open the wine . . . and we'll talk."

He did. And they did.

"I've sold my share of the Appaloosa, El. I've got nearly four thousand dollars and the things you see in this room. I'm leaving Gilead."

"So am I."

"But . . ."

"No, wait. You summed up your situation. It won't take long for me to sum up mine."

"All right."

"It's Homer Keeler's turn to be sheriff of Gilead. I've had mine, so I'm quitting. After sharing that reward with you and Homer—by the way, you can add another five hundred to that four thousand— plus the reward from the Garden City Bank and what I've saved up, I've got about half as much as you, and the suit you see on this body. Question number one . . ."

"Go ahead."

"Which direction are you heading?"

"Not east."

"Me, neither."

"Certainly not south."

"Me, neither."

"North?" She shook her head, answering her own question. "Too cold."

"I agree. Well, that only leaves one direction. West. So it looks like we're traveling in the same direction. At the same time."

"Anyplace in particular?"

"Ever hear of a pueblo called Los Angeles?"

"Yes."

"Well, that's just about as far west as you can get on this continent."

"But why that particular place?"

"Because there's prime ranch land there, and Diego O'Brien."

"Diego O'Brien? What kind of a name is that?"

"His father married a señorita. It happens out there."

"What's Diego O'Brien got to do with you?"

"He thinks I saved his life in the war."

"Did you?"

"Well, let's put it this way. I didn't kill him."

"Northerner?"

"Yep. Took him prisoner instead. When he said good-bye he offered me a piece of prime ranch land in appreciation. I'm going to buy it instead."

"How do you know he's still there?"

"He keeps in touch. His father's the mayor of Los Angeles, so if ranching doesn't work out he's already offered me the job of sheriff. A nice peaceful little community. So we might just as well get married and go out there."

"Suppose we just go out there without getting married?"

"Nope."

"Why not?"

"Because I want to introduce the most beautiful and the best woman in Los Angeles to Diego O'Brien as my wife . . . and to everybody else. That's why not."

"El . . ."

"What's the matter? You think I'm marrying you for your money?"

"El, what if we have children?"

"It happens." He nodded.

"What if . . . ?"

"They're yours and mine and ours. There's nothing more to be said. Diego O'Brien can be godfather to the first one . . . if it's all right with you. Now, will you do me a favor?"

"What?"

"Will you let me know before Christmas?" He took the watch from his vest pocket and looked at it. "You've got a little less than a minute to decide."

"Deek."

"What?"

"Merry Christmas."

"What?"

"I said, merry Christmas." Bart pointed to the gold watch he held in his palm. "According to my gold watch here, it's one minute past midnight. That makes it Christmas Day, so . . ."

"All right, all right."

Deek Keeshaw was looking out of their hotel room window across the dark street to the bank. Tom lay on the bed, balancing a half-filled glass of whiskey on his forehead. The hotel room was illuminated only by a kerosene lamp on a stand close to the bed.

"Tom." Deek turned from the window.

"Yo!"

"How much of that stuff you been drinkin'?"

"Not hardly any. Been nursin' it, like you said, big brother."

"Good."

"That all you want to know?"

"No, that's not all. You got the stuff set?"

"Yep." Tom took the glass from his forehead, placed it on the bed stand, and lifted three sticks of dynamite bound together, with a fuse, from beside him on the bed.

"Looks good enough." Deek nodded.

"More'n enough." Tom smiled.

"Well, we don't want to blow the whole building apart, just the safe. Don't want to be accused of destroying real estate." Deek also smiled.

"Just the safe . . . and maybe a few odds and ends."

"Should we get going?" Bart put the watch back in his pocket.

"Give it another half hour." Deek turned to the window.

Tom set the dynamite beside him on the bed, lifted the whiskey glass, and balanced it on his forehead again.

"Want to make sure nothing's moving out there," Deek said.

The window moved upward without a sound. When it was raised sufficiently, Austin crawled out of the bedroom window of Reverend Groves's house. He helped Davy, who was carrying the small carved Christmas tree, come out after him. Then Peg came through.

After listening to Reverend Groves recite the supper prayer, the children ate the best meal that the three of them could ever remember. Reverend and Martha Groves were astonished at the capacities of their three young visitors. But the hosts kept offering more and the guests never once refused, right down through the dessert.

The children were in bed by nine. They spoke the nightly words from Psalm 91. Mrs. Groves retired by ten. Austin heard the reverend tell her that he was going to work on his sermon for a while. "I'm going to revise it so as to include the plight of the orphans," he said.

The reverend went to bed before eleven. Both Peg and Davy had fallen asleep. But not Austin. Austin had a plan and he was determined to carry it out. When he was sure that the Groveses were asleep he woke up Peg and Davy and whispered for them to get dressed. They did, grudgingly.

"I'm sleepy," Davy said as his feet touched the ground outside the Groveses' house.

"Ssshhh," Austin admonished.

"Austin," Peg whispered, "where we going?"

"Where they'll never look if they miss us."

"Where's that?"

"The cave."

"Austin." She stopped as they walked through the darkness. "Are you crazy?"

"See! That's just the way they'd think. That's why they'd never look for us to be there. We'll leave in the morning when we can see where we're going. Now, come on."

"I liked it here," Davy said, not whispering.

"Ssshhh, be quiet."

It was quiet outside of Shad Parker's cabin. And inside. It was so quiet that he could hear, as well as feel, the beating of his own heart as he sat in the chair with the whiskey bottle in front of him.

And then he no longer heard his heart beat. Shad Parker had fallen into a deep, senseless sleep.

Chapter 33

Tom Keeshaw, with the bundle of dynamite, knelt at the safe. Deek and Bart stood next to him, black shadows outlined against the glistening windows.

"Goin' good, so far, huh, Deek?" Bart grinned.

"Gettin' inside the bank's no hard knot," Deek replied. "That safe's somethin' else again."

"Not for long." Tom went confidently about his preparation.

Getting into the bank was the second illegal entry of the operation. The first had been to secure and saddle their horses from the livery. The animals were off the street, tied to a post in the alley behind the bank.

"Hey, Deek," Bart tapped his brother on the shoulder, "we forgot to pay the hotel bill."

"Got nothing left to pay it with."

"We'll have plenty in a minute," Tom said.

"Bart," Deek whispered.

"Yeah?"

"Get out there and hold them horses so's they don't spook when she blasts."

"You bet!" He nodded and left.

"Get behind that desk," Tom said as he struck the match.

Deek ducked behind and as close to the desk as he could. Tom lit the fuse and dove next to him.

Outside, it was still silent. Until the dynamite went off. The big window of the bank shattered, spraying the street with glass, wood, and sundry debris.

Bart came from the alley behind the bank, holding on to the reins of three fractious horses. He stood out in the street waiting for what seemed a long time, too long. Long enough for lamps to be lit in the hotel rooms and other places. Along with the lighted lamps came sounds and voices:

"What the hell's going on!"

"What happened?"

"Jesus Christ!"

"Son of a bitch!"

"Son of a bitch!" Bart, himself, said out loud. "Come on! Come on! Get outta there!" he hollered while trying to hang on to the reins.

Deek, with gun drawn, ran out of the bank, then Tom. Tom carried a heavy canvas bag. A man in underwear appeared from around the corner of a building.

"They're robbing the bank!" he yelled, then repeated even louder. "They're robbing the bank!"

Deek fired twice, missing the man with both shots, but coming closer with the second. The target dove back around the corner. Deek and Bart managed to saddle up, but the gunshots had skittered the third horse and Tom, with the heavy money bag, couldn't get the horse to hold still so he could mount.

Sheriff Elwood Hinge, still dressed in his Sunday suit, but carrying a shotgun, appeared out of the darkness. He leveled the shotgun toward the man with the money bag and squeezed, then swung the weapon and fired again at the two mounted men, who spurred their horses.

Tom had taken the full impact of the shotgun blast in the back and collapsed, still gripping the money bag.

"They got Tom!" Bart screamed.

"To hell with him. Let's go!"

"He's got the money!" Bart hollered, but galloped off beside his brother. They disappeared into the black night.

Sheriff Elwood Hinge walked to the crumpled form lying atop the shards of glass and debris and picked up the money bag. By then dozens of townspeople had realized that the shooting was over and materialized from every direction.

Amos Bush pushed his way through the crowd, followed by Deputy Keeler.

"Who was it, Sheriff?" Bush asked. "Did they get away?"

"One of 'em didn't." Hinge, still holding the bag and shotgun, rolled the dead man faceup with his boot.

"That's Mr. Keeshaw!" Bush pointed to the body.

"The late Mr. Keeshaw," Hinge corrected.

"The money!" Amos Bush exclaimed. "What about the money?"

"Here's part of it." The sheriff handed Bush the bag.

Amos Bush grabbed at it with both hands and started to examine the contents. Rosalind DuPree in her evening gown stood at the edge of the gathering looking at Elwood Hinge.

"Why, that's all of it!" Bush announced. "It's all here!! Eighteen th . . ." Amos Bush decided not to continue.

"You sure, Amos?"

"I ought to know, Sheriff. That's all that was in the safe. It's all here!"

"Sheriff." Deputy Keeler took a step forward.

"Hello, Homer. You enjoy your dinner?"

"Yuh," the deputy nodded, "but . . ."

"But what?"

"Well, ain't we goin' after 'em?"

"Homer, you want to get shot in the dark?"

"No, sir," Keeler answered directly.

"Then we'll wait till morning."

"Huh?"

"We got the money, didn't we?"

"Yes, sir."

"Then go get the undertaker."

"I'm here." A solemn voice responded out of the night.

Elwood Hinge walked to where Rosalind DuPree was standing and smiled.

"Are you all right, Sheriff?" she asked.

"Yes, ma'am," he answered, then lowered his voice. "We never did finish that bottle of wine."

Chapter 34

Deek and Bart rode west through the cold, dark night, Deek a considerable distance ahead.

"Deek!" Bart hollered out in pain. "Deek, hold up a minute!"

Deek reined his horse to a stop and waited as his remaining brother came alongside.

"That second blast tore into me."

"Bad?"

"Bad enough," Bart groaned. "Damn! Everything went wrong. They got Tom and we didn't get the money."

"Yeah."

"I got to get patched up. I got to. I'm bleedin'."

"All right. I know where we can do that and get some money besides."

"You do?"

"Yeah, a lot of money."

Shad Parker still slept in the chair, with the tin box and the letters on the table next to the whiskey bottle.

* * *

The cave was lit only by a single candle and provided no warmth. Austin, Peg, and Davy harbored close to one another. Davy shivered and still held on to the small, carved Christmas tree.

"Austin," Davy said, "I'm cold. Can't we build a fire?"

"No."

"I'm cold," he repeated.

"I told you he'd see the fire and come up here. You want him to do that?"

"I don't care. I'm freezing."

"Here, Davy." Peg tried to comfort him. "I'll put my arm around you."

"I'd ruther have a fire."

"Go to sleep," Austin said.

Deek and Bart dismounted about twenty yards from the cabin.

"There's a lamp lit." Bart reached back and rubbed at his ruptured coat.

"Yeah, hand me those reins." Deek tied the reins from both horses to the limb of a tree. "Come on."

Both men lifted their guns from their holsters and walked toward the shack.

A couple of minutes later the latch to the door inside the room lifted slowly without any sound. The door opened an inch at a time and the barrel of a six-gun appeared.

Suddenly, the door burst open, slamming against the wall. Shad Parker's head snapped in the direction of the sound as Deek and Bart stepped into the room, aiming guns at the man in the chair.

"Sit still, friend," Deek said. They both walked farther into the room and looked around. "Anybody else here?"

Shad shook his head *no*.

"Good. Well, it looks like we're not gonna be neighbors after all." Deek grinned. "Me and Bart'll be moving on directly. Just the two of us."

"Where's the other one?"

"He's dead. And we're what you call 'desperate.' So be careful what you do, friend."

While his brother talked, Bart spotted the whiskey bottle on the table. He walked over, picked it up, and took a long pull.

"Go easy, Bart."

"Easy, hell. Take a look at this." Bart turned his back toward his brother. A part of his jacket and shirt were ripped by scatter shot, and blood oozed through.

"We'll get around to that." Deek raised the gun toward Shad's head. "All right, friend . . . up! Slow and easy!"

Shad Parker rose slowly from the chair, trying to clear his brain of sleep and whiskey, and to formulate a plan.

"Just right," Deek nodded. "Now, we'll have your money."

Shad studied the position of the two intruders, but they were too far apart from each other for him to take any action. He wanted to maneuver them closer together so he would have a chance to take them both at once.

"The money," Deek repeated.

"My pocket."

"Lift it out."

Shad reached into his pocket, removed a wad of bills. He held the money straight out ahead of him.

"We ain't gettin' that close, brother." Deek smiled and pointed the gun for just an instant. "On the table."

Shad let the money drop onto the table.

Deek continued to point the gun. He walked to the table, took up the money, and put it in his pocket. Bart swallowed another mouthful from the bottle.

"That's a start," Deek said to Shad. "Now we'll have the rest."

"What rest?"

"The rest of the money. Nobody carries it all on him."

"I do."

"It don't float." Deek shook his head. "Now, where's the rest of it? We got no time for games."

"Maybe it's in there." Bart pointed to the metal box and took a step.

"Keep away from there." Shad moved forward.

"Aha." Bart laughed. "You see, it *is* there!"

"Back off," Deek warned. "Do it!"

Shad Parker retreated a few inches. Bart thrust his hand into the metal container, lifted out the contents, searching for money. Parker stared at the man digging at the letters as if he were desecrating something sacred. Bart threw most of the letters onto the floor, shook his head negatively toward his brother, then looked at the letter he still held in his hand.

"Jesus Christ!" Bart said.

"What?"

"A bunch of damned love letters." He laughed and haltingly started to read aloud. "'My . . . dearest . . . dar . . . ling.'" Bart looked up toward Shad. *"Him?!"*

"Put that down." Shad was shaking. He started to lunge.

Deek fired. Shad Parker staggered.

"Hold it!" Deek growled.

The slug had shattered Shad's left thigh.

"Now I ain't Bill Hickok, but I hit pretty much where I aim, mister."

"Deek." Bart nodded toward the door. "Maybe somebody heard that."

"Like who?"

"Posse, maybe."

"On Christmas night? And them with the money. There ain't no posse, Bart. Ain't nobody here but us and the chickens."

"Austin!" Peg had bolted upright first, then Austin and Davy. "Did you hear?"

"Yeah."

"It came from his house."

Austin nodded.

"You think we ought to go down there, Austin?"

"What for?"

"He could be drinking again. Maybe the gun went off. Maybe he's hurt."

"You know he'll turn us in if he gets the chance."

"I know."

"And you still want to go down there?"

"Austin, that's the same gun that saved Davy."

"All right, mister." Deek pointed the gun at Shad Parker's chest. "It's one thing to be crippled . . . something else to be dead."

"I'm already dead."

"I'm in no mood for riddles. Where's it hid?"

"You can look all night. You won't . . ."

"I ain't got all night. Now, *where*?!"

Austin, Peg, and Davy had scrambled down the hillside and were making their way across the dark yard.

"I'm . . . I'm scared," Davy muttered.

"You should've stayed up there like I told you," Austin said.

"I'd be scareder."

"Look," Peg pointed, "the door's open."

"I'll look in the window," Austin said. "You two stay here."

But before Davy stopped walking he fell over a tin tub.

"Somebody's out there!" Bart reacted to the noise.

"Keep him covered." Deek went to one side of the window and looked out. "Damn! It's them kids. Musta been in the barn."

The three children stood in the yard, looking toward the open door, waiting to see if the man would appear.

A man did appear, but not the man they had

expected. Deek stepped halfway out, keeping the gun in his hand hidden.

"Hey, kids! Come on in here." He beckoned in a friendly voice. "It's all right. Come on in. Your friend had a little accident."

"You," Bart pointed the gun at Shad and whispered, "don't say nothin'. Not a word. Just stand still."

Deek Keeshaw smiled and continued to conceal the gun as the three children came to the door.

"Come on in, kids. Like I said, your friend had a little accident. Been hurt a little but we're takin' care of him."

Shad's leg bled from the bullet hole in his thigh. Bart stood to the side so the children couldn't see his gun yet. But it was pointed at Shad's heart.

As the three entered the room Deek slammed the door shut behind them and no longer concealed his gun.

"All right, kids. Welcome to the party," Deek said.

"Yeah, welcome." Bart grinned.

"Mister." Peg looked at blood on Shad's leg. "What happened?"

"I told you," Deek said. "He had a little accident. And he's liable to have another one. Fatal."

"What you doing down here?" Shad asked Austin.

"We ran away."

"I mean *down here*!"

"We thought maybe . . ." Austin paused. ". . . maybe you was hurt. Maybe you needed help."

Shad Parker blinked and breathed a deep breath in a pretense that he was affected only by the pain in his leg.

"Now, ain't that touchin'!?" Deek said, then nodded. "You're right about one thing, kids, your friend does need help. Maybe it's a good thing you're here. You see, he's being stubborn. Won't tell us where his money's hid. Now, maybe you can reason with him."

"Yeah, that's right," Bart agreed. "That's a good idea, Deek. "You kids wouldn't want nothin' worse to happen to your friend, now, would you?"

"All we want is the money," Deek said. "You tell him to give us the money and we'll ride off and leave you all to have a merry Christmas. Otherwise . . ." Deek slowly raised the gun upward, directly at Shad Parker's head.

"Please, mister," Peg pleaded to Shad, "tell him where it is!"

Shad Parker closed his eyes and gritted, fighting at the weakness creeping deeper into his body and brain.

Deek came a step closer with the gun pointing at Shad Parker's temple. Davy sobbed and turned his head away, into Peg, as she put both arms around him.

"Now, you got one minute," Deek snarled. "Then I'll blow your head off . . . right in front of them . . . starting *now*."

Shad Parker's eyes looked directly at the barrel of the gun. He stood straighter, no longer seeming to suffer from the effects of the wound, letting the seconds slip by.

"Tell him, mister," Austin implored.

"Please." Tears came out of Peg's eyes. "Please tell him."

"Forty seconds," Deek said, and waited.

"*Tell* him!" This time Austin shouted.

"Oh, he will." Deek cocked the gun. "He will. Because every living thing wants to go on living. It's the law of nature. Thirty seconds."

"I got nothing to live for."

"Sure, you have," Deek spoke evenly. "Everybody's got something. Me, I got Bart. And you . . ." he looked from Shad Parker to the children, then back, ". . . you got ten seconds."

Bart took another drink from the bottle. Shad Parker did not move, nor speak.

"Seven seconds," Deek said, then . . . "five."

"Mister," Austin begged.

"Four."

Peg turned her face away.

"Three."

There was no doubt. Deek was going to squeeze the trigger.

"Two . . . one."

Peg screamed. Austin sprang at Deek. His gun fired, shattering a window. Shad swung at Bart, caught him on the side of the head, dropping him cold.

Deek got control of the clawing Austin and slung him against the wall. He swung the gun toward Shad again, but Shad had lifted a chair and crashed it across Deek's face. As Deek collapsed, dropping the gun on the floor, Shad fell on top of him, grabbed the gun, and wheeled around.

"Get clear of them," he said to the three children. Slowly, and with what could have been a grimace, or a smile, he got to his feet and moved toward a chair.

Austin, Peg, and Davy came away from the two

fallen men and stood behind Shad Parker as he eased into the chair.

"Now . . . Austin, can you ride a horse?"

Austin nodded.

"Good. Get on one of their horses. Ride into town and fetch the sheriff."

Austin nodded again.

"And see if you can find a doctor."

The boy smiled, opened the door, and ran out.

"Peggy."

"Yes, sir?"

"Get me something to wrap around this leg." With the gun he pointed toward a drawer. "There's some towels in there."

Peg nodded and hurried toward it.

Davy was staring at the blood on Shad Parker's leg. Then he looked up at the man's face.

"Are you gonna die?" Davy asked, and waited a moment for the answer.

"Hell, no."

Chapter 35

On Christmas morning many of the citizens of Gilead were at the church services singing hymns, with Martha Groves at the organ, and then listening to a sermon by the reverend. But not all of the citizens.

Amos Bush stood in front of his bank watching a crew of workmen boarding up the front window. Bush had taken the money recovered by Sheriff Hinge home last night and left it there in a second, smaller safe up in his room. And there most of the money would stay until he could order a new strongbox from Chicago. The Keeshaw brothers nearly got away with a stack of one hundred hundred-dollar bills, a stack of one hundred fifty-dollar bills, a stack of one hundred twenty-dollar bills, a stack of one hundred ten-dollar bills, and a stack of one hundred five-dollar bills. Eighteen thousand, five hundred dollars. But they didn't. One of them was dead. The other two occupied cells in the sheriff's office next door.

Inside his office Sheriff Hinge, drinking from a

mug of coffee, sat in his chair by the rolltop. Also in the room, with coffee cups, Deputy Homer Keeler, Kathy Lewis, and Rosalind DuPree.

"Well, Homer." Hinge took another swallow. "I wouldn't be surprised if in the next batch of dodgers you find the ugly faces of the brothers Keeshaw. If so, that'll be your responsibility . . . and your reward."

"How so, Sheriff?"

"I'm resigning. Leaving town." He smiled at Rosalind DuPree.

"When?" the surprised deputy asked.

"Pretty soon."

"But . . ."

"But what?"

"Well, sir, Kathy and I . . . that is, I thought, well, I was hoping . . . Elwood, I'd be honored if you'd stand up for me. Be my best man."

The office door swung open, and Amos Bush stepped inside and closed it behind him.

"Good morning." He smiled an expansive smile. "Ah, Miss DuPree, good morning, and Miss Lewis. Miss DuPree, I'm told you're going to be leaving us. Is that true?"

"Yes, it's true."

"I'm sorry to hear that but may I wish you Godspeed."

"Thank you, Mr. Bush."

"Not at all." He turned his attention toward Hinge. "And, Sheriff, I want to thank you also. As a token of my appreciation, I've drawn up this draught," he removed an envelope from inside his coat pocket, "for one thousand dollars, redeemable at my bank, or any other bank, after the Christmas holiday, of course. I trust that that will be satisfactory, sir."

"It will and I thank you, Mr. Bush." Hinge reached out and accepted the envelope without rising.

"Yes, well, if you'll excuse me, I've got to get home to Mrs. Bush. She wasn't feeling well at all this morning. Not at all. Well, good day." He smiled even more expansively as he was leaving. "And merry Christmas, everybody."

Nobody replied.

"That son of a bitch, pardon me, ladies," Homer said after the door closed. "Elwood, how much do you suppose was in that bag you handed him?"

"Over fifteen thousand, easy." The sheriff smiled.

"And you're supposed to get fifteen percent of that for recovering it, aren't you?"

"I guess so."

"Well, what about it?"

"Forget it, Homer."

"That fella owns just about everything in town worth owning. Why, he's the richest and luckiest . . ."

"I said, forget it, Homer. Things have a way of working out." He rose and went to Rosalind DuPree. "Don't they?"

She smiled.

"Now, about that wedding." Hinge turned back to Homer and Kathy. "When's it come off?"

"New Year's Day, right, Kathy?'

"Yes."

"Will you stay and do it, Sheriff? I mean, be my best man."

"On one condition."

"Sure, anything. What is it?"

"That you will, too."

"I will, too . . . *what*?"

"Be my best man. We'll make it a double wedding. If that's all right with the both of you . . . and you, too . . . Miss DuPree."

"I think," Rosalind DuPree took the sheriff's hand, "that would be . . . splendid."

Chapter 36

The man on the mule came to a stop not far from the NO TRESPASSING sign.

He had passed the place many times before. Never before had he seen anyone there except the man who owned the property. This time it was different, and so was the man who owned the property.

Shad Parker stood, supported by a pair of crutches, in the middle of the yard. But he was not alone. A boy chopped firewood. An even younger boy, holding a small, carved Christmas tree, stood close to the man on crutches. A girl, wearing a kitchen apron over her dress, stepped out of the cabin door.

"Good morning," Shad Parker said to the man on the mule.

"It is a good morning," the man answered. He looked at the children. "A very good morning." The man glanced at the NO TRESPASSING sign then back to Shad Parker. "Well, sir. See you again. And . . . merry Christmas."

Shad Parker nodded. Then the man rode east.

"We'll need some eggs to go with that bacon." Peg took a step forward, wiping her hands with the apron.

"Well," Shad's head motioned toward the chicken coop, "go get 'em."

She smiled and walked across the yard past Shad Parker, Davy, and Austin, who looked up from his chore.

"Set that log on its end," Shad said to Austin. "Be easier to split."

Austin took the advice. Davy came a little closer. He shifted the small, carved Christmas tree from his left hand to his right.

"Are we gonna live here?"

Austin and Peg paused to hear the answer.

"Well, you're here, aren't you?"

Austin split the piece of wood with one blow. Peg continued toward the chicken coop.

"What can I do?" Davy asked.

"Feed the chickens."

Davy nodded and started to walk away. He hesitated and then turned back. He looked at the man on crutches.

"Is it gonna be the same as if you was our daddy?"

"No," Shad Parker answered. "It won't be the same." Then added, "But it'll be . . . something. And, Davy . . ."

"Yes, sir?"

"Happy New Year."

"Yes, *sir*." The little boy grinned and hurried toward his brother and sister.

"Austin, look!" Peg pointed to the sky just above the cave on the hill.

"I see it," Austin said.

"What is it?" Davy asked.

"An eagle," Peg said. "It's an eagle."

Shad Parker started toward the cabin. He took a few steps, stopped, and looked back at Austin chopping wood, Peg and Davy by the chicken coop. He watched for a moment, then walked on, past the NO TRESPASSING sign. He spoke just above a whisper.

"It's time we all quit running away."

THE WISE OLD MAN
OF THE WEST

Back . . . and Forth

To paraphrase Shakespeare's *Othello*: "Soft, you, a word or two (maybe a mite more) about the Wise Old Man of the West."

The first effort was a short story entitled "The Wise Old Man of the West and The Fountain of Youth."

It was written as, what we used to call in the olden days of television, a "pilot" for a series of short stories, and published as a bonus addendum to the novel *Black Noon*.

Well, it appears that quite a few people enjoyed reading it almost as much as I did writing it.

Pinnacle Books received a passel of letters, and what nowadays is called e-mail, with a positive slant.

So, here are three more to add to the collection about the dapper, mysterious stranger, a salient phantom of the night, who appears in unexpected places, tells unrecorded stories about a time and place that can never happen again.

A wise old man, who knows more about the West than Frank and Jesse knew about banks and railroads.

The Stranger Who Limped
Blazing Guns of the Bible
The Bravest Soldier

—Andrew J. Fenady

THE WISE OLD MAN
OF THE WEST
and THE STRANGER WHO LIMPED

For
JOHN CARRADINE
We will never see
his like again

and of course
for
MARY FRANCES

"It was a time to commemorate. For some to celebrate. For others to contemplate. Winners and losers. The war was over and we were the survivors. But winners or losers, we would never be the same."

So began the story of the Wise Old Man of the West and The Stranger Who Limped.

A warm, windless April night in Nevada, 1875, a decade after the cessation of hostilities . . . some called it the Civil War, others, the War for the Confederacy.

The Wise Old Man appeared at the small camp of what might have been a separated section of a wagon train, but turned out to be something undeniably different.

"Good evening, night walker," the tallest, most notable member of the camp greeted him. "Are you alone?"

"Not anymore," the Wise Old Man replied as his

glance scanned the eight members of the group, five men and three women of assorted ages and sizes.

"Allow me to welcome you to the Crown Players Theatrical Company," the tallest, most notable, man proceeded. "We are currently touring the Southwest in a modified, more modest production of *Hamlet.* We play mostly mining camps, rail camps, wagon trains, women's clubs, and sometimes even on actual stages. No need to employ our proper names . . . They are hardly proper, or relevant. I am Hamlet." He pointed, in order, to each of the cast. "Queen Gertrude, Horatio, Laertes, King Claudius, who also appears as the ghost, old Polonius, youthful Ophelia, and Miss Supernumerary, on the road to Saguaro to perform in a former saloon, now a theatrical house of questionable repute. And how shall we address you, squire?"

The Wise Old Man looked up briefly at the sparkling sky, then toward the cast.

"'Stargazer' will suffice."

"In all due modesty, we're hardly stars, more like cinders, but with still a slight glow."

Through the glimmering light of the campfire, Hamlet appraised the aspect of the night walker; clear-eyed and clean-shaven except for a neatly trimmed military mustache, sartorially impeccable in his three-piece dark gray suit, holding a malacca walking stick in one hand and a curved meerschaum pipe near his mouth in the other.

Polonius could not resist mouthing one of his quotations.

"'The apparel oft proclaims the man.'"

"And what is your destination, Mr. Stargazer?" Hamlet inquired.

"Here and there."

"Where from?"

"There and here."

"Very good . . . and from your mien and manner, likely one of us, I presume."

"Oh," Horatio proffered, "I'd say more of a military man."

"Possibly both," young Ophelia opined.

"A man in his time," the Wise Old Man replied, "plays many parts, someone once said."

"You're old enough to play my part." Polonius stroked his bearded chin.

"And he has a better resonance," chimed the queen.

"The trouble with you, dear lady," Polonius retorted, "is that you've let failure go to your head. Be thou familiar, but by no means vulgar. To thine own self be true and . . ."

"Now, children, let us not squabble in front of Mr. Stargazer," Hamlet rebuked. "Are you a drinking man, stranger?"

"An occasional brandy . . . and on rare occasions . . . beer."

"Will coffee satisfy?" Hamlet indicated the pot over the campfire.

"Verily," the Wise Old Man smiled.

"Does it seem most strange to you, Mr. Stargazer," Hamlet also smiled, "that a theatrical company, even such as ours, would lack so much as a modicum of alcoholic libation?"

"I am not an authority on such quandaries."

"The truth is," Polonius once again stroked his

hirsute chin, "that some distance after Lordsburg we ran dry, but intend to replenish our larder in Saguaro."

"In the meanwhile," Hamlet picked up the cue, "let us make do with a nightcap of mocha java, before we scent the morning air."

They did.

Hamlet raised his tin cup.

"What shall we drink to?"

"Birthday? Death? Anniversary? Special occasion?" Laertes proposed . . . "A memorable event?"

"What about you, Mr. Stargazer? Suppose tonight, for a change, we are the audience," Hamlet suggested, "and you come up with some memorable event to entertain us . . . fact or fiction . . . that might compensate for the coffee . . ."

"And your hospitable companionship," the Wise Old Man added.

"Thence pray thee proceed with the libretto, Mr. Stargazer." Hamlet waved.

"Very well." The Wise Old Man inhaled a puff from the meerschaum, then proceeded.

"Ten years ago, this month, this week; it was a time to commemorate. For some, to celebrate. For others, to contemplate. Winners and losers. The war was over and we were the survivors. But winners or losers, we would never be the same. It seemed as if there was not enough land to bury the dead, but buried they were. There was land enough for all the dead, and for all who lived. But the living had a choice. The dead would stay forever in their little plot of land they fought for."

"So be it, Mr. Stargazer," Hamlet nodded, "but the play's the thing. Where do you come in, make your entrance?"

The Wise Old Man sipped from the coffee cup, relit his meerschaum . . . and went on with his story.

"It had been almost a week since the surrender at Appomattox. That night I made camp alone. A strange thing happened.

"For days I had drifted aimlessly, not far from what had been battlefields, and before that, villages and farms. I wanted to be away from everyone and everything. I was tired. For the first time in a long while I realized just how tired I was. Of being on the alert for an enemy who might have broken through the lines. But now there were no lines. And there was no enemy. I told myself I could relax. I had survived, unlike so many who fought on either side, more than half a million casualties.

"The night was cool and becoming cooler. I had built a small fire, even before unsaddling my horse. And for the first time in years I was not in uniform. Even though I was proud of it, I wanted to be myself again. Not a soldier . . . but soldier, or not . . . it happened.

"I had relaxed too much. In trying to wipe away too many memories, too soon, too hard. Victories and defeats. While looking into the yellow flames of my little fire, I was unaware until the man on horseback was too close.

"Another time, another place, if the man on

horseback had worn a uniform different than mine,
I might already have been dead.

"But the man wore no uniform. He was dressed in
civilian clothes, fine, expensive clothes but now dirty
from what had to have been a long, hard ride. The
horse, a buckskin, was lathered and seemed hardly
able to stand.

"Against the glimmering firelight, the man looked
ghostly. His garments and face were spotted with dirt,
but a face still handsome, and finely chiseled, though
thoroughly exhausted from the ride. The eyes were
like living jewels, black and weary. Hatless, his long,
dark hair curled down his formidable forehead. Re-
flexively, my hand went toward the sidearm I still
carried, but stopped short as the man spoke. His
voice, deep and cultured.

"'You here alone?'

"'Not now.'

"'Were you Blue, or Gray?'

"'The war's over.'

"'Is it?'

"The man smiled, a warm, charming smile, but I
wanted to talk about something else. 'That animal
looks beat.' I pointed to the buckskin.

"'It is.'

"'So do you.'

"'I'm . . . not.'

"He said the two words slowly, emphatically, and
once again I chose to steer the conversation in a different direction.

"'Well, would you like to step down off that horse
and have something to eat?'

"'I would.'

"The man nodded and began to dismount. But it wasn't easy. It took great effort. He strained and grimaced. I started to move toward him as if to help, but he shook his head and waved me away.

"'I would,' the man repeated. 'I would like to stay and enjoy your hospitality, but I'm afraid it was not meant to be.'

"'Why not?'

"His aspect suddenly changed.

"'Because of this.'

"The man had removed a six-inch derringer from his pocket and pointed it at me.

"'And because I need a fresh horse and need it now. To avoid any bloodshed, yours or mine, I must ask you to remove your sidearm . . . with your left hand . . . slowly.'

"I complied, then looked back at him, still pointing the derringer.

"'I wouldn't have marked you as a horse thief.'

"'I'm not.'

"'I paid eighty dollars in gold for that animal as it stands. Four double eagles.'

"The man's left hand dug into another pocket. He held the contents in his fist for a moment, then let them fall to the ground. They glinted by the firelight.

"'Five double eagles and my buckskin in the bargain.'

"He pointed toward his horse.

"'He'll be fit to ride by morning.'

"The man limped as he moved toward my horse, but with the derringer aimed directly at me. He was drained, but not too drained to squeeze the trigger.

"'And now I have an appointment to keep.'

"'Unless it's with a nearby doctor I don't think you'll make it, but I won't try to stop you.'

"'I'll make it . . . just as I made a prior appointment with destiny.'

"I watched as the man struggled, then finally boarded my horse, and spoke dramatically.

"'All good soldiers must fight for their cause.'

"'Most good soldiers are dead.'

"'But not all, and not all wear uniforms. We all have different roles to play. Good night and Godspeed.'

"The man wheeled the horse and rode into the night, south."

The Wise Old Man took a breath, relit his meerschaum, removed his gold watch by its slim gold chain out of his vest pocket, snapped the lid open, and noted the time.

"Nearing midnight."

"Dear fellow," Hamlet intoned, "are you telling us a story, or telling us the time?"

"Birthday? Death? Anniversary? Special occasion? Memorable event?" Laertes smacked his lips. "And you speak of a horse thief . . ."

"He didn't even steal the beast," the queen exclaimed. "I'd say you got the better of the bargain."

"Hear! Hear!" Supernumerary blinked and nodded.

"It's past my bedtime," Ophelia yawned.

"Depends on whom you're bedding," Hamlet amended, then turned to the Wise Old Man. "Mr. Stargazer, if there's more to this tale, kindly hasten thy story . . . 'So shall my anticipation prevent your discovery, and your secrecy to the king and queen moult no feather.'" Then, almost as an aside: "Whatever the hell that means."

"'Tis so, my liege," Polonius was at his beard again, "The wind sits at your shoulder. Pray, set sail."

"There is a final chapter to this memorable event," the Wise Old Man went on. "It had occurred on April 14, 1865, shortly before my meeting the man who limped, but I was unaware of that event at the time.

"In Washington, at Ford's Theatre during the performance of *Our American Cousin*, President Abraham Lincoln, his wife, and their guests sat in the Presidential Box of the theatre. Every seat was filled since it had been announced that President Lincoln would be in attendance.

"An hour earlier, John Wilkes Booth, the actor and fervent Southern sympathizer, had left the National Hotel. At nine p.m. he arrived at Ford's Theatre, where he, himself, had previously performed. The actor made his way along a back corridor with which he was familiar to the unguarded Presidential Box.

"Within, Lincoln, drained of most of his energy, sat in a rocking chair, nearly asleep, as the others in the box were enjoying the stage play. During the laughter and applause Booth silently opened the door and stood for a moment behind the occupants.

"Booth quickly took aim with a derringer at the back of Lincoln's head and fired. One of the guests, an officer in the box, sprang at Booth, but the assassin managed to free himself and leap from the box onto the stage, breaking his leg as he landed.

"Amid the confusion and shock of all the spectators, Booth turned to the audience and proclaimed:

"'*Sic semper tyrannis!*' and then declared in English, 'The South is avenged!'

"Most in the theatre were not completely aware of what had happened, and Booth ran limping through the wings to a horse he had stationed in the alley.

"The other conspirators and would-be assassins were unsuccessful in their attempts to kill Secretary of State Seward and the other human targets.

"But the dreadfully wounded president was carried across the street to a private residence, where several doctors did all that was humanly possible to save Lincoln's life.

"Their efforts were in vain.

"At 7:22 the next morning, Lincoln's secretary of war, Stanton, spoke the words, 'Now he belongs to the ages.'

"Abraham Lincoln was dead.

"On April 26, twelve days after having killed the president, the end came for John Wilkes Booth in a tobacco shed in Port Royal, Virginia.

"After a frantic two-week search by the army and secret service forces, and during which time, Booth had received medical aid from a Dr. Mudd, Booth had been discovered hiding in a barn by a man named Garrett. The barn was set afire, and Booth was either shot by his pursuers or shot himself rather than surrender."

* * *

The Wise Old Man's story of the stranger who limped had ended. During the telling he had captured the attention of the group of actors, but at the first mention of the name John Wilkes Booth there had been a silent, but visible, reaction from his audience of play actors.

In a way, they were kinfolk, all related by profession, and all aware of the great theatrical reputation of the Booth name, from the paterfamilias, Junius Brutus Booth, to his sons, Edwin Booth, the greatest, most renowned Hamlet of his time, and John Wilkes, who, himself, had been famous until that fateful night when he had become notorious by a shot fired at Ford's Theatre.

The reaction and excitement of the players around the campfire was palpable.

They didn't want the story to end. They all wanted to know more.

One by one, stepping on one another's lines, they fired questions at the Wise Old Man without waiting for answers.

"At your campfire, did you have any suspicion, or inkling, as to the limping man's identity?"

"On which side did you fight? Blue or Gray?"

"Did you ever see Edwin Booth's performance as Hamlet?"

"Whatever happened to Booth's horse—the buckskin?"

"Were you ever aware that there was a hundred-thousand-dollar reward for the capture of John Wilkes Booth?"

. . . and more questions that were jumbled together.

The Wise Old Man puffed on his meerschaum and shook his head, smiled, and spoke slowly.

"Some questions are better left unanswered."

Hamlet rose and took a step forward.

"Every play has to have an ending with a closing curtain."

"Life," the Wise Old Man said softly, "is not a play, and are we really certain that the curtain ever goes down?"

The actors gazed at the Wise Old Man, who, now, was looking at his watch again.

"As for John Wilkes Booth, he, too, was a great actor, but the most memorable, historic, and devastating role he ever played . . . was offstage.

"And now methinks I scent the morning air."

The next morning when the actors awoke, the Wise Old Man of the West had already made his exit.

THE WISE OLD MAN
OF THE WEST
and BLAZING GUNS OF THE BIBLE

For
STEPHEN LODGE
Gentle Buckaroo
of Western Writers

and of course
for
MARY FRANCES

"Indians don't attack at night," said Lieutenant Kevin Connors.

"Too many white men, thinking just that, died in the dark," a voice responded from out of the purple gloom.

Soldiers around the campfire snapped guns from holsters while others grabbed rifles and pointed toward the voice that came from the direction of the unseen intruder.

"Step out here by the light of the fire, *mister*!" Lieutenant Connors's voice converted into harsh command.

The man and the voice obeyed as a silhouette moved closer.

"A pleasure, Lieutenant. I welcome the warmth of the fire and the company of the United States Army."

For an instant the soldiers stood mumchance at the anomalous sight of the nocturnal trespasser— age, indeterminate, but older than each of them. Dressed, in mufti, but more like a stage actor, complete with malacca walking stick, high-toned homburg, tailored suit coat—clear blue eyes, and clean-shaven, except for a speckled military mustache, with cultured bearing and utterance, in response to Lieutenant Connors's next question.

"Who the hell are you, and how'd you get here undetected?"

"As for the first part, just an old man, and as to the second—the way our red brothers would, past your semisomnolent sentries."

"A wisenheimer," Connors rasped.

"Not all that wise, and quite harmless," he smiled and lifted the cane, "except for this trusty crosier, as you must've already gleaned."

"What are you doing out here all alone?"

"Nothing—except hoping for a cup of coffee from your commissary."

The old man pointed the tip of his walking stick toward the oversized coffeepot half settled on the grate of the fire.

Private Nicholas Adamchock, who served as cook of the expeditionary platoon, glanced at Lieutenant Connors, who nodded almost imperceptibly.

Adamchock poured the steaming black liquid into a tin cup and extended it toward the old man.

"Thank you, Private . . . and you, too, Lieutenant . . ."

"Connors."

"A fine old Hibernian nomen." He sipped from the cup. "And good strong brew."

"Are you afoot?" Connors asked.

"For the nonce." The old man sipped again. "But I've journeyed from donkey to canvas to Conestoga."

"You headin' to Fort Concho?"

"No, I don't think so."

"Where, then?"

"Wherever the wind is at my back."

"Excuse me, Lieutenant," Sergeant Seth Coolidge said. "I think I've heard tell of this jasper from time to time . . . full of tall tales and highfalutin confabulation . . . showed up onc't at a prayer meetin' where my Uncle Hawkins was attendin' . . ."

"You a preacher, mister?" Connors asked.

"I do not have that distinction," the old man smiled.

"Uncle Hawk said he was known as the Wise Old Man in some parts."

"That true?" Connors persisted.

"'Wise' is a nebulous appellation."

"Just the same," Connors pointed to one of the troopers, "Davis, check the sentries. Make sure they're okay . . . and awake."

"Yes, sir." Davis was already on his way.

Connors's attention again turned to the Wise Old Man.

"You see any signs of those red-coated coyotes out there?"

"I presume you're referring to the native tribal inhabitants. The answer is negative; but there's no assurance they haven't seen me . . . or you gentlemen."

"That's why I'm checking the sentries."

"A sensible precaution." The Wise Old Man nodded and proceeded to remove a curved meerschaum pipe and tobacco pouch from his pocket. "May I inquire as to your mission, Lieutenant?"

"Routine scouting expedition. We'll be back to Fort Concho in three days."

"And nights," the Wise Old Man added as he lit the meerschaum.

"You intend to spend this night with us, ol'-timer?"

"If I may presume upon your hospitality, sir."

"Don't 'sir' me. You're not in the army. Hungry?"

"No, thank you."

"Armed? Beside that cane?" Connors smiled.

"I carry a revolver . . . unloaded at the moment."

"Why?"

"Why is it unloaded? I expended my last cartridge into a jackrabbit I consumed some hours ago."

"Maybe we can refill your pistol . . . just before you leave."

"I would appreciate it even if some other jackrabbit out there won't."

Connors smiled again.

"Sit down and enjoy your smoke while we check the sentries."

"I'm beholden again for your hospitality."

A breathless trooper Davis soon returned and reported.

"All sentries okay . . . and awake, sir."

"Good. I guess we can relax a mite for the time being."

The troopers seemed to unflex and some of them lit up cigar stubs, rolled up cigarette papers, and fired up their pipes.

Connors's Irish blue eyes were aimed at the Wise Old Man.

"Coolidge said you had a bagful of tall tales. It's early yet. You want to pull one out of that bag and spin it . . . maybe one we'll enjoy in this situation?"

"Well," the Wise Old Man inhaled from the

meerschaum, "I don't know how much you'll enjoy it, but it does rather put me in mind of another group and another fellow . . . some call it 'Blazing Guns of the Bible.'"

"How the hell can that be?" Sergeant Seth Coolidge remarked. "There wasn't any guns during Bible times."

"No, not exactly, but did any of you hear about a man called Jason Evers . . . sometimes known as the 'Silent Gun'?"

There was a negative response from the troopers.

"Go ahead and tell us about this so-called Silent Gun," Connors nodded.

"Well, Jason Evers had a reputation as what is known as a gunfighter, or pistolero, or shootist. And that reputation was somewhat unsavory. Evers's gun was for hire, sometimes as a bounty hunter on the side of the law and sometimes on the other side . . . more often than not.

"Every story's got to have a start and finish. This one may well have begun in a flyspeck of a Kansas town when a young lad named Jason Evers walked into that town carrying all his earthly possessions in a bag slung over one of his broad-beamed shoulders. It was evident that he had walked a long way.

"Three brothers swaggered out between the bat-wings of a saloon. It was easily discerned that they were brothers by their pig eyes imbedded in their porcine faces. They were the dregs of the Casper clan—in descending order: Rafe, Ralph, and Rodger, each over six feet and weighing fifteen or sixteen stone.

"Rafe stepped in front of Jason, while Ralph and Rodger flanked him.

"'Who you, boy?' Rafe grunted.

"No response.

"'Never seen you before,' Ralph noted.

"Jason didn't speak.

"'We're the welcomin' committee,' Ralph barked.

"'Talk to the "welcomin' committee."' Rodger grinned. Even their voices sounded the same as they taunted.

"'Hey, boy, you look at your betters when they're talkin'—you hear?'

"'Maybe he can't hear. Maybe he don't talk. Maybe he's a dummy.'

"'What you got in that bag, dummy? Let's have a look.'

"Rafe took a step closer and grabbed for the bag. But Jason brought up a lightning fist and knocked him flat on his back. The other two jumped in swinging at the youth, and they became a whirlwind of flailing knuckles and hammering fists that sent them both bleeding to the ground. But Rafe rose, drew his gun, fired near the boy's feet, aimed at his midsection, and jeered as a considerable crowd gathered round.

"'Maybe the dummy can dance.'

"He fired another shot near Jason's boot.

"'Go ahead and dance, dummy!'

"Two more shots even closer, but Jason stood statue still, unmoving, as Rafe aimed again.

"'This one's going right through your knee.'

"A shot rang out but not from Rafe's gun, which flew from his hand onto the ground in shattered pieces.

"A tall man on horseback moved his pistol slightly toward the other two Caspers.

"'Believe you've had enough fun for the day, fellows. Drift.'

"They did, as the tall man dismounted and approached the youth.

"'You're not short on grit, son. What's your name?'

"'Evers. Jason Evers. Yours?'

"'Just call me J.B.'

"'Thanks, J.B.'

"The youth picked up his bag, turned, and started to walk away.

"'Just a minute. Jason, you don't waste many words.'

"'No, sir.'

"'Put up quite a fight and didn't back down; but the odds were against you. There's something that would at least tilt those odds. What do you do?'

"'Worked in a stable, mostly.'

"'It's one thing to be born in a stable; it's another to go on working in one. You remind me of me sometime ago—and about balancing those odds . . .'

"'What about it?'

"'Come with me, Jason.'

"'Why?'

"'I'll introduce you to a friend.'"

The Wise Old Man adjusted the pipe in his mouth and struck a match to relight it.

Connors's eyes, and ever so slightly, his head, moved from Adamchock to the coffeepot, to the Wise Old Man, and back to Adamchock, who lifted his hand toward the kettle.

"Say, Old Man . . . care for a redo on that java?"

"No, thanks, I seldom indulge my vices—or virtues—two at a time."

"Well," Coolidge nodded, "in that story you're

tellin', J.B. sounds like the gunslinger and that Evers fella more like a fistfighter."

"Patience, Sergeant C, that's just the first act. The next finds the two of them in a field just outside of town where J.B. is removing something from the saddlebag on his mount. Evers looked around and then spoke for the first time since they left the village.

"'I don't see that friend you talked about.'

"'He's right here in my hand.'

"J.B. extended a gun, holster, and cartridge belt.

"'Mr. Evers, meet Mr. Remington. He's got a cousin, Mr. Colt, but Remington's a lot smoother and faster on the draw. You ever shake hands with one of these before?'

"Evers moved his head negatively.

"'Well, it's about time you did. Strap it on.'

"Not much later J.B.'s voice was calm, but instructive, terse, and deadly serious.

"'There's them that keep the hammer on an empty chamber. I'm not one of 'em. Don't you be, either. Might need that extra bullet. Now, this is important. Never . . . never squeeze the trigger unless you're willing to kill . . . and I mean kill without compunction or hesitation. Got that?'

"'I got it, J.B.'

"'Good. Because an instant of hesitation could cost you your life on account of the other fellow won't hesitate and that's the difference between the quick and the dead. And you'd better be quick or else you'll be dead . . . and if you miss once, shoot again . . . fast. Follow me?'

"'I follow, J.B.'

"'And don't do anything dumb, like aim to wound. That lets him get off a shot, a shot that could kill you. And never aim for the head. Know why?'

"'Too small a target.'

"'Partly right. The other part is that the head moves quicker than the rest of the body. The chest, lad, that's the place . . . broader and slower . . . and that's where the most vital target is . . . the heart. Now, speaking of that, don't give him a broad target by standing square on. The less he has to aim at the better your odds of coming out alive. Got that?'

"'Got it, J.B.'

"'And forget that crap about watching his eyes. He shoots with his thumb and trigger finger. When that hand starts to move, you move faster . . . unless you decide to move first . . . and don't worry about being fair . . . worry about being alive. That's why I say don't squeeze unless you're willing to kill . . . just like war. Only difference is a gunfight is a war between two people. Hook. Draw. Fire. Three elements in one swift, sure, motion. Hook. Draw. Fire. Repeat that.'

"'Hook. Draw. Fire.'

"'Good. Now, there's just one other element. Accuracy. All the rest is bullshit unless you hit the target. Part is natural. The other part is practice. See that tree over there with that knobby trunk?'

"'I see it.'

"'That's a man who's willing to kill you . . . unless you kill him first. That apple-sized knob in the center is that son of a bitch's heart. When I say "now" his hand is starting to move. You move, too. Hook. Draw.

Fire. Fast, but not too fast or the barrel won't be level. You ready?'

"'Ready.'

"'Let's give it a go . . . NOW!'

"Hook. Draw. Fire is what Evers did. Once. Twice. The first shot was a close miss. The second split the knob.

"'Sweet. Sweet and smart. Your hand was made for the trigger. So are your reflexes. Good beginning. A couple more hours today, and we'll keep at it tomorrow . . . and then some.'

The Wise Old Man held out the meerschaum as if it were the Remington.

"Hook. Draw. Fire. Scores of cartridges later the day's lesson was done except for what J.B. had to say as they moved toward their horses.

"'Practice, practice, practice—rehearse, rehearse like an actor rehearses a stage play; but this is no stage play. It's life or death. His or yours.'

"'I see you wear two guns; you always carry a third one in a saddlebag?'

"Evers began to unstrap the Remington.

"'Not *my* gun. But leave it on and I'll tell you about it while you ride back on that horse we rented.'

"'Not *we, you* rented. I don't have any money except for a little loose change.'

"'You want to hear it?'

"'Sure.'

"'Then, mount up.'"

"Adamchock," Connors pointed, "throw a couple more pieces of mesquite on that fire; it's burnin' low."

"Yes, sir."

"Go ahead, stranger, tell us about that Remington pistol."

The other soldiers nodded and even voiced approval.

"All right, Lieutenant, but I'll tell it in my own fashion and version, as I, myself, heard it told."

"Shoot." Connors smiled.

"Yes." The Wise Old Man returned the smile. "And so the next chapter begins during a saloon card game. Of the six players who began, three had dropped out and quit the game. That left the youngest player, Jimmy Sanders, and a fellow, Truscutt Jones, with a disarming Southern lilt to his voice, who looked like a riverboat gambler because that's what he mostly had been . . . and J.B. was the third.

"J.B. had been a heavy winner but didn't like what he had seen the last couple of plays. Consequently, he dropped out of the current hand as Truscutt Jones was dealing. On the table a sizable pot with just about an even amount of currency in front of the two remaining players.

"'Cards, young man?'

"'I'll play these.'

"'Dealer takes a single. Your bet.'

"'Table stakes. That's an even hundred here.'

"'I'll see the hundred,' Jones drawled.

"'And I'll see the top card in the deck because you drew from the bottom.'

"'Repeat that!' he ordered not with a drawl.'

"'I repeat that you cheated. You drew an ace from the bottom, and . . .'

"That's when J.B. spoke up."

"'I never volunteer an opinion, but if you ask for mine, youngster . . .'

"'You stay out of this, Mr. Butt In,' Truscutt Jones snarled.

"'Thank you, sir,' Sanders smiled at J.B., 'but I'm old enough to take care of myself and . . .'

"Truscutt Jones reached across and slapped young Sanders.

"'Suppose we settle it outside in the tradition of the South?'

"'Suppose we do.'

"Sanders rose and in the next few minutes a town crowd had gathered to observe a death duel.

"Both drew simultaneously. Sanders was fast; but Truscutt Jones was a crack-second faster. His shot hit the young man's midsection and he fell mortally wounded but still alive.

"To everyone's surprise the gunman swiftly turned his pistol in J.B.'s direction and spat.

"'Here's yours, Mr. BUTT IN . . .'

"That's as far as he got. J.B.'s first bullet hit Truscutt Jones's heart, the second bullet hit the first bullet.

"With his fading breath the young man spoke to J.B., who leaned over him.

"'Thanks . . . my gun and rig . . . do you hear?'

"'I hear.'

"'Take it . . . give it to someone who'll be better with it . . . than I was . . .'"

And the Wise Old Man tapped out the burnt pipe tobacco in his palm.

"Well, that's how J.B. told it to Evers, but in his own way . . . with just one more addition."

"What was that?" Lieutenant Connors inquired.

"A short, bald-headed gentleman approached J.B. and introduced himself.

"'Sir, I'm Stacy Spencer, local barber and undertaker. Can I be of service?'

"J.B. handed the bald-headed gentleman two double eagles.

"'They won't be needing any haircuts. But you can bury the two of them up in boot hill . . . not too close together.'

"And as for Evers, the Remington tutelage went on . . . until—"

"'Well, Jason, that's as much as I, or anybody, can teach you. The rest is up to you, yourself. But you're a natural. Like I said, your hand was made for the trigger, you've got keen-seeing eyes and a sharp instinct.'

"'J.B. . . . I . . . I want . . .'

"'Don't start getting talkative now, son. Keep the gun. You can sure as hell use it better than the last owner. And that horse and rig is yours . . . paid for.'

"It was difficult for Evers to speak . . . or even swallow.

"'Besides teaching me . . . how to use a gun . . . you . . .'

"'Everybody ought to have some kind of a teacher—even with a gun. I had one.'

"'Who was that?'

"'Not much older than me. In a way we sort of taught each other. Name of William Frederick Cody.'

"'You know, J.B., I don't even know what your initials stand for . . . J.B.'

"'James—and—Butler.'

"'Butler. That's your last name?'

"'Middle name. Last name's Hickok. James Butler Hickok.'"

At the mention of Hickok the verbal reaction of the troopers ranged everything from "Great Caesar's Ghost!" to "Holy shit!" And the words "Hickok" and "Wild Bill" echoed across the campfire in surprise, astonishment, and even awe.

As the reaction receded Lieutenant Connors turned to the Wise Old Man.

"What is it that would make a man like Hickok take such an interest in a young stranger?"

"The Bard of Avon wrote, 'There's no art to find the mind's construction in the face.' Who can tell? Perhaps it was watching the 'young stranger' as you call him, stand unflinching against insuperable odds, or as Hickok mentioned, the lad reminded him of his own young self in less fortunate times. Or perhaps to make up for one of his own less fortunate misdeeds. Maybe for not interfering more overtly on behalf of the young card player. But it happened."

"Well," Sergeant Coolidge questioned, "what happened after that . . . to the two of 'em? That ain't the end of the story . . ."

"No, it's not. Hickok and Evers parted company. Wild Bill proceeded north toward the Black Hills and Deadwood in the Dakotas. Evers, to the Southwest, Arizona, New Mexico Territories, where his Remington became a gun for hire . . . and so was he.

"At first his workload was mostly legitimate, bank guard, payroll delivery, sheriff's deputy, in the course of which he was sometimes challenged, or drawn into a gunfight where his 'Hook. Draw. Fire.' capability rendered him victorious and the challengers dead.

But as time went on and his reputation grew he became less particular about what he was hired to do. And as his reputation grew so did his fee. He would hire out on either side in a range war depending on where the double eagles were stacked higher. He became known as the 'Silent Gun,' because he was spare with words and let his gun do the talking.

"Years later, the story goes, Jason Evers was commissioned by a cattle baron to go up against a pistolero with an even greater reputation, hired by an opposing cattle baron. An ice-blooded gunfighter called Wilson.

"Shortly before the appointed time, midnight, Evers sat at a table in a customerless saloon, his waist-coat hung on a nearby peg on the wall, while he sipped a glass of sarsaparilla.

"Jason Evers whirled, gun drawn, as the batwings swung open.

"No. It was not Wilson, but a frock-coated man holding a Bible, who paused a second, then approached slowly.

"'May I sit for just a moment, Mr. Evers?'

"Evers looked up at the saloon clock . . . Eleven forty.

"Evers nodded.

"'My name is Reverend Thomas Kinkaid.'

"Kinkaid placed the thick Bible on the table and sat.

"'Haven't got much time, Reverend, for Bible reading.'

"Evers noticed a fresh bruise on the side of the reverend's face.

"'What is it you want?'

"'Peace. I want to urge you to leave town instead of . . .'

"'Meeting Wilson?'

"'Killing or being killed.'

"'Have you talked to Wilson about this?'

"The reverend lowered his head.

"'Yes.'

"Evers pointed to the bruise.

"'Did he do that?'

"The reverend nodded.

"'I see you didn't turn the other cheek.'

"'I came here to reason with you.'

"'Here's my reason, Reverend. I was paid to do a job. I'm going to do it. Or die trying.'

"'Mr. Evers . . .'

"'My time's running out. You tried, Reverend. Your conscience is clear.'

"'I hope yours is, Mr. Evers.'

"Reverend Thomas Kinkaid rose with his Bible and walked toward the front of the saloon, paused near the peg with Evers's coat, as Evers looked again at the clock . . . Eleven forty-five.

"At midnight exactly the street was empty except for spectators shielded behind posts and whatever cover afforded them a view to whatever was going to happen. And that twelve-o'clock street was as silent as sweat, except for a dog barking and snapping in some dark alley.

"Neither of the two cattle barons who had hired the gunfighters was within a hundred miles of the imminent encounter. The sheriff and his son-in-law deputy were coincidentally and conveniently out of town.

"Two figures faced each other at gunfight distance.

"One was taller than the other.

"Wilson. Frigid blue eyes, his face a mask immune to emotion, whose stock-in-trade was tailor-made death, with no regard for life or afterlife. When the deed was done the doer traveled on to another place and another piece of work.

"The other figure.

"Jason Evers. Not as renowned or quite as experienced, but with a swelling reputation in the use of his Remington. Evers felt an unusual weight as well as a bulge in the left inside pocket of his waistcoat; but there was no time to do anything about it. His concentration was cemented on the figure he faced.

"Who drew first no one could tell.

"The shots were simultaneous.

"Evers felt the impact in his chest and staggered somewhat, but before he could fire again he saw Wilson drop his gun and fall forward, a deadweight.

"One more vacancy was filled in hell.

"The street was no longer empty . . . or quiet, as scores of citizens left their shelters and swarmed amid shouts of congratulation toward the standing survivor.

"Later, Evers sat next to Reverend Thomas Kinkaid. Just the two of them.

"There was a bullet hole through his waistcoat as he reached inside and withdrew a Bible.

"He held it in his hands as he flipped open the pages until he came to the slug lodged at the far side.

"Jason Evers held the spent slug in one hand and the Bible in the other.

"'Thank you, Reverend, I . . .'

"'It was the Lord's will, my son.'

"'The Lord's?'

"'God? Fate? Destiny? Call it what you will. It was an impulse as I was leaving you in that saloon.'

"'An impulse?'

"'Like Lazarus, you have a second chance at life. Please keep the Bible.'

"'And the slug?'

"'That, too. Nobody knows what Lazarus did with the rest of his life. Maybe this will help you change the rest of yours.'"

This time the troopers around the campfire remained silent.

But not for long.

"Well," Sergeant Coolidge broke the silence, "did it?"

"Ah, Sergeant C . . . that's the third act . . . until the final curtain falls . . . or does it?"

"Go ahead and tell us," Lieutenant Connors waved.

"I'll tell you what I know . . . after I refuel my friendly hookah."

The Wise Old Man refilled his meerschaum, lit it, rubbed his chin, and proceeded.

"No one knows how many hours, days, and nights Jason Evers spent reading the scarred Bible, or exactly when the transformation took place, but take place it did. He was a changed man, in more ways than one. His eyes were just as keen, but somehow softer, his manner somehow gentler, and his voice richer and more self-assured with an emotional depth.

"And his gun was now truly silent, but Jason Evers kept the Remington and gun belt, along with the Bible and slug, in a leather satchel he carried as he spread the gospel that he memorized. At first there were only a few curious people gathered to listen.

"'. . . *The Lord is good to all: and his tender mercies are all over his works.*
"'. . . *The righteous shall flourish like the palm tree.*'

"At Sunday picnics where families celebrated the birth of a nation.

"'. . . *Bear ye one another's burdens, and so fulfill the law of Christ.*
"'. . . *Let your light so shine before men, that they may see your good works and glorify your Father which is in heaven.*'

"Outside of saloons where wives and children of patrons gathered to listen.

"'. . . *Blessed are the poor in spirit: for theirs is the kingdom of heaven.*'
"'*Blessed are ye that hunger now: for ye shall be filled.*
"'*Blessed are ye that weep now: for ye shall laugh.*'

"In town hall meetings of a place in need.

"'. . . *The Lord give mercy unto the house of Onesiphorus: for he oft refreshed me, and was not ashamed of my chain.*
"'. . . *Surely goodness and mercy shall follow me all the days of my life: and I will dwell in the house of the Lord forever.*'

"Then as guest speaker of churches in the wilderness of the West.

"'. . . *Open thine hand wide unto thy brother, to thy poor, and to thy needy, in thy land.*
"'. . . *But they that wait upon the Lord shall renew their strength; they shall mount up with wings as eagles; they shall run, and not be weary; and they shall walk, and not faint.*'"

The Wise Old Man continued.

"And somehow even those who came in doubt, came to scorn, fell under the spell of this mystifier called Jason Evers.

"And then it happened. Jason Evers came upon a wagon train traveling west through hostile Indian territory, where renegade Chiricahua Apaches had decimated other trespassers.

"It became his nightly habit to stand before a makeshift pulpit, with the open Bible on it, but to sermonize from memory.

"After several nights, the wagon master, Pete Steele, turned impatient, even jealous at the rapt attention the travelers were showing Evers, but the sermons continued as the stranger addressed the tired congregation while a cold winter wind whipped through the camp.

"'. . . *Cast thy bread upon the waters: for thou shalt find it after many days.*
"'. . . *For a good tree bringeth not forth corrupt fruit; neither doth a corrupt tree bring forth good fruit.*'

"At this moment the night wind swelled across the camp, caught up the pages of the scarred Bible on the makeshift pulpit, then ceased, as Jason Evers looked down on the open page and the words.

"'. . . *The righteous shall rejoice when he seeth the vengeance: he shall wash his feet in the wicked.*'

"Another gust of wind, another page.

"'. . . *and I will execute the vengeance in anger and fury upon the heathen, such as they have not heard.*'

"Again.

"'. . . *for the rod of the wicked shall not rest upon the lot of the righteous.*'

"The eyes of Jason Evers blazed, no longer those of the sermonizer, but those of the gunfighter of before.

"An impulse had seized him, as the Reverend Thomas Kinkaid was overtaken long ago . . . but a different impulse.

"He reached down and drew the Remington and gun belt from the satchel. His voice barked commands to the stunned viewers.

"'Get to your guns and rifles!'

"'Women and children to cover!'

"'You men . . . be ready to fire!'

"'An ATTACK! They're GOING TO ATTACK!'

"The wagon master's voice rang out.

"'He's gone crazy . . . they don't attack at night.'

"But they did.

"A whirlwind of renegade Chiricahuas on horseback; they stormed out of the night rocks with ebony eyes out of flat red faces, and green paint, yelping and screaming.

"But the camp was ready, and Winchesters and Henrys . . . Colts and Remingtons spat their deadly messengers with blistering rapid fire into the charging bodies of the startled Apaches.

"For every galloping Apache there seemed to be a hundred shots tearing toward them from the blazing guns of the wagon train, until the remnant Apaches disappeared into sheltering darkness.

"The night ambush failed.

"The desert was silent.

"The wagon train had survived."

"We heard tell," Connors said, "that Indians don't attack at night."

"Apaches are a different breed of Indian," the Wise Old Man noted, "and Fort Concho is in Apache territory."

He settled back and drew again from the curved meerschaum as the troopers looked at him and one another.

"Well," Sergeant Coolidge tossed the stub of his cigar into the dimming fire, "I guess you could call it 'Blazing Guns of the Bible' at that. Must've made Evers quite a hero."

"Not for long."

"How come?"

"Because, came the dawn and Jason Evers was gone, along with his satchel."

"We get the point of the story, mister," Lieutenant

Connors said, "but tell us what you know about him after that."

"Not much, neither does anybody else. Just speculation. Some say he was seen moving south toward Mexico . . . others, that he boarded a sailing schooner to the Sandwich Islands, or some; that he ventured to Alaska, or a monastery in India. Probably none of those."

The Wise Old Man tapped out the dredges of his cold pipe and smiled.

"Well, it's getting late and most everywhere they've played 'Taps' a long time ago, so, gentlemen, I'll bid you good night."

"Good night." Connors smiled. "But, Sergeant, see that this gentleman gets those cartridges for his revolver before we turn in."

"Much obliged." The Wise Old Man smiled.

"So are we," Connors nodded.

The next morning Sergeant Coolidge reported to Lieutenant Connors.

"Sir, that stranger, so-called Wise Old Man, is gone . . . disappeared before first light."

"The sentries?"

"Seen hide nor hair of him."

"How could he have . . . ?"

Connors left it unfinished, but Sergeant Coolidge replied.

"Beats me."

"Yeah. Sergeant, the next two nights, till we get to Fort Concho, double the sentries."

"Yes, sir."

"And if you catch any of 'em sleeping, or even blinking . . . shoot 'em."

Sergeant Coolidge knew that Connors wasn't exactly serious, but he wasn't exactly kidding.

"Yes, sir . . . and, sir . . ."

"What?"

"I was just thinking . . ."

"Well, go ahead and think out loud."

"Sir, he never did tell us his name . . ."

"So?"

"So . . . sir, he did have blue eyes . . ."

"And so have a lot of people, including me."

"But . . . you think he might *be* Jason Evers?"

Lieutenant Connors paused.

"I don't know. But after last night . . . that Wise Old Man could be anybody."

THE WISE OLD MAN
OF THE WEST
and THE BRAVEST SOLDIER

For
WILLIAM BRYANT
Friend, Actor, and
WWII Hero—
Belly Gunner, B-17
The Bloody 101st

and of course
for
MARY FRANCES

"I was to the Little Big Horn with Custer."
—JIM HUNTLY

"The bravest soldier I ever knew was not a soldier."
—THE WISE OLD MAN

After decades of warfare, the vastly outnumbered Apaches were defeated and exiled from their native highlands to the faraway marshlands of Florida.

Since the departure of Colonel George Crook and General Nelson Appleton Miles, Fort Bowie wasn't much of a fort. The cantina inside the decaying walls was even less.

Along one side, wide wooden planks on six heavy barrels served as the bar. A couple of crude wooden shelves beneath the warped mirror served as backbar stocked by liquor bottles with assorted labels. Amalgamated ashes from cigars, cigarettes, and pipe tobacco mixed with other matter graced the wooden floor that hadn't been swept the night before or week before.

There were half a dozen round tables with Douglas chairs, most of them occupied by bleary-eyed soldiers. A haze of stale smoke wafted toward the low ceiling.

Among them all, at a corner table, sat a human

anomaly known as the Wise Old Man of the West, in immaculate contrast to the four slovenly soldiers at his table who had been listening to the old man's tales for the past three hours.

Sartorially impeccable, his three-piece dark gray suit might have been tailored for him at Savile Row. Clear-eyed and clean-shaven, except for a meticulously trimmed salt-and-pepper military mustache. His ubiquitous malacca crosier leaned against a nearby wall with his high-toned homburg capped over the curved handle of the cane. His near-hypnotic voice was caramel coated and deeper than expected of a man his average size. The four soldiers involuntarily leaned in closer, anticipating that the raconteur was nearing the climax of his tale.

Also trying to listen while bartending, but catching only snatches of the Wise Old Man's stories, was the cantina's owner, who had a much weatherworn face for an indoor laborer. It was difficult to determine his age because he was bald as a peeled egg, but less difficult to determine was the loss of his left leg now substituted for by a wooden peg. His surname was MacBaldwin, but he was invariably addressed as "MacBaldy."

As the four soldiers sat in rapt silence, the Wise Old Man finished his story with an actor's stage whisper just before the curtain came down, ". . . and that was the last Tom Horn ever saw of his blood brother, the Apache Kid."

The Wise Old Man took a draw from his meerschaum pipe, set it on the table, and with his thumb, then forefinger, stroked his trim military mustache. He reached toward his vest pocket and gently withdrew the Elgin hunter case gold watch by the slim gold chain, pressed the stem, and the lid snapped open, revealing both hands of the watch directly on the number twelve.

At that exact instant there resounded through the cantina the clattering dissonance of an alarm clock prominently stationed on the backbar to the accompaniment of MacBaldy's raspy voice.

"MIDNIGHT!"

As if reacting to some officer's command all the soldiers in the room rose wordlessly and filed out of the cantina.

The Wise Old Man also started to rise but was restrained by a wave from MacBaldy, stomping toward the table with a bottle in one hand and two large glasses in the other.

"Hold on, old fella. You're not a soldier here and there's no curfew for you. Besides, I wanted to hear one of those yarns you been spinning from start to finish along with the companionship of the best bottle of rye for the both of us. Agreed?"

"Agreed," the Wise Old Man smiled, and sat down.

MacBaldy managed to sit, pour two fingers of rye into one glass, and half fill his own tumbler.

"You know, I used to be a soldier myself, but the army don't have much use for a one-legged cavalryman—and vice versa—so I won this here cantina in a crooked poker game. The owner held four deuces and a jack. I held four kings and an ace. The game was crooked because I was dealing. Didn't lose my limb in battle . . . damn horse fell on it and smashed it all to hell."

"Sorry."

"Don't be. Shot the horse and it was the best

thing ever happened to me . . . I mean, owning this cantina . . . make a tolerable living."

"Congratulations."

"You bet. How about that yarn? Sounds like you met quite a few soldiers in your time."

"Quite a few."

"Then, tell me about the bravest soldier you ever met." MacBaldy took a deep swallow from his tumbler. "Closest to danger I ever come was seeing ol' Geeroneemo himself from about ten yards away after he surrendered, right here at this ol' fort."

The Wise Old Man sipped from his glass and relit his meerschaum.

"The bravest soldier I ever met was not a soldier."

"How could that be?"

"His name was Jim Huntly, and he told me about it when our wagon train was lost in the snows of the Oregon Trail and we had suffered an attack from renegade Sioux. It was a small caravan composed of six Conestogas, with mostly women and children, led by a behemoth of a wagon master named Sam Waters. We knew they were going to hit us again, but Jim Huntly commenced to tell me his story."

"'I was to the Little Big Horn with Custer.'"

"Impossible! How could he tell you? Everybody was killed at Little Big Horn."

"Not everybody. It was the night of June 24, 1876. Huntly was called into Colonel Custer's tent. In his own words he spoke of the unlikely beginning."

"It was past midnight. Colonel Custer sat behind a small desk, his long yellow hair curling over his buckskin jacket, with our regimental red scarf around his throat. 'You sent for me, sir?'

"'Tomorrow, more likely than not, there will be a remembered battle involving the 7th.'

"'I know, sir.'

"'There's something *I* know, just found out in the last dispatch from Fort Lincoln; that's why I'm sending you back before first light. Mount up on that prize hammer-head of yours . . . what do you call him?'

"'Buckeye, sir.'

"'Yeah, Buckeye. Mount up and get damn seldom in a hurry.'

"'But, sir, you'll need every soldier for the fight.'

"'In the first place, you're not a soldier . . .'

"'But, sir . . .'

"'You don't qualify . . . years too young. In the second place, you wouldn't make the difference. Besides, you're about the same age our son would've been if Libbie and I hadn't lost him at birth.'

"'But, sir . . .'

"'That's three 'but sirs.' Be mounted by four a.m.'

"'Sir, I'm big for my age.'

"'You're big, for any age, but mount up.'

"'Is that a direct order, sir?'

"'When, and if, you get to be a soldier—three or four years from now—you'll know there's no such thing as an "indirect order."'

"'I was born in Ohio, sir . . .'

"'So was I. Good farm country. Go back to Ohio and farm.'

"'Besides growing it, we had to hunt for our food. I'm a good shot, sir.'

"'So are the Sioux . . . and as I said, you wouldn't make the difference. If I kept you with us knowing you're underage it'ud be my ass in a sling again, and I don't want to go through another court-martial.'

"'But, sir . . .'

"'Good night and good luck, *Mister* Huntly.'"

"*Mister* Huntly went on to tell me that the next morning he and his horse, Buckeye, watched the battle of the Little Big Horn from Crow's Nest Bluff, a distant hill, but close enough to see it wasn't a battle. It was slaughter. The 7th was outnumbered by more than fifty to one, maybe a hundred to one. The entire command, including Custer, killed and mutilated. He thought of going back but trembled and threw up, thinking of Custer's words, '*You wouldn't make the difference.*'

"Like one seared with an invisible branding iron of dismay, he watched until the carnage was done with . . . the dead Custer's words ringing in his fevered brain—'*You wouldn't make the difference.*' But still, he couldn't help wondering:

"*Why was I spared?*
Like Lazarus why was I given
a second chance to live?
What did Lazarus do with the rest
of his life?
What would Jim Huntly do
with the rest of his life?'

"Somewhere, somehow, he vowed that the time would come where and when he would make the difference.

"Years later on that lost and beleaguered wagon train, where we knew that the Sioux would charge again with the dawn, he thought this place and time might be the chance for him to make a difference, and breathlessly talked to me about it.

"'Some miles back, before the storm hit, we passed an army outpost. If I could make it there and bring back enough troopers . . .'

"'Like hell!' It was the barking voice of Sam Waters, wagon master, that broke through the blistery night. He had been listening. 'I need every gun and sonofabitch who can pull a trigger right here!'

"'Mr. Waters,' I spoke in a soft but firm voice, 'there aren't enough of us "sonsofbitches" to stop the Sioux.'

"'We can die trying, old-timer.'

"Sam Waters was furious. I do believe partly because he blamed himself for taking the wrong turn in the snowstorm and getting us lost. He had to vent his fury on someone, and at that time young Jim Huntly was his target.

"'Huntly, you're a damn coward who wants to leave the women and children and save your own rotten skin.'

"'Mr. Waters,' Huntly pleaded, 'you say you need guns. I'll leave my gun here, but let me try. It's our only chance.'

"'You got no chance. We're surrounded. It's still snowing. With this weather you'd never get through.'

"'With this weather I *can* get through; they'd never expect anybody to try.'

"'He's right, Mr. Waters,' I nodded. 'We've got more, much more to gain than lose. Otherwise, as Jim said, we've got no chance at all.'

"There was silence except for the whistling wind through the falling snow.

"Sam Waters wiped the flakes from his mouth and chin.

"'All right, but take your gun. You might want to shoot yourself before they catch you and . . . well, you know what would happen then.'"

"The upper Northwest is untrustworthy, especially in the winter months. At noon the sky is clear blue and relatively warm with a rugged horizon visible for miles. Within minutes it is overcome by a whirlwind of fierce, blinding snow making it impossible to see the palm of your hand inches in front of your quivering face. The storm might last a short spell, or stretch into a frozen hell. For us, either way was hell enough, but what would follow by the savage Sioux was worse. With the Sioux there was no mercy, only death, or capture, torture, and mutilation.

"Almost miraculously, Jim Huntly, on his mount, Buckeye, somehow made it through the swirling snow as the hostiles had found refuge and rest in a tree-lined dale more than a mile from the wagon train. And somewhere ahead lay the army outpost if he could find it in the infinite no-path terrain.

"As he spurred Buckeye, Huntly was hit hard from

above. In that split second he thought it was a heavy tree branch, but instantly realized it was something alive and deadly. A Sioux warrior slammed into Huntly, and they both tumbled from Buckeye onto the ground, as the warrior's knife hand lashed at him with one arm and his other hand clutched hard at the young man's throat.

"Over and over they twisted and turned with a piercing pain throbbing at Huntly's side where the knife had struck.

"Thunder. Then a bolt of lightning split a nearby tree and as the warrior instinctively reacted, Huntly in one swift motion slid out his Army Colt, pressed it against the Sioux's temple, and squeezed the trigger. Bone and brain matter sprayed from the dead warrior's shattered head as the shot reverberated through the night.

"Then silence.

"If there were any other Sioux in the vicinity they must have thought it was more thunder.

"Huntly's movement was no longer swift. There was that knife ache along with the leak of blood slipping down his side. He managed to find the stirrup with his boot, straddle onto the saddle, then rein the animal toward what he hoped was the right direction to the outpost.

"For how far, how long, he wasn't sure. Buckeye breathed hard as cold wind penetrated its nostrils, invaded its innards, challenging its heartbeat in a heart that seemed ready to explode. But the great animal's heart kept beating.

"On they struggled, with Huntly squinting for the

sight of some familiar landmark he might recognize to be near the outpost. But if there was one, it would have been camouflaged in a white blanket with snow still falling through the endless night.

"Eyes bleary and unfocused, Huntly, close to comatose, suddenly seemed to make out a blanched wall.

"Buckeye whinnied, then reared, and Huntly fell hard into a deep petrified pit of oblivion.

"The next thing he remembered was comparative warmth, voices, then the forms of uniformed men tending to him, while he tried to regain his senses.

"'Army outpost?'

"'Yes, Captain Jeb Hawkins. We patched you up . . . Who are you?'

"'Jim Huntly . . . wagon train . . . attacked . . . Sioux . . . going to hit again . . . soon . . . need help . . .'

"'Where?'

"'You won't find it . . . I'll take you . . .'

"'You're hurt . . .'

"'I'll make it . . . their only chance . . . for God's sake . . . got to save them . . .'

"'You can't ride . . .'

"'Yes, I can . . . I've got to . . .'

"There was a suspended moment with Captain Hawkins's critical decision.

"'All right. We'll get you a fresh mount . . .'

"'No! *My* horse! Help guide us . . . please . . . for God's sake . . . hurry . . .'

"'All right . . . Sergeant, sound 'Boots and Saddles'!'

"Through the icy open outpost gates, Huntly mounted on Buckeye, and Captain Hawkins riding beside him, Company C, with two color guards bearing the U.S. flag and regimental guidon, hoofed into the still storm-stricken dawn.

"As Huntly's eyes and head cleared, he sensed that he was moving in the right direction and pressed his mount into a strained gallop through the snow-clogged terrain. The troopers followed.

"Even though the weather had not subsided, Huntly knew the Sioux would attack as the rising sun provided light enough to outline the besieged Conestogas and their doomed defenders.

"Through the intermittent drum of thunder and crack of lightning, the company made its way in an ever-increasing pace as Huntly waved them on in spite of the stabbing ache in his side.

"Company C relentlessly plowed ahead until the sound of thunder and crooked white streaks of lightning clashed into the eruption of . . . gunfire.

"'CHARGE! CHARGE!' blared Captain Hawkins, and the troopers obeyed.

"The Sioux had encircled the Conestogas. Guns from both sides blazed until the Sioux realized what was happening.

"'Fire at will!' Hawkins commanded.

"A fusillade of gunfire from the troopers felled almost a dozen warriors.

"The Sioux broke their circle and re-formed into a charging brigade.

"Cheers from the relieved wagon train were barely audible as the Sioux and troopers clashed in close combat with both Company C's regimental standards snapping amid swirling snowflakes and falling bodies.

"The tide quickly turned toward defeat for the

Sioux. Rifles, pistols, and drawn sabers of the troopers overwhelmed the warriors. The regimental guidon was still fluttering. But the color guard of the United States flag had suffered a deadly wound. He wobbled, about to drop the banner.

"Jim Huntly fired his last shot, threw away his pistol, rode to the flag bearer, and grasped the flag pole, then, leading the charge, turned Buckeye toward the retreating, but still-firing remnants of Sioux. A final streak of warriors' gunfire tore into the troopers, targeting the bearer of the United States flag.

"Buckeye and Huntly both fell. Buckeye dead. Jim Huntly barely alive, still clutching the bullet-riddled flag."

The Wise Old Man concluded his story.

"Inside one of the wagons Jim Huntly lay on a cot with the tattered, bloodstained flag folded lengthwise beside him.

"Captain Hawkins, the wagon master, Sam Waters, and I looked down at him with moist eyes. Mortally wounded, Jim Huntly struggled to speak . . .

"'I'm going . . . to . . .'

"But I spoke for all of us. 'Rest easy, son. Your wounds were torn from the cloth of the flag you fought for. Rest easy.' But Huntly went on.

"'I'm going . . . to meet Colonel Custer and the 7th . . . and tell them . . . that maybe . . . this time . . . I . . .'

"He never finished his last sentence."

* * *

The Wise Old Man reached for his hat and cane, walked to the cantina door, opened it, then turned back to the bartender, who never had touched his drink.

"We didn't know much else about him, but I had an inscription put on his grave marker."

"What did it say?"

"It said:

> *"Jim Huntly*
> *He made*
> *The difference"*

The Wise Old Man closed the door and disappeared into the deep blue Arizona night.

**Keep reading for a special excerpt of *Black Noon*
by award-winning author
ANDREW J. FENADY.**

When their wagon breaks down in the desert,
Reverend Jon Keyes and his ailing wife, Lorna,
find themselves at the mercy of blistering heat,
punishing thirst, and circling buzzards. On the
brink of death, they are rescued by Caleb Hobbs
and his beguiling daughter, Deliverance, who take
them to their home in San Melas. It's a strange little
town, built to resemble the New England village
they left behind. Everyone in the community is
convinced that Jon's been sent from heaven—that
he's capable of healing their sick and saving their
flock. But can he save these God-fearing folk from
the gunslinger Moon, who descends on the town
like a bloodthirsty vulture? Can he explain the
robed figures who gather and chant after midnight?
And finally, can a good man wage war with evil
itself . . . without losing his life . . . or his soul?

**Look for *Black Noon*.
Available now from Pinnacle Books.**

Preamble

As when a misty dream unfolds—out of the darkness of the mind; black, impenetrable, until—the face of a cat appears, lambent, saffron eyes glinting, mouth distended, then twisted.

The cat screeches.

An unearthly sound.

The cat creeps noiselessly on its pads, then stops in front of something burning; the flames fling leaping towers, yellow and blue, behind the hunched feline as it looks at something, or someone, and emits an audible purr of contentment while its gaze travels ever slowly upward—the length of a human figure.

The figure of a young woman—she wears a gossamer white gown that slithers across her long and sinuous body, and her face is the fulfillment of the promise of the upward journey. Silver-blue eyes illuminated by the flames, flowing flaxen hair, a claret mouth, and sensuous alabaster skin all molded into a living mask of mythic perfection. She watches, fascinated by the trident flames.

The cat leaps effortlessly, and just as easily, the beautiful young woman catches the purring animal, presses and softly strokes its flanks. The cat purrs even louder as it is stroked by tapering white fingers, while ascending flames, glowing against the chocolate night, reach up to a burning cross atop the tower of a church that is on fire.

The curling flames turn to sable.

AND THE BLACK FLAMES RISE INTO THE STARLESS DESERT NIGHT.

Reverend Jonathon Keyes woke abruptly, stared at the ribbed top of the Conestoga, then at the stirring figure of his wife, Lorna, lying next to him.

"What is it, Jon?"

"Nothing, dear."

"Nothing?! You're trembling . . . was it that dream again? The war? The battle of Yellow Tavern? The wound?"

This was not the first time since he had come home from the war with a head wound that his sleep had been breached by a bad dream. She reached out and gently touched the back of his head as she had done before.

"No, Lorna. It was a dream, but not about the war. Something different this time," he tried to smile.

"Then tell me about it. They say that dreams often have some meaning . . . sometimes about something that's happened, or even about what's going to happen . . ."

"Or," he said smiling, "as Dickens's friend, Scrooge, said, 'the result of an undigested bit of beef, a fragment of underdone potato.' Let's just forget about it."

"But, Jon . . ."

"Actually, I thought I heard something, something out there. Probably the cry of a lonesome coyote."

"Well, I'll never be lonesome, Jon . . . so long as we're together."

"That makes two of us." He moved and kissed her forehead. "Now, go back to sleep. It's only midnight, and we've still got a long way to Saguaro."

Chapter 1

It was a long way from Monroe to Saguaro, much longer than they had anticipated as they journeyed by creaking wagon—pulled by a two-up team, through Missouri, southwest into Kansas, across the one hundredth meridian, to the panhandle of Texas, then the desolate New Mexico Territory and its arid, unforgiving terrain.

There had been a few respites such as Amarillo and Santa Fe, too few and too far between, and they had so far averted sudden, deadly threats from hostile red natives, who resented trespassers coming into their ancient domain.

This was Dry Tortuga—although they didn't know it—and no one really knew where it began and ended—a worthless span of earth where God had stomped the dirt and dust off his boots, with little or no water to provide nourishment, no game to provide food, or no fertile fields to provide crops.

And so they faced the vast emptiness between the winds—grassless, barren, rock hard, boiling windles.

days under a blistering sun, and relentless freezing nights under the worn canvas of the Conestoga.

Still, there were forced smiles, mostly from the young bride, unaccustomed to such trials.

"Jon, tell me more about Saguaro."

"There's not much I can tell except what was in the letter from the retiring reverend that we served together in the war . . ."

"Served gallantly."

"Most of those who served gallantly are dead."

"But not all, those medals you . . ."

"The war's over, Lorna. That's all in the past."

"But not our honeymoon. That's just beginning." She smiled.

"Some honeymoon." Keyes barely smiled. "Hundreds of miles in nowhere, to a place we know little about . . ."

"Except they need a minister named Jon Keyes."

She rested a soft white hand on his muscled arm that held the reins.

After a strained silence, he spoke without looking at her.

"But, Lorna . . ."

"What, Jon?"

"I've been thinking . . ."

"About what?"

"You and me. You mostly . . . did you make the right choice? You could have had your pick of rich young men in Monroe, of the elite society you were born into, with all the comfort you're used to, with everything . . ."

". . . Everything except the man I love . . ."

". . . Maybe your family was right . . ."

"As you said, Jon, about the war . . . all that's in the past. Our future's in Saguaro."

"Saguaro . . . you know what's been said. 'There's no God in Saguaro.'"

"Reverend Jonathan Keyes can do something about that."

"We'll see." Then he added, "If we ever get there."

"We'll get there. I have no doubt about that . . . or you."

But after what seemed like infinite days and nights, the prospect of Saguaro became less likely and more doubtful—much more doubtful.

The parched earth of the desert had claimed countless pilgrims wasted into dried-out meatless bones, picked clean by ravenous, far-seeing blackbirds who preyed on those who had prayed in vain—until they could pray and breathe no longer.

After scores of unnumbered days and nights lost in the no path terrain, with far away mountain peaks that never came closer—but vultures that circled ever nearer, it seemed inevitable that two more bodies and souls would soon surrender to the fate of those who had gone before.